"You want to know why I try to look and act like a man?"

Ann's tone was hard as she continued. "Well, I'll tell you. A woman has to be tough to be a cop. Any show of softness hurts her effectiveness and her career. If I want to be soft, I do so out of the public eye."

Diaz's voice had the velvet undertone she'd heard him use on other women, but never her. "I'm not the public."

"You're one of those people who questions how tough I am every day."

"What in hell gave you that idea?"

"Do you remember what you said to me after I was assigned to work with you?"

Brown eyes wary, Diaz shook his head.

"'Here's hoping you have half your old man's goods.'" She quavered inside, having spent a lifetime wondering whether she did. "You put me on notice. My father was known for being tough. So what do you think? Do I have his goods?"

His jaw muscles spasmed. "You're a better cop than he was."

"What?"

"You use your head. He didn't always." He raised an eyebrow. "Close your mouth."

S0-AGF-614

Revelations

Janice Kay Johnson

HARLEQUIN®

TORONTO • NEW YORK • LONDON
AMSTERDAM • PARIS • SYDNEY • HAMBURG
STOCKHOLM • ATHENS • TOKYO • MILAN • MADRID
PRAGUE • WARSAW • BUDAPEST • AUCKLAND

ISBN 0-373-71228-6

REVELATIONS

Copyright © 2004 by Janice Kay Johnson.

This edition published by arrangement with Harlequin Books S.A.

® and TM are trademarks of the publisher. Trademarks indicated with ® are registered in the United States Patent and Trademark Office, the Canadian Trade Marks Office and in other countries.

www.eHarlequin.com

Printed in U.S.A.

ABOUT THE AUTHOR

When not writing or researching her books, Janice Kay Johnson quilts, grows antique roses, spends time with her two daughters, takes care of her cats and dogs (too many to itemize!) and volunteers at a no-kill cat shelter. *Revelations* tells the story of Ann Caldwell—first introduced to readers in Janice's previous Superromance book, *Mommy Said Goodbye*.

Books by Janice Kay Johnson

*Patton's Daughters
**3 Good Cops
°Under One Roof

CHAPTER ONE

STANDING AT ATTENTION, shoulder to shoulder with her fellow police officers, Ann forced herself to look at the gleaming cobalt blue casket resting on a framework above a dark hole.

A funeral in all its solemnity was the worst of all places and times to become mired in self-pity.

"Comfort us in our sorrows at the death of our brother. Let our faith be our consolation, and eternal life our hope."

She tried to make her mind a blank. If she let herself think, she either remembered her father's funeral, so much like this one, and tears threatened, or she felt sorry for herself because she had no idea how to look pretty or flirt or make men feel protective and was therefore achingly lonely.

Spring sunlight didn't yet bring much warmth to the cemetery grounds, but leaves budded on the maple and sycamore trees and on old lilacs. A bird twittered in the tree behind Ann and the phalanx of other solemn, uniformed police officers who had come to see one of their own laid to rest. Just as they had come to her father's funeral last August.

"This joy that one we love has entered into the

nearer presence of our Lord does not make human grief unchristian,'' the pastor promised the grieving.

Did anyone truly grieve? Ann wondered. She'd known Leroy Pearce for most of her life—he'd been a crony of her father's—and she couldn't honestly say she'd liked the man. He'd been bigoted, crude and sexist. When Ann had transferred to Major Crimes, he'd refused to work with her.

''Sorry, babe,'' he'd said with an insincere grin. ''Can't think of you as anything but a little girl.''

Huh. *Girl* was the relevant word. If she'd been her daddy's son, he would have been thrilled to show him the ropes. But not her.

Okay, Leroy's widow and daughter seemed to be genuinely grief-stricken. Ann was trying not to look at them, because her very own partner was hovering over the gently sobbing daughter, a divorcée in her late twenties, Ann's age. He had one arm around her, while he held her elbow with his other hand. When Ann stole a look, Eva turned her head and cast a tear-drenched look up at Diaz.

It was enough to make Ann want to puke. Or go home and cry, she wasn't sure which.

Her mind had wandered earlier, too, during the church service. She'd struggled to remember the words to hymns. She wasn't the churchgoer she should be. When she was young, her mother had taken her, but later her father couldn't be bothered. Maybe it was *because* her mother had been the one to take her that now Ann had no interest in sliding into a pew every Sunday morning. Besides, she'd spent too many of those Sundays crouched beside a body assessing blood spatter patterns. She'd quit thinking of Sunday morning and church as connected. Saturday night was too popular for committing murder.

"Sometimes mid scenes of deepest gloom," had sung the mourners at the church.

Almost everyone here to honor Leroy was a cop, and they'd sure seen scenes of deepest gloom. Ann had had to hustle to get home, shower and change into dress uniform for the funeral. Her morning had been spent in the parking lot of a biker bar, where a regular had been stabbed upwards of a hundred times and left to bleed any remaining life out on the pavement in a bronze slick.

Her partner had been there, too, scribbling notes and seeming unaffected by the remarkable amount of blood pooled on the pavement.

Now, at graveside, Diaz was a lot more moved by the grieving daughter, who just then sniffed and turned to lay her cheek on his shoulder. He patted her back.

Ann tried to remember if he'd even been at her father's funeral. Maybe. Probably. But he hadn't been at her side, prepared to blot her tears on his uniform front. The captain had been beside her, she remembered, but several feet away. She had stood staring down at the casket and the large hole beneath, icy with shock and grief and the paralyzing realization that she was truly alone now.

She'd always wished she had a sister or brother. Now she heard other officers complain about huge family get-togethers and their packs of nieces and nephews and their interfering mothers and brothers-in-law and what have you, and she was jealous. All she had left in the world were grandparents, and she hardly knew them. Because they didn't live in the Northwest and hadn't made much effort to stay close to her after her mother died, her relationship with them consisted of polite Christmas cards.

Ann's eyes burned, and she tried to sniff without being audible. Damn it, why had her father had to die? Sure, he'd had a beer or two before he drove home that night, but not so much he should have missed a curve. But he had, and in his arrogance he hadn't bothered with a seat belt. Investigators told Ann that he'd hit a tree with such force, they weren't sure he would have survived even with the belt. His old pickup truck didn't have an airbag, the only thing that might have saved him.

Don't think about Dad, Ann ordered herself. *Don't think about the fact that his grave is only a hundred yards or so uphill. Or you'll cry, and you can't cry now, in front of everyone.*

She was good at not crying. Her father had been disgusted when she cried. If she hurt herself and bore it stoically, he might nod with approval and say something like, "That's good. You're toughening up now."

She used to think she *had* toughened up. Now she thought maybe she'd just been pretending all along, that inside she was still all girl.

On the outside…well, she had no idea how to be a girl. She was neither fish nor fowl, woman nor man. Her entire social life revolved around other cops, and it was limited. She had drinks with fellow officers on occasion, but there was always a barrier separating her from the men, and an even bigger one yawning between her and their wives and daughters and even the few other women cops she knew. They might wear a uniform and pack a gun during the day, but they also liked to shop and get makeovers and go dancing and crochet or quilt or "do" memory books. She would stand there with a smile frozen on her face and have no idea what they were talking about. She liked jewelry, but when would she wear it? She couldn't imagine decorating the pages of a photo album filled with images of her father with metallic gel pens and cute stickers. She didn't want mud all over her face or cucumbers slapped on her eyeballs. The reason women seemed to enjoy wandering the mall even when they didn't need anything was as foreign, even unknowable, to her as the age-old hatreds in countries like Israel and Ireland. Her few friends were misfits in their own ways as much as she was, and therefore incapable of guiding her.

Depressed, she murmured, "Amen," with the rest of the mourners, watched as the casket was lowered into the ground and the symbolic clod of earth thrown atop it. The widow let out a piercing cry that made Ann shudder and remember not just personal grief but also that morning's visit to the biker's girlfriend, who had dissolved right in front of them, her cry gurgling in her throat.

The crowd broke into small clumps of people who spoke in murmurs. Ann started toward the parking lot. Ahead of her Diaz walked beside the daughter, while their captain supported the sobbing widow.

Lucky she'd brought her own car, Ann thought. Separating her partner from the beautiful blonde would be a trick.

As if he knew she was thinking about him, he looked over his shoulder just then, scanning the crowd until his eyes met hers. For an instant she thought his expression was beseeching. She dismissed the idea immediately; Juan Diaz was plenty able to handle any woman. Still, she hesitated, then grudgingly started toward him. She ought to offer some condolences to Leroy Pearce's widow and only daughter, she supposed. Their fathers *had* been friends.

Although he hadn't looked back again, Diaz must have felt her approach, because he turned when she was only a few feet away.

"Ann. Do you know Eva Pearce?"

So she'd gone back to her maiden name after the divorce.

"Yes, since we were children." Ann hesitated, trying to decide whether she should offer a hand or a hug or some other form of physical expression of sympathy, none of which came comfortably to her. "I'm very sorry for your loss."

"Thank you." Eva's blue eyes filled with tears again. "Damn it, I can't quit crying, and Daddy was such a…" She wiped her cheeks. "Forget I said that."

Huh? What had she missed? "Forget you said what?"

Eva gave a choked laugh. "Bastard. He was such a bastard. He might have been my father, but I hated him half the time. That's what you never heard me say."

Ann shocked herself by admitting, "I felt the same

about my father. You knew him. He was a bastard, too."

Diaz had been gaping at the beautiful blonde. Now he gaped at Ann.

"There was a reason they were best friends." Eva sniffed. "We played together when we were little. Do you remember?"

"You wanted to play Barbies, and I thought anything but Cops and Robbers was dumb."

The blonde looked down at herself in her high-heeled pumps and chic black suit, then at Ann in her blue uniform and sturdy, brilliantly polished dress shoes, and laughed. "Neither of us has changed a bit."

Ann grinned back. "Apparently not."

"Can we get together and have coffee?" Eva asked. "We can bitch about our fathers and cry a little."

"Yeah. I'd like that." Somewhat to her surprise, Ann realized she would. She and this very feminine divorcée might not have much in common, but their fathers were a link.

"I'll call you." Eva gave her a watery smile, then offered Diaz a more charming one. "Thank you for your shoulder, Officer."

"You're more than welcome." His voice was deep velvet.

"I suspect you were assigned the job of tending me, but I appreciate it anyway." She sighed. "Speaking of tending, I'd better join my mother."

Ann and her partner murmured appropriate things and watched her walk away, heels sinking into the grass so that her stride had more lurch than sway.

"Were you assigned the job?" Ann asked.

"I've had worse ones."

"What?" She turned her head sharply. "You really were ordered to hover over her?"

"Yeah." His mouth tilted. "'Hovered' wasn't the word the captain used. 'Make sure she's all right' is closer to what I recall him saying."

They started walking.

"Nobody hovered over me when Dad died." She hoped she didn't sound petulant. "Did somebody fall down on the job?"

Amusement crinkled the skin at the corners of his dark eyes. "I wouldn't know. I doubt anyone was ordered to lend his shoulder to you. You're a cop."

And therefore too tough to cry, at least in public. Her father had been born to be a cop. Ann wished she had been, that she didn't have to pretend her nonchalance when she shrugged.

"Wouldn't have known what to do with a shoulder if one had been offered."

His smile vanished, and he studied her face for a long, uncomfortable moment. "That's a shame," he said at last. "Nobody would have thought less of you if you'd cried."

"I'm a woman, or haven't you noticed? A burly male cop makes the front of *Time* magazine when he cries over a wounded child. The public is moved by his tenderness. When a woman cop cries, everyone says, 'See? She's too softhearted. Should have been a teacher.'"

He shook his head. "The times, they are a'changing."

Ann said something succinct and heartfelt.

Diaz laughed again. "You're wrong. Most people accept women in damn near any profession. They don't have to be manly to do the same job."

"Damn straight they don't!"

"Then why do you try…" He swallowed the rest of that sentence when he saw the storm clouds building on her face.

Rage had her hands shaking. Shame made her go for flippancy. "To hide my raving beauty? Gosh, I'm just inclined to think lashes weighted down with mascara—" she batted her eyes "—might blur my vision at a crucial moment. And lipstick…" She pursed her lips. "Well, bloodred isn't my favorite color at the moment."

"I didn't—"

"You did," she snapped, flippancy gone. "I'm just not girlie, okay?" Or beautiful, and no amount of mascara or lipstick would change that.

"Damn it, Caldwell, don't put words in my mouth and thoughts in my head!" He stopped at his car and glowered at her. "You're a good cop, and you're a woman. So what?"

"So what" was about all she'd ever gotten in the way of sexual or romantic interest. Hearing the words said aloud stung, even if that wasn't what he'd meant.

In a hard tone, she said, "You want to know why I try to look like a man, and act like one? Well, I'll tell you. A woman has to be tough to be a cop. It's a fact. Any show of softness hurts her effectiveness and her career. If I want to be soft, I do it off the job and out of the public eye."

His voice went quiet, with that velvet undertone she

had heard him use toward other women but not her. "I'm not the public."

"You're a colleague. You're one of those people who questions how tough I am every day."

"What in hell gave you that idea?"

She jutted her chin. "Do you remember what you said to me after I was assigned to work with you?"

Brown eyes wary, Diaz shook his head.

"'Here's hoping you've got half your old man's goods.'" She'd quavered inside, after spending a lifetime wondering whether she did. "That's what you said. You put me on warning. My father was known for being tough. Tenacious. Hard-assed. Not kindhearted, not soft. So, what do you think? Do I have my father's goods?"

His jaw muscles spasmed. "You're a better cop than he was."

"What?"

"You heard me. You use your head. He didn't always." He raised an eyebrow. "Close your mouth."

Her teeth snapped together and she felt a flush creep up her cheeks.

"Are we going to go back to work, or stand here chatting all day?"

"I have to run home and change." As if he didn't know.

"I'll pick you up there." Juan Diaz nodded, opened his car door and got in.

Ann took the hint and headed for her own vehicle.

Just as well, because she had to blink hard to stop tears. She felt like mush inside, because…

Because he'd given her an unexpected accolade, shinier than any medal. *You're a better cop than he was.* She'd spent a lifetime trying to measure up to her father. Better? She didn't believe it. Couldn't. The words warmed a cold place in her chest anyway.

But she also wanted to cry because her father was gone and she'd never have the chance to win his complete approval. Her eyes were tearing up because she'd discovered she wasn't the only one who hated her father at the same time as she loved him.

And, damn it, she wanted to cry because she knew damn well that Diaz would never see her as a woman. Whatever he said, he didn't imagine her out of uniform, legs tangling with his, mouth soft under his, voice sexy in the darkness. It wasn't him—she didn't care about him. But she wished desperately some man would notice that, cop or no, she was a woman, with a woman's needs and vulnerabilities.

But she also knew that would never happen. Women had to advertise, and she didn't know how. Or even if she really wanted to.

Because what if she discovered that beneath the pretense she was too soft to be a cop? It was who she was, her only identity!

Behind the wheel of her car, Ann looked at herself in the rearview mirror. Blue eyes, brows she knew were too thick, brunette hair drawn tightly back from a pale, severe face.

Who are you kidding? her inner voice jeered. *You have to have a product to advertise. Why bother?*

With a steady hand, Ann started her car. Well, wasn't it lucky she hadn't grown up *wanting* to play Barbies.

JUAN DIAZ was in a lousy mood.

For starters, he hated funerals. He saw too much

death in its rawest form to be fooled by the ceremony and glorious hymns and grand words into thinking angels had anything to do with man's last moments.

Leroy Pearce had fallen off a ladder and broken his neck. His house was on a hillside. Apparently his ladder wasn't tall enough to reach the gutters from the downhill side of his plunging lot. So, like an idiot, he'd wired two aluminum ladders together and climbed them, unsteady as they must have been. As bulky as Leroy was, you'd have expected the wire to fail, but it hadn't. Instead, he'd leaned too far or shifted his weight wrong, and the ladders, still rigged together, had fallen outward, crashing at last far down the brushy canyonside.

Leroy would have had plenty of time on the way down to know he was going to die. His skull had been crushed when he hit a tree.

Death was not pretty, and despite his Catholic upbringing, Diaz doubted God had had anything to do with the time or occasion.

He had also spent the entire graveside service trying to keep an eye on Caldwell. An echo of her father's, this funeral had to be dragging grief to the surface even if she'd tried tying cement blocks to it to keep it buried deep. He knew her well enough to be sure she wouldn't burst into noisy sobs. He also knew she'd refuse to acknowledge feeling any upsurge of sadness. Ann Caldwell had spent the winter trying to convince him that she was as hard as her old man. He hoped she was lying to both of them.

Today, her face might have twitched a few times when the preacher talked about grief; could be she'd blinked more than normal. But when she'd walked up to him and Pearce's daughter afterward, her eyes were dry. She'd surprised him, though, with her admission that she'd had mixed feelings about her father. He'd seemed to loom so large in her world, Diaz was sometimes tempted to turn on his flashlight to find his way through the gloom of Sgt. Michael Caldwell's shadow.

Diaz was pissed by her attitude, too, her assumption that she constantly had to scramble to measure up. She was a good cop; she'd won awards, and risen to detective at record speed. Maybe she believed all good things had happened because of her name, not her own competence. Who the hell knew why she had such a chip on her shoulder?

He and Ann had had a few rough patches their first month together. She'd inherited from her father an obsessive determination to see a man named Craig Lofgren behind bars for murdering his wife despite the fact that her body had never been found. The whole thing had made Diaz uneasy. With no new evidence, there had been no justification for reopening the case, but her father had been unable to let it go and she'd seemed to feel a sacred duty to finish what he couldn't.

Well, she'd done that without much help from Diaz, and Daddy wouldn't have been happy, given the way he'd frothed at the mouth at the mere mention of Lofgren, a well-to-do airline pilot. Ann Caldwell had found the missing wife—alive and seemingly oblivious to the turbulence left in the wake of her disappearance.

By careful, solid police work, she'd cleared Lof-gren's name.

She didn't want to talk about the fact that Craig Lofgren never would have been under suspicion if her father had conducted an investigation anywhere as careful and impartial as hers.

"We all make mistakes," was all she'd say.

Ignoring witnesses and evidence that didn't fit your theory wasn't making a mistake, in Diaz's book. Every cop had prejudices. Keeping them on a short leash was part of the job.

Diaz had worked with a woman partner before. He'd been sorry when Melanie Najjar had decided during her second pregnancy that she wasn't coming back to work. Maybe because she was married he'd been able to damn near forget she was a woman. It was funny, too, because Najjar had been considerably more feminine than Ann Caldwell. Petite, fiery, with a taste for bold colors in makeup and everything else. Perps sometimes surrendered just for the charge of being cuffed by her.

In six months of working with Caldwell, Diaz hadn't forgotten for a single minute that she was a woman. Most of the time the knowledge didn't get in the way. It was just *there,* a tiny irritant like a piece of grit in his sock or the twinge of a sore muscle. The kind of thing he could ignore, all the while knowing he was ignoring it.

He wouldn't say he was attracted to her. How could he be, as plain as she managed to make herself despite vivid blue eyes, milk-white skin and hair the color of just-brewed coffee? She was either stocky or wore clothes that made her look that way, walked and talked like a man, refused to wear even a hint of lipstick and kept her hair drawn back so tightly he had no idea whether it was thin or thick. A man could pretty well assume she didn't *want* anyone to be attracted to her.

She wasn't his type, anyway. He wasn't interested in marrying again. Cops weren't good at ever after. Their wives—or husbands—started noticing they never seemed to make it home for dinner. When they were home in body, they tended not to be in spirit: they were too busy brooding over the mysteries of why people did the cruel or stupid things they did to notice that little Elena had hung a new picture she'd painted in kindergarten on the fridge and was eagerly waiting for Daddy to notice.

He'd been a crappy husband and an inadequate father. He didn't watch reruns of failed TV shows, and he wasn't going to act in his own.

Which meant he confined himself to women who wouldn't want or expect a marriage proposal down the line. Pretty women out for a good time, cynical women who wanted dinner table conversation, good sex and no whiskers left in their bathroom sink.

Repressed, complicated women who didn't know the meaning of a good time were off-limits. So, although he felt that irritating twinge now and again, like when he glanced at her beside him in the car and noticed the pure line of her throat or the delicacy of her cheekbones, or when she got ticked at him and her eyes flashed blue, or when she turned so that he couldn't avoid noticing how full-breasted she was... Damn it, when he felt anything at all toward Ann Caldwell that had a sexual connotation, Diaz ignored it. And he intended to keep ignoring it.

Just as he had to shut off this protective streak. If she were a male partner, he wouldn't have been watching her during the damn funeral, worried about her fragile emotional state. He'd have given her the credit of assuming she could handle renewed grief.

So why couldn't he let it go where Caldwell was concerned?

Diaz scowled at the red light holding him up.

Because she was a woman, he concluded. And his gut instinct told him she *was* emotionally fragile, despite her kick-ass persona.

He didn't want to worry about someone else. He could hardly deal with his own problems.

Ask for a change of partner, he thought, but knew he wouldn't. If she found out he'd put in a request, he'd wound her, and he never wanted to do that. Besides, they worked well together now that they'd straightened out a few kinks.

He was exasperated to realize he'd worry about her even if they weren't working together. Maybe especially if they weren't. She was bullheaded sometimes. She needed him to moderate her tendency to charge ahead.

Uh-huh, his inner voice taunted. *She needs you to protect her.*

He swore out loud just as he pulled to the curb in front of her apartment complex. The piece of grit irritating his instep felt like a jagged chunk of gravel right now.

Caldwell stirred up something...brotherly in him.
Yeah, that was it.

He was just damn grateful she was as plain as the
cream-colored facade of her building, and that his
flashes of awareness were few and far between.

Brotherly. Okay, he could be brotherly, even though
he didn't need another sister.

Diaz leaned on the horn.

CHAPTER TWO

"I'VE BEEN THINKING." Seat-belted in, Ann took a cautious sip of the hot coffee she'd poured into an insulated cup just before she left the house.

After a glance to check for traffic, her partner accelerated away from the curb. "Yeah, me, too. I'm thinking we'll find the slug who went berserk with the bowie knife holed up at his mama's house. Hell, she's probably doing his laundry, wondering why the water is running red."

"Come on. He must have been soaked with blood. She isn't wondering anything. If she's doing his laundry, she knows she's washing evidence." Ann took another, more confident swallow of coffee. "But that's not what I was thinking about."

"No?" Diaz gave her an odd look before returning his attention to the road ahead.

She frowned, hoping she wouldn't sound wacko. No, part of her wanted him to tell her she was just that. Convince her to drop the whole, creepy line of speculation.

"What I'm thinking," she said, "is that two cops have died in really stupid accidents."

"Two?" Another surprised, then speculative, glance. "Your father?"

"You don't think not wearing a seat belt was stupid?"

"Yeah, I think it was stupid. Just…"

"Normal stupid? Instead of unbelievably stupid?"

"Right." He slowed as a light turned yellow ahead. "Wiring two aluminum ladders together and then climbing damn near to the top of them, especially when you aren't a lightweight… That's unbelievably stupid."

"Okay. Yeah. I agree." She continued to frown. "Still…"

"Still, two cops have died in stupid accidents. Which took place six months apart."

"That's true. But do you remember a few months ago, when Reggie Roarke told everybody who'd listen about how someone tried to kill him?"

Diaz snorted. "Because he was on his back under a car raised by two flimsy jacks?"

"Uh-huh. Doing something stupid."

Braked at the stoplight, he was silent. When she stole a glance, she saw that her partner was frowning, too.

"Something," Ann added, "between normal stupid and unbelievably stupid."

"Damn stupid," Diaz supplied, but automatically, as if he was thinking hard.

Ann waited.

The light turned, and he started forward with the other cars. She wondered where they were going. No, she knew: the berserk biker's mama's house. At least this murder, hideous as it was, held no mystery. Half a dozen witnesses had seen the assault. Two, to their credit, had tried to stop it, and had gotten their hands and forearms sliced viciously for their efforts.

"He was high," one of them said, shaking his head. "Crazy high."

"On?" Ann had asked.

"Crack. But he might've had some other stuff, too."

Unbelievably stupid seemed to be going around.

Now, still frowning, Diaz asked, "What was it Roarke claimed? That the car rocked, like someone was pushing it?"

"He said he heard footsteps. Thought it was his wife and started talking to her. Then the car rocked and he told her to knock it off. But it rocked harder, and he started scooting out. Didn't make it before the first jack collapsed."

"Yeah, yeah," Diaz said thoughtfully. "I remember his face."

With a bulbous nose, thick jowls and a bull-like neck, Big Reggie Roarke wasn't a candidate for a calendar of hot law enforcement guys at the best of times. With a black eye, plaster across his nose and a cheekbone blossoming purple and puce, he'd probably scared his own grandkids.

She gave a quiet grunt of amusement. Yeah, okay. He probably scared them without the added beauty treatment. When she was a kid, he'd scared *her* when he came to the house.

"He was lucky," Diaz ruminated. "Damn near got his skull crushed."

Ann waited some more.

"You're saying...what? That someone pushed the

car off the jacks? That he wasn't making it up to hide how damn careless he'd been?''

Trying not to sound tentative, she said, ''Maybe.''

''And that your father and Leroy Pearce's 'accidents' weren't.''

''A little shove would have taken care of Leroy.''

Diaz made a sound of disgust. ''A belch would have catapulted the idiot into space.''

''But what if you were watching, waiting for them to do something stupid? How much easier could murder get?''

He was shaking his head before she finished. ''You're reaching. What if we looked county-wide at accidental deaths in the past six months. You know what we'd find.''

She knew. ''Amazing idiocy.''

''People who let their kids ride a dirt bike down a rocky, forty-five degree slope with no helmets on. I guarantee we'd come up with at least one mother who killed her baby because she was holding it on her lap in the car instead of using an infant seat. She thought she could hold on to him. How many times have we heard that?''

Too many.

''Remember the five-year-old killed because his dad tied his plastic saucer to the back of his truck when the roads were black ice? The truck went into a spin and slid right over him?''

''Who could forget?''

He was on a roll. ''Oh, yeah. There were the sixteen-year-old jocks playing chicken on an empty road, both with too much testosterone to lose.''

They'd hit head-on, neither, apparently, having braked or turned the wheel.

"Okay, okay," she conceded.

Diaz's fingers flexed on the steering wheel. "Your dad. What are you suggesting? Somebody cut the brake lines?"

"No, the truck was checked over. I'm thinking he was forced off the road. Or tricked somehow—35th makes that sharp bend there."

"Any dents on the side of the truck?"

"One long, deep scrape. But the cab crumpled, so it was hard to tell. Anyway, we all just figured someone had hit his truck in a parking lot."

"He'd have bitched loud and long if something like that had happened."

Yeah, he would have. He'd have ranted and raved. Thinking aloud, Ann said, "I don't know if they checked for paint flakes in it or not."

"We can find out," her partner suggested.

"You don't think I'm crazy?"

His grin was wry. "Probably. I shouldn't encourage you. But…hell. We can ask a few questions."

"Damn it," Ann muttered. "I was hoping you'd say I was wacko. Then I could forget the whole idea."

"You're wacko," he obliged. "Let's forget it."

"Now it's too late." She scowled. "Speaking of too late, do you suppose they looked for footprints at Leroy's? Ground was soft."

"I can't imagine. By the time his wife and half a dozen neighbors rushed over, and the EMTs trampled the hillside bringing him up, what were the chances?"

Resigned, she made a face. "None. Of course."

''Still, we could talk to neighbors. Maybe one of them saw somebody go around back, figured it was a friend, didn't think anything of it.''

''And no one ever asked them.''

''Happens.'' His tone was utterly expressionless.

Ann glanced at him, knowing darn well what he meant. Her father hadn't asked some questions when he was investigating the disappearance of Julie Lofgren. If he'd asked them, he would have found her and saved her husband and kids an excruciating year and a half.

''Okay,'' she agreed, then realized they were stopped.

The neighborhood on the fringes of Puyallup was run-down: paint peeling, lawns ragged, driveways filled with cinder-blocked wrecks. She'd been on domestic disturbance calls here when she was a patrol officer.

''Which house?''

''Two blocks down.''

''Do we want backup?'' she asked.

''We're waiting for it.''

''My, aren't we efficient.''

He gave her another crooked grin, and Ann had one of those moments she hated, when something turned over in her chest and she had to admit he was an attractive man.

His dark hair and eyes went with the Hispanic name. He was half a head taller than she was: six foot one or two, she guessed. She'd found out he was eight years older than she was, which put him at thirty-six. Rumor said he'd been a state champion hurdler in college, which she could believe after seeing him run down a suspect.

Grooves bracketed his mouth, deepening when he was tired, adding puckish charm to his smiles. And damn it, his smiles were what got to her, with the glint in his eyes and the skin crinkling beside them. A face that was usually impassive became sexy.

He was probably a lady-killer. If she called him during off-hours, she often heard laughter and a feminine voice in the background. Unlike her, he apparently had an active social life.

He also had kids, she knew. A couple of times he'd offhandedly mentioned having them for a weekend. When she'd asked once what happened to his marriage, he'd only shrugged.

"I'm a cop."

That couldn't be the whole story. Plenty of cops did stay married, even seemed happy. But she had tried hard not to speculate; Diaz's personal life wasn't any of her business. They worked together. Period.

She just wished...oh, that he was fifty-five instead of thirty-six. Squat, or pudgy, or stringy, instead of lean and athletic. Maybe that he chewed tobacco, so his teeth were stained. Or...heck, she'd forget he was sexy-looking if he had a crude sense of humor and down-deep disdain for the pathetic excuses for humanity they often met in their jobs.

No such luck. As far as she could tell, Diaz was smart, occasionally funny, basically kind and dedicated to his job. She'd looked hard for faults and was irritated by how few she'd found.

He interrupted her reverie. "You're thinking again."

"What?" She knew she flushed. "I'm supposed to empty my mind while we sit here?"

He glanced in the rearview mirror. "Sitting's over."

A patrol car pulled in behind their unmarked blue sedan. The four police officers got out to hold a brief conference. The two uniforms nodded when told their role in the upcoming drama.

Minutes later, Diaz and Ann pulled up to the curb in front of a shabby white house. The squad car slammed to a stop in the driveway. The uniforms raced to the back of the house, while Ann followed Diaz to the front door.

She stood back while he took the lead, knocking hard and calling, "Police!"

The woman in the stained housecoat who came to the door tried to pretend she had no idea where her son was, but she was a lousy liar. Shouts in back told them their quarry had tried to make a break.

When the uniforms shoved him, handcuffed, unshaven, barefoot and screaming obscenities, around the house, she broke into tears.

"Don't hurt Eddie! It's not his fault. Those drugs, they got him by the throat and make him crazy! You gotta help him!" she begged, tears tracking a face aged by a life that couldn't be any picnic.

"He's in police custody. He won't be hurt," Diaz said, in a voice gentle enough to make her sag.

As the day unwound, damned if they didn't find she *was* washing Eddie's blood-soaked clothes. The vest, though, was black leather, and she hadn't wanted to ruin it, or his good leather boots. It apparently hadn't occurred to her that rusty streaks of dried blood on her pink plastic laundry basket might be hard to explain, too.

Dinner was sandwiches at Subway, with Diaz and Ann companionably sharing cookies and chips. She figured she'd gotten her daily vegetables in the lettuce, tomato and green pepper on the six-inch sub.

Their knees bumped under the small table. They talked in short bursts, until Diaz suddenly swore. "I was supposed to call Elena and Tony before eight."

"Your kids." She vaguely knew their names.

"Crap." His shoulders slumped. "I'm always doing this."

"They must understand."

He gave a sharp, incredulous laugh. "They're seven and nine. Of course they don't understand."

She bit her lip and said in a quiet voice, "I did at that age."

"Your mother wasn't telling you that your dad couldn't be bothered with you."

"My mother died when I was eight." Her mother's death was something she didn't let herself think about, and mentioned only when it seemed unavoidable. Even then, she kept the statement matter-of-fact. No how or why; that was nobody's business. Ann crumpled up her sandwich wrappings.

Mercifully, Diaz didn't say, *Oh, what happened to her?* Instead he stared at her. "I didn't know. Is that why…"

When he stopped, she said, "Why what?"

His big shoulders jerked. "I don't know. Why you're a cop."

She heard the pause after "you're." He was thinking something else. Fill in the blank. "Like one of the guys." When what he meant was, "Why you're so unfeminine."

The knowledge stung, as every such suggestion did. Especially lately.

"Yeah, Dad wasn't much help at picking out a prom dress." Flippancy seemed to be her best defense these days.

"You went?"

"Sure," she lied. "Pretty in pink."

He took a last swallow of soda, then rattled the ice cubes. "Pink isn't your color. You should wear blue. To match your eyes."

Rarely without a comeback, Ann didn't have the slightest idea what to say. She couldn't take offense at a casual observation. "Thank you" wasn't called for. He hadn't said, "You'd be beautiful in blue."

He didn't remark on her silence, only gathered up his wrappings and said, "Ready?"

In the car, she said, "Do you want to try calling your kids now?"

Diaz shook his head. "Cheri would just claim they're asleep even if they're not. I'm not in the mood for her digs."

"I'm sorry," Ann heard herself saying. "You've never said…"

"That my ex-wife hates my guts?" He made a sound in his throat. "That's the way it is."

Ann let the silence ride for a minute. She wasn't

real good at this interpersonal stuff. Would she seem uncaring if she didn't ask questions? Nosy if she did? But she was curious, so finally she said, ''You want to talk about it?''

His fingers tightened and loosened, tightened and loosened a couple of times on the wheel. He sighed, long and ragged. ''Maybe another time, okay?''

She shrugged as if she didn't care. ''Sure.''

Conversation died there. When he dropped her in front of her complex, Ann said, ''See you tomorrow.''

He nodded. ''Yeah. Tomorrow.''

He waited at the curb, as he always did on the rare occasions when he took her home, until she let herself in the door of her ground-floor unit. Chivalry, she had wondered before, or a cop's paranoid belief that creeps lurked in every dark corner?

Damn it, she thought, standing in the middle of her living room, why was she obsessing about stuff that would never have occurred to her a year ago?

She knew the answer, and was shamed by it.

A year ago, she'd been so focused on winning her father's approval, she hadn't had time to sit back and wonder whether she was happy with herself or her life.

Now she did. And she wasn't.

She liked being a cop. She just wished she had something, someone, else. She wished she knew how to have fun, how to flirt, how to feel pretty. A hobby would be good. Maybe a sport, like tennis. She jogged regularly, to stay in shape, and it did relax her. But jogging wasn't *fun*.

The trouble was, she had no idea where to start to make changes. Her apartment needed something, for

example. Okay, a lot. It had no character. But…
decorating. How did you do that? She'd bought stuff
before. Some of the furniture was hers. But whatever
she brought home just never melded. A print would
look lost on the wall where she hung it. A throw pillow
on one end of the couch, bought in a rash moment,
looked like an orphan from some exotic species, kindly
taken in by a plain Jane mom.

Ann wandered into her bedroom, stripping as she
went. She felt lighter the minute she laid her shoulder
harness and gun on her bedside table. Unbuttoning her
shirt, she eyed with equal disfavor the contents of her
closet. What if some day she had call to look elegant,
or flirty and sexy, or even just like a woman?

Out of luck. Even she could see that almost everything hanging in there was ugly. She never wore any
of it anyway, except the blazers, Oxford cloth shirts
and slacks that were her plainclothes uniform. She
ought to bundle the rest up and give it to the Salvation
Army. If they'd take it.

Still brooding, Ann changed into flannel pajama bottoms and a sacky T-shirt.

She could afford a new wardrobe, and to refurbish
her apartment. Or even to buy a house. She'd been
thinking of doing that. With what she'd saved and
what she'd inherited from her father, money wasn't an
issue. She just didn't want to waste it—buy a bunch
of stuff and be as dissatisfied with it as she was by
what she already owned.

Maybe she should hire a decorator. Of course, then
the place would have character; it just wouldn't
be hers.

Depression hit her in a wave. What difference did it make what her apartment looked like? She hardly ever had anyone over anyway. She kidded herself when she said she had friends. Her ''friends'' were people she met to see a movie. Acquaintances was probably closer to the truth.

What she needed was someone to decorate *her*. In the act of getting her toothbrush and toothpaste out of the medicine cabinet, she stopped. Actually, it wasn't a bad idea. You could get makeovers. Couldn't you? And maybe go to some store like Nordstrom and find a friendly-looking clerk and say, ''Help?''

She studied herself carefully in the mirror and wondered if she'd have the courage to appear in public wearing a short skirt or a tight top and with makeup on her face. What if she sauntered into work someday thinking she'd achieved chic, and everyone busted a gut laughing?

Ann made faces at herself in the mirror: bared her teeth, tried for a radiant smile, tilted her head this way and that to see herself at every angle.

She wasn't *that* bad-looking. At least, she didn't think so. Her skin was good, if too pale. She couldn't seem to tan, no matter what she did. Her teeth were white and straight—her father had seen to that, when one front tooth started trying to cut in front of the other. Braces were a hideous memory, but she was grateful for the result. Her forehead was high—maybe too high, especially with her hair pulled back the way it was. Blue eyes, check. Normal lips, not pouty but not thin, either. Wavy dark hair that tumbled well past her shoulders when she let it free.

Below the neck…well. She was too buxom for her short stature, giving her the look of a fireplug. Ever since she turned eleven and started to develop, she'd been trying to hide her breasts. Her hips were wider than she liked, too; the uniform had never fit her right. Why couldn't she be tall and lean? She was pretty well on the other end of the spectrum from the ethereal models men and women alike seemed to admire these days. But she was no Playboy bunny, either. She was too…compact. Too strong, despite a build that didn't match who she really was.

But maybe, with the right clothes—whatever they were—she could look curvy instead of squat. She'd settle for that. If she could figure out what the right clothes were.

She grimaced at herself and stuck the toothbrush in her mouth. Like she was going to go waste a bunch of money on clothes.

But maybe, she could spend a *little* money. Just…oh, go to Nordstrom and wander around. Maybe try some clothes on, just for fun.

She'd done that once, when other girls were shopping for prom dresses. Ann had pretended she was, too, trying on long dresses sewn with glittery sequins or simple satin slip dresses. But they hadn't looked right on her, and she had suddenly, in the dressing room at the Bon, felt so inadequate she'd ripped off the slinky royal blue number and scrambled into her own clothes, rushing out of the store.

The memory almost made her jettison the plan, but she was beginning to think she had to do something instead of just feeling miserable.

She wasn't sixteen anymore. So, okay, her idea of shopping was usually marching into the store and buying a new pair of the same pants she always bought. But she could browse.

Ann made one last face at herself in the mirror.

It wasn't like she had a whole lot else to do on her days off.

"DO YOU USUALLY use bold colors, or soft ones?"

Ann sat on a tall stool at the cosmetics counter feeling as if she were at the dentist. The makeup consultant, or whatever she called herself, even reminded Ann of the dental technician who cleaned her teeth. Blond, perky, relentless.

"Uh… Surprise me," she improvised. "I'm here because I want a change."

"Oh, what fun!" chirped Britny.

Yeah, that was how her name was spelled, according to the tasteful tag she wore on her bright blue lapel. Ann had almost asked if someone had made a mistake, but decided poor Britny's parents had just decided to be creative. Make her stand out from the crowd.

Preparing her tools, Britny assured Ann, "You were smart to come with your face bare. Most people don't, and then we have to start by washing off the old makeup."

Ann made a noncommittal sound and warily watched the hand approaching her face with pale goop on a cotton ball.

"You have fabulous skin!" Britny spread the cool liquid across Ann's cheeks, chin, upper lip. Ann almost asked why she had to cover her skin, if it was so fabulous, but was afraid if she opened her mouth her tongue would get coated, too. "Alabaster is our palest shade of foundation. It's blending in beautifully."

She continued to chatter as she outlined Ann's lips with a colored pencil—to "define them" she explained—then filled in with lipstick. "Your brows could use some shaping," she suggested. "They have a lovely arch, but a more delicate line would bring out your eyes." She tilted her head and studied Ann as if she were a half-done canvas. Nodding, she agreed with herself. "Definitely. Jeannie down at Salon Francine does a wonderful job. I know she takes drop-ins."

Keeping her eyes open while that hand approached with a sharp implement was all Ann could do. Grimly she gripped the edge of the seat, stared straight ahead, and let Britny draw lines on her lids, then "accentuate" her lashes with mascara. Eye shadow was "blended" and blush applied to cheeks. At last, Britny caroled, "Let's see how you like this look!"

She tilted a round mirror on the glass top of the counter until Ann could gape at herself.

"Ohmygod."

Britny beamed.

Another doll stared back at her. One with huge, mysterious blue eyes, mysteriously enhanced cheekbones, a mouth that...well, almost *was* pouty.

It also felt stiff. In fact, she was afraid if she smiled or raised an eyebrow or drew her lips back from her teeth the facade would crack.

Britny was suggesting that if she liked the "look" she could buy all this stuff. Ann wasn't sure she'd be able to apply it—heck, if she'd ever have the nerve to try—but she nodded.

"Sure," she said, moving her lips a minimal amount. "Fine. Put together what you think I'll need."

Ann admitted to being low on eye makeup remover—who knew you needed it? she'd have just used soap—and half a dozen other things.

In a state of shock, she wrote a check for more than she'd spent on her entire wardrobe in the last year, then obediently presented herself at the salon, where Jeannie happened to have an opening.

Ann had seen that Mel Gibson movie where he waxed his legs, so she knew the procedure hurt. She didn't know it would be excruciating until she strangled a scream, her body levitating from the chair.

"Goodness, you've let these grow out!" Jeannie chided.

By the time she was done, Ann's eyelids and entire forehead were in flames. She moaned when Jeannie laid a cool compress over her forehead and told her to relax for a few minutes.

Once the raging pain had subsided to sharp throbs, Jeannie was kind enough to take the bag of makeup from Ann's nerveless hand and deftly apply foundation to cover the inflamed skin.

"Perfect!" she declared, turning the salon chair so Ann could stare dully at the new her.

Wow. Half her eyebrows were gone. The puffy red skin where the other half had been couldn't be totally disguised. The effect was…she didn't know. Maybe good when she healed.

Having a vision of how she'd look when the stubborn hair roots recovered and sprouted stubble, Ann asked suspiciously, "How often do I have to do this?"

She barely refrained from a moan at the answer. She had to put herself through this every few weeks so she could feel feminine?

"The price of beauty..." she muttered.

Jeannie laughed merrily. "If you don't let them go, it doesn't hurt nearly as much."

"Okay," Ann vowed. "I won't. I promise."

When she stood, she swayed, and Jeannie had to grab her arm. "Are you all right?"

"Sure." Ann gave her head a little shake. "I'm fine." She gave blood on a regular basis with less trauma.

She paid, ditched the idea of clothes shopping, and walked almost steadily out to her car. There, she stared with amazement in the rearview mirror at the new her, started the engine, and drove home.

Maybe she'd take this campaign to redo her image a little slower. She could put off shopping until next week. Or even the week after. She had to get used to the new eyebrows first. Figure out how to use all that stuff she'd just wasted a week's salary on. How to wash it off if you couldn't use soap.

Baby steps, she decided. Nothing radical.

In her slot at the complex, she bowed her head and pretended to be hunting for something in her purse when the young couple who lived in 203 walked by, bickering. Ann wasn't ready to be seen.

Her stomach knotted, and she stole another look at herself in the mirror. Oh, God. Everyone would notice, wouldn't they?

What would she *say* if someone—Diaz, for example—commented? Would she tell him fliply that they'd
needed pruning?

With a whimper, she locked her car and raced for
the safety of her apartment, the expensive bag of tricks
she wouldn't have the courage to use clutched in her
hand.

CHAPTER THREE

SOMETHING WAS DIFFERENT about her. Diaz just couldn't put his finger on what it was.

Driving again today, he kept stealing glances. It seemed every time he did, Caldwell averted her face.

He felt like he had when his ex had started striking poses the minute he'd walked in the door from work, and he'd known she must have a new hairdo, clothes, *something*. And he was supposed to notice.

Only, Caldwell didn't want him to notice.

"You're staring," she snapped.

"You've done something to your face."

She looked directly at him for the first time, defiance in her tight mouth and the jut of her chin. "Yeah? So?"

"Your eyebrows." At a stop sign, he studied them—her—more closely. "Where the hell did they go?"

The minute the words were out, Diaz knew he'd blown it. *You look great,* was the all-purpose, correct remark.

Caldwell's vivid blue eyes narrowed and her teeth showed. "I had my brows waxed," she snarled. "That is, I believe, a normal thing for a woman to do."

"Yeah, but you're…" He cleared his throat.

"Not normal?" she inquired.

Knowing danger when he saw it, Diaz ignored the honk of some idiot who was in a hurry.

"You don't do stuff like that," he blurted.

"Because it's a waste of time for me? Are you suggesting I'm hopeless?"

"Because you just don't do it!" he all but shouted.

Somebody rapped on his window. "Hey, buddy, you want to quit arguing with your girlfriend and get a move on?"

Diaz hit the down button and fixed an icy stare on the red-faced Yuppie who thought the world would end if he was held up two minutes.

"Maybe you want to rethink interfering with law officers in the performance of their duties."

"You're cops?" His stare took in the grill between front and back seats, the radio and the gun that Caldwell displayed as she bent forward, casually letting her blazer fall open. "And you're sitting at the stop sign...why?"

"I'm afraid that's not your concern, sir." Caldwell had a gift for cool dismissal. "Please return to your car."

Diaz zipped the window back up, glanced both ways, and started across the intersection. His mouth began to curve into a grin before they made it across.

He turned his head to see his partner's mouth twitch.

"God knows what he thought."

A laugh bubbled out of her. "That we were conducting a stakeout?"

"Squabbling like a long-married couple is more like it."

She drew back instantly without seeming to move a muscle. He just felt it; her contracting into her space, a turtle making sure its shell was ready and available. Diaz thought a faint flush touched her cheeks, too.

"You made me mad."

"Yeah, I wasn't very tactful," he admitted. He took another glance. Definitely pink cheeks. And the eyebrows... Much as he hated to admit it, the shaping had the effect of opening her face, emphasizing eyes he'd always known were spectacular. "Actually, uh, I like what you did. It looks good."

"Really?" She couldn't know how uncertain she sounded.

"Yeah," he said. "I'm just not used to my partners having a makeover."

"I didn't go that far," she said, really quickly, the pink in her cheeks deepening. "I only did my eyebrows."

Uh-huh. She was hiding something. God. Had she had a bikini wax, too? Was that why she was embarrassed?

He felt a surge of lust that shocked him. It was all he could do not to let his gaze lower to her crotch. Just for a second, he'd imagined her naked, a thatch of silky dark hair at the vee between smooth thighs and a flat, pale belly.

He looked away from her so fast, something cracked in his neck. *Don't think of her that way,* he ordered himself. *She's a cop, your partner. Never, ever, imagine her naked again.*

Keeping himself from thinking anything at all seemed to be the only way he could prevent pictures from forming before his mind's eye. But sustaining a giant blank like a dry-erase board where he normally had a tangle of thoughts and plans and images took an enormous effort. His palms grew sweaty.

"I made a few calls," she said, breaking the silence and bailing him out.

"Calls?"

"About Dad. And Leroy Pearce."

"Right." He relaxed fractionally. He could think about this. "What'd you learn? Wait." He put on his turn signal. "Let's stop for a cup of coffee."

No espresso here. The truck stop café had padded booths patched with duct tape, middle-aged waitresses in starched pink uniforms who willingly refilled white china mugs whenever the level dropped, and French fries that tasted so good, they were probably still being made in beef fat.

Reluctantly, he skipped the fries. Breakfast hadn't been that long ago. But he figured a piece of pie would settle.

One of the things he liked about Ann Caldwell was her appetite. Most women were on a perpetual diet. She never seemed to give a thought to calories.

When he said, "Pie sounds good," she agreed.

"Make mine cherry," she told the waitress. "Warm."

"À la mode?"

"Why not?"

"Boysenberry," he said. "I'll take the ice cream, too."

"Okay," he said, once the waitress had left them

alone in a booth in the far corner. "Find out any-thing?"

"That scrape along the driver's side door and fend-ers bothered the mechanic who looked at the truck after the accident. He mentioned it in his report, but no one picked up on it."

"Who would remember if the scrapes were there before that night?" Diaz frowned. "Where was your father going?"

"He was on his way home from The Blue Moon." The tavern was a popular hangout for the older cops. "He had a blood-alcohol level that would have gotten him in trouble if he'd been pulled over, too. That's one reason 'accident' was the obvious answer. He was speeding, lost control on the curve..." She shrugged.

"What do you think?"

Her voice was clipped. "Dad liked his beer. But I never knew him even to wander across a center line when he was behind the wheel. He carried it well. You know?"

"That's what they all say," Diaz reminded her.

She grimaced. "Yeah, I know. But, see, he drove me places a lot when he'd had as much as a six-pack. And, if anything, he'd slow down. Get more cautious. He never speeded. He said he'd picked up too many body parts off highways. When I got my license, he told me that if I was ever ticketed for speeding, I wasn't driving again for a year. If I was lucky."

"He wasn't, um..." Diaz tried to think how to phrase his question without offending her. "He hadn't been feeling low about anything?"

His meaning sank in and her voice rose. "Low?"

The waitress brought their pies, but neither of them picked up a fork or broke their locked stare.

"You're asking if he was depressed?" She flattened her hands on the table. "You think he might have committed suicide?"

"He drove at high speed into a tree. Yeah, the thought occurred to me."

Her face worked, and he braced himself for the blast.

"No! He'd never do that!" She breathed heavily. "How can you even suggest...?" She broke off with a lurch, as if a sob had torn at her throat.

In alarm, he said, "Jeez, Caldwell. Don't get worked up. I just figured I should throw the possibility on the table."

"It's a horrible thing to say!"

"I'm not making an accusation. I just asked. Cops commit suicide, just like other people."

"Not my father!" she yelled.

Heads on the other side of the diner turned.

"Okay, okay," Diaz soothed. "Had you seen him in the week before he died?"

"I talked to him the day before." She glared at him as if he was going to argue. "He was feeling good about an arrest, and he claimed he had a break in the Lofgren case. He wanted to know why my arrests were so low for the month." She swallowed. When she continued, she'd stripped her voice of emotion. The change was so stark from her passionate defense of a moment before, he knew the memory must burn in her belly. "Dad said if I couldn't do the job, he'd seen an ad for a new session at the cosmetology school. Then he—'' She stopped again. Deliberately relaxed, but Diaz saw the effort it took. She stirred her coffee, although the half a teaspoon of sugar she'd added had long since dissolved. ''He was his usual supportive self. That was just his way.'' She shrugged again. ''He wasn't any different than ever. If anything, he seemed to be in a good mood.''

Suddenly furious for reasons he hardly grasped, Diaz asked, ''Then he what?''

She stared at him.

''Tell me.''

''What difference does it make?''

''I want to know,'' he said, rough and unyielding.

Just audibly, she said, ''He laughed. 'Hell, they wouldn't take you once they got a look at you.' That's what he said. But by God, if I couldn't use the advantages he'd given me to do the job, I'd better start exploring other career paths.''

Diaz wished the son of a bitch was alive so he could plant a fist in his face. ''He just couldn't admit you might be his equal.''

''But why?'' she whispered, as much to herself as to him. ''Did he hate me?''

Diaz couldn't remember ever hearing Sgt. Caldwell talk about his daughter. ''Maybe,'' he suggested, ''he desperately had that urge men sometimes do to live on through a son. He couldn't see himself in you, so you wouldn't do.''

''I tried.'' The two small words were as desolate as anything he'd ever heard.

''If he wasn't proud of you, he didn't deserve you.''

She looked at him with those vivid, desperate eyes. "You have a son and a daughter both, don't you?"

"Yeah." Picturing his kids, dark-haired and bright-faced, smart, mischievous, all bony elbows and knees and warm cuddly bodies at the same time, Diaz knew his voice softened. "Can I live again through my son but not my daughter? Is that what you're asking?"

She glanced down, saw the ice cream melting in pale rivers around her pie, and picked up her fork. "I guess."

"No." He couldn't imagine the concept, not the way she meant. "Actually, I see more of myself in Elena than Tony. He looks like his mom, loves to talk like she does. He's creative, too, like she is. Elena's more for mulling things over before she gives an opinion and takes action. Tony's the rash one."

Around a bite, Caldwell asked, "You were a cautious kid?"

"Yeah, I hung back." Damn, this was good pie. "I can remember every time Mom served a new dish, I'd watch my sisters' faces as they tried it before I put a bite in my mouth."

Caldwell laughed, and he saw that some of the misery had left her face.

"Back to your father. We need to hit up his drinking buddies. Find out if anybody knows about the scrape on his truck."

She nodded. "I can do that. I know his friends."

"While you're talking to Roarke, see if his story about the car that landed on his face has changed."

Another nod.

"I'll tackle Leroy's neighbors. Talk to the widow,

the EMTs. You never know. Someone might have noticed something.''

''Okay,'' she agreed. ''Do we tell the lieutenant what we're doing?''

''Not until we have something to go on. He'd say the whole idea is wacko and tell us to drop it.''

She laughed. ''I told you I'd have let it go if you'd just said that in the first place.''

''The way you let the Lofgren thing go when I didn't back you?''

His honest answer to their superior that he didn't think the case justified reopening had been a betrayal, as far as Caldwell was concerned. Partners backed each other, she'd said. In general, Diaz agreed. Truth was, he didn't think they'd find anything this time, either, in investigating the two deaths and the one near-miss. But Caldwell would feel better if she wasn't left wondering, and that was good enough for him.

''That was different,'' she said.

''This matters, too.''

Pushing her empty plate away, she cleared her throat. ''I didn't say it the other day, but I want you to know I appreciate you taking me seriously.''

''Yeah, yeah.'' They were descending into Hallmark territory, which made him uncomfortable. If he'd talked about his feelings more readily, he might still be married. ''Good cops have hunches. I figure this one might be legit.''

''Yeah.'' She looked grateful. ''I mean, I hope it's not, but I'd like to be sure.''

Grateful. That stuck in his craw. Her bastard of a father had never respected her opinions or worth, so she was pathetically grateful when someone did. He almost liked it better when she snarled.

"You done?" he asked abruptly.

"What? Oh. Sure." She drained her coffee and slid from the booth. "Pit stop."

He made his own, taking a second to frown at himself in the blotchy mirror above the sink in the men's room as he washed his hands. The face that looked back at him was older than he remembered being, grimmer. Every one of his thirty-six years showed today. He wondered how Ann Caldwell saw him, whether she ever...

No, damn it. He wasn't going there. He didn't want to know if she ever had moments like he'd had in the car, when she felt a flash of intense sexual awareness. Hell, he'd rather not know if she *didn't,* either. A man had some pride.

NOT UNTIL late that afternoon could Diaz get over to Pearce's house.

His widow answered the door, her eyes puffy and red-rimmed, her stare vague.

"Mrs. Pearce, I'm sorry to disturb you," he began. "But I wonder if I could ask you a few questions."

"Questions?"

"About your husband's accident."

"But...why?"

He came up with something slick about tying up loose ends, and she finally nodded and stood back.

The living room was dim with drapes drawn and only one lamp on. She sat in the large brown recliner that dwarfed her, and he guessed it had been her husband's. A basket at her feet overflowed with crumpled tissues.

She wrapped an afghan around her shoulders as if she were chilled despite the warm room. "What do you want to know?"

Diaz flipped open his notebook and held his pencil above a blank page. "Were you home at the time of the accident?"

"Yes, but I didn't know what he was doing. I was sewing in a room on the other side of the house. I heard a few thumps and vaguely wondered what he was up to."

"I understand he had somebody stop by to speak to him?"

"Did he? I guess he might have."

"Were both ladders his?"

She nodded, her mouth crimping. "I told him to call a service. Those gutters were so high off the ground, but he was determined…" She groped for a tissue.

Diaz gave her a moment to blow her nose and compose herself. "Did you hear him fall?"

She sniffed and shook her head. "I…I had the sewing machine running. I thought I heard a bellow and I stopped to see if Leroy was calling for me, but then when he didn't again, I finished the seam."

"You couldn't have done anything," he said gently.

Tears overflowed. "I'd have held the ladder if he'd asked. He was so stubborn!"

That was one way of putting it.

"How did you learn that he'd fallen?"

Mopping her cheeks, she said, "The doorbell rang. It was Ron Blackman from next door. He said…he said there'd been an accident, that he'd called 911 already.'' Her voice faltered. ''That Leroy had fallen.''

By the time she got out there, neighbors had gathered and several had slid down the bluff to Leroy. She didn't actually remember who was there.

''Except Ruth Blackman. She had her arm around me.''

''But you knew everyone there?''

''All I could see was Leroy, crumpled against a tree.'' Fresh tears filled her eyes. ''I kept thinking he'd swear and sit up.''

Feeling cruel for making her relive her husband's accident, Diaz thanked her and made his escape. He was glad that in her grief she hadn't noticed the tenor of his questions.

The Blackmans, an older couple, were home next door. Their house, too, backed on the canyon.

Mrs. Blackman offered him coffee, which he accepted, and they talked readily about the tragedy.

''I heard him yell.'' A tall, gaunt man with stooped shoulders and close-cropped white hair, Ron Blackman shook his head. ''I was on the computer doing some research on a company I'm considering buying stock in. It took me, oh, a couple of minutes at least to get up and go out to the back deck.''

''As stiff as your back is,'' his wife put in, ''it might have been longer than that.''

''You saw him right away?'' Diaz asked.

''I might not have noticed him at all, if the ladders hadn't been lying on the rhododendrons.''

''Were you the first to see him?''

He considered. ''Well, I don't know. I heard a shout

from the other side of the Pearces'. Jack Gunn. I guess we met at the top of the bluff. Got there about the same time.''

"So you were the first two on the scene?''

Unlike Mrs. Pearce, he was putting two and two together and making four.

"Do you mind my asking why the questions?''

Diaz shook his head. "You've probably answered every one of these questions already. I apologize, sir. But even a simple accident gets investigated pretty carefully when it's a police officer who died.''

His expression cleared. "I understand.''

Diaz got the Blackmans to come up with a list of who had gathered in the Pearces' narrow backyard. They hemmed and hawed and went back and forth before agreeing, with only slight hesitation, on a final list of names.

"I wish we knew whether he had just reached too far, or whether something distracted him.'' Diaz closed his notebook. "Someone said they thought they'd heard him talking to someone a little earlier.''

"I did think I heard him talking,'' Ruth Blackman said, a little timidly.

"Really?'' Diaz hid his intense interest, keeping his tone casual. "Do you remember how much earlier?''

"Well…right before. I mean, I didn't think anything of it. The day was a little chilly and damp, so not that many people were outside working, but the mail had come in the past hour. I said hello to Margie across the street when I fetched ours.'' She added apologetically, "I can't swear it was him. Somebody might have been talking in another yard.''

"You didn't hear a second voice?"

"I don't think so. I just vaguely wondered who'd made Leroy mad this time."

So the voice wasn't conversational. "Obviously, you didn't glance out."

She shook her head, her expression regretful. "If I'd seen Leroy up there like that, I would have called for Ron to go insist he get down. What was he thinking?"

"His wife thought she'd talked him into hiring a service to clean the gutters. She knew it wasn't safe for him to do it."

Mr. Blackman spoke up. "When he hired someone to work for him, he was never satisfied. A couple of years ago, he was working so much overtime he hired a lawn service, but he said they didn't edge the lawn the way he liked and they overfertilized, so he's been taking care of it himself since."

There was a moment of silence as they all reflected on the fact that Leroy's widow would now be hiring out all those jobs he would have been doing if only he hadn't been an idiot and for all practical purposes killed himself.

Unless, of course, someone had given him a push.

Some neighbors weren't home. Others hadn't been home when Leroy died. Diaz did talk to Jack Gunn, who lived on the other side of the Pearces'. He came up with a different list of names of who'd been gathered to witness the tragedy. He shook his head and insisted that a couple of the people the Blackmans thought had been present weren't there, and added a few of his own. Diaz knew from experience that every other person present would remember the scene dif-

ferently, too. Neither, however, remembered anyone
being there that they didn't know.

Gunn, a beefy fellow in his forties, hadn't heard
voices before the accident, but admitted he'd been running a circular saw in his garage. "Stopped for a
smoke. That's when I heard Leroy yell and then fall."

"Did you see or hear anyone leaving the scene?"

His gaze was sharp. "Leaving? Didn't see anybody." He frowned. "Thought I heard a car engine
start up, though. Can't swear to it. Just an impression."

Back in his car, Diaz made notes of which neighbors
he had yet to interview. He'd do better to come back
on Saturday morning, when more people were likely
to be home.

He hadn't learned anything to prove Ann's hunch,
but he hadn't disproved it, either. Pearce might have
talked to someone in angry tones right before his fall—
or he might not have. Someone might have started a
car and driven away just as the neighbors were rushing
to the Pearces', but people did get in their cars and
drive away for legitimate reasons.

He wouldn't give up yet, but he wasn't convinced.

"THIS POT ROAST is wonderful, Mary." Ann sighed in
pleasure. "I don't do much real cooking."

Mary Roarke, a comfortable, motherly woman,
shook her head in disapproval. "You wouldn't be so
skinny if you did."

Ann grinned at her. "Actually, considering my
usual diet is Winchell's for breakfast, McDonald's for
lunch and frozen meals I can microwave for dinner,

my guess is I might actually lose weight if I started cooking good stuff.''

Mary shuddered. "My dear! I know you're young, but you need to think about your health.''

"I was kidding." Honesty compelled her to admit, "Partly. I eat more junk food than I should, but I actually start most mornings with a banana sliced on cereal, and I do have a vegetable with dinner." Sometimes. Occasionally. "And I keep fruit around.''

"Are we going to have dessert or not?" her husband interrupted.

Mary stood as if invisible wires had lifted her. As cheerful as if her husband wasn't glowering at her, she said, "Lemon meringue pie. Of course you'll have a slice, Ann?''

"Couldn't stop me," Ann assured her. She waited until the plump woman in her fifties had disappeared into the kitchen before she said to her father's old friend, "Reggie, I have something I wanted to ask you about.''

"Got to do with the job?''

"Uh…maybe. I don't know," she admitted.

Despite the couple of beers he'd downed, Reggie Roarke's gaze sharpened. "Is this something we want to talk about in front of Mary?''

"I don't know that, either. I was hoping you'd tell me more about your accident.''

His eyes bored into hers. "You got a reason?''

She hesitated. "I think I'd rather hear you tell me what happened first, if you don't mind.''

He took a long swallow of beer from the can, his

eyes never leaving hers. "All right. But let's leave Mary out of it."

His wife bustled back in with slabs of pie, dunes of meringue quivering above lemon filling. From the first bite, Ann forgot her purpose in being here. This pie was manna, the tart and sweet melting into a paean on her tongue.

Her husband ate his piece, grunted and pushed the empty plate aside. It was no wonder that Mary seemed so pleased at Ann's heartfelt compliments.

"I made two. I'll send you home with some. No, don't argue," she insisted, when Ann opened her mouth to make a polite if feeble protest.

"Ann's here to talk business," Reggie said brusquely. "We'll take our coffee into the living room."

Leaving Mary clearing off the table, Ann followed her dad's partner to the front room, dominated by his and hers recliners and a big-screen television set. He sat in his recliner and waited while she took his wife's. Ann found the effect rather strange. With both pointed at the TV, she had to turn her head to see him. She set her coffee cup to one side and saw that he'd brought a new can of beer instead.

"I remember hearing you talk about the accident once you were back at work," she began. "But the details didn't stick."

Popping the top off the beer, he said, "I've got a '71 'Vette out in the garage. Been restoring it for a while."

That day, he explained, he'd jacked it up so he could roll under it to perform some task that went right over

Ann's head. To her father's disgust, she had never become fascinated by the workings of a combustion engine. Car talk, a staple of poker games with his friends, had bored her so completely she hadn't even pretended to share his interest to please him.

"I was under the car when I heard footsteps coming into the garage."

"From the street?" she interrupted.

"Right. Thought for a minute it was Mary and I wondered why she hadn't come through the kitchen door, but she might have been out gossiping with a neighbor. I asked her what she wanted. Didn't get an answer."

"So this person was standing where your feet would have been sticking out from under the Corvette."

He shook his head before she finished sketching the scene aloud. "No. See, that was a strange thing. Whoever it was went to the other side of the car. I tried to twist my head to see the feet, but I couldn't. Whoever it was must have been behind the wheel. But I realized the footsteps hadn't sounded like a woman's. They were heavier than that. So then I started thinking, maybe it was Hank from two doors down. He likes to see how I'm coming. So I said, 'Hank, that you?'"

She nodded, watching his face to judge whether he was telling the truth and nothing but. So far, she saw only outrage and residual fear.

"That's when the car moved just a little. Scared the bejesus out of me, I can tell you!" His face flushed as he remembered. "'Hey!' I yelled. Something like that. Then I felt it rocking above me. I tried to shoot out from under there, but I didn't want to use the under-

JANICE KAY JOHNSON	61

carriage to move myself in case my push helped the bastard knock the 'Vette off the jacks. I was probably swearing.'' He took a gulp of beer. The hand that set the can down might have had a tremor. ''I didn't make it. Turned out Mary was at the grocery store and I'd forgotten. She found me when she got home.''

Ann nodded. ''You never did see feet, and the person didn't say anything.''

''Not a word.'' He shook his head. ''Nobody believed that someone pushed the goddamn car off the blocks. They figured I was a dumb-ass who didn't know how to jack up a car.'' He glared at her as if she'd expressed that exact opinion. ''But let me tell you, little girl, I've been working on cars since I was a kid. I know what happened.''

She wanted him to lay it out in blunt words. ''What did happen?''

''Somebody tried to kill me.'' His voice grated. ''And they damn near succeeded.''

''Pretty unusual way to commit murder.'' She pursed her lips and shook her head. ''Somebody happening to wander by, seeing you in a vulnerable spot.''

He didn't like doubt. ''The scum watched for his chance, that's all.''

''You have any ideas at all about who might want to kill you?''

He snorted at her naiveté. ''I've been a cop for thirty-two years! I've put away my share of slugs. They'd probably all raise a glass if they heard I was dead.''

''Okay. Let me put it another way. Who would want you, Leroy Pearce and my dad all dead?''

He stared at her, a man who downed too many beers every night but was still a cop, could still draw a line from A to B to C. Reggie Roarke breathed a word as ugly as his nose.

''You're thinking he murdered two of us and tried to kill me.''

Ann studied his expression of bafflement, anger, fear and something else she couldn't quite put her finger on. Something that interested her because it was secretive.

''And I'm thinking he might not be done. Someone else might be on his list. Depending on why he's mad. Also…'' Ann paused to be sure she had his full attention. ''I'm thinking he failed to kill you, which means he'll be back.''

Aluminum crackled and tore as he crushed his empty beer can in his meaty fist. In a hard voice, he said, ''And I'm thinking I'm done talking until you tell me what you know.''

CHAPTER FOUR

"So, what did you tell Roarke?" Diaz asked.

Today's lunch consisted of burgers, fries and milk shakes. Deserted when the two cops came in, the burger joint had filled like magic at noon. Empty booths on each side of theirs were now occupied by a pair of mothers with whiny toddlers and a morose teenager dressed in black and wearing a spiked dog collar around his neck.

In answer, Ann said, "Not much." She bit one end off a fry.

Her partner grunted in amusement. "In other words, you told him the truth."

"I was a little evasive. As if I knew more than I was saying."

Although he'd been about to slurp strawberry milk shake through a straw, Diaz lifted his head and frowned. "Was that smart?"

Surprised, she set down her fries. "Why wouldn't it be?"

"Let me ask this—why weren't you straight with Reggie?"

While she tried to find words to describe her unsettling feeling that her father's old friend had been hiding something, Ann watched the teenage boy in the next booth unwrap his second bacon cheeseburger. His world-weariness appeared not to be inhibiting his appetite.

"I don't know," she said after a minute. "There was something about the way Reggie got suspicious. As if…"

When she didn't finish, Diaz did. "As if he wondered whether you might be working with Internal Affairs."

"Yeah. He gave me this once-over, and I knew he was looking for a wire." She'd actually been afraid for a minute, until she remembered that Mary was in the kitchen loading the dishwasher and wrapping pie in plastic for Ann to take home.

Diaz balled up a wrapper. "If you asked me a few questions about who might hate me, I wouldn't get antsy. Because I'm not hiding anything."

"You think Roarke is."

He raised his brows. "Isn't that why you went to talk to him?"

She narrowed her eyes, not liking where he was going. "Maybe."

"If the two deaths weren't accidents, if somebody tried to kill Roarke and all three of these incidents are linked, odds are these aren't random attacks on cops."

"They could be." She scowled at him.

As relentless as an oncoming freight train, Diaz said, "If I'd been killed, and Pearce and…oh, hell, say, Dennis Fassett had been attacked, *that* might suggest random." Fassett was a fresh-faced recruit who had puked at the sight of the bloodbath in front of the biker bar last week. "Random doesn't hit three cops who've known each other and worked together for twenty-five years.''

She knew he was right, but she hated what he was suggesting. ''Dad wasn't dirty.''

''Didn't say he was.''

One of the toddlers in the next booth lost patience and started to wail. Voice sharp, the kid's mother tried to quiet him. When she didn't succeed, the two women, still gossiping over the sobs, collected their garbage, bundled their children in parkas and gloves and hats with earflaps as if this was Juneau in January, and finally left. The kid's face was turning purple as he screamed all the way to the door.

Ann muttered, ''Talk about an argument for abstinence. They should borrow that kid as an object lesson for sex-ed classes at the high school.''

Diaz laughed, real amusement crinkling the skin beside his eyes. ''I take it your biological clock isn't ticking.''

She didn't even know if she had one. She was still trying to figure out how girls got guys to ask them to the prom.

''Not if it means taking one of those home from the hospital.''

''They have their moments, you know.'' His smile had changed, become tender.

Ann's heart felt too big for her chest. Surreptitiously, she pressed her rib cage.

''Kids let you see the world fresh, through their eyes. When your baby smiles the first time, just for you, or you hear this giggle of pure glee, or you see understanding dawn on your little girl's face…'' He hunched his shoulders suddenly, as if embarrassed.

Damn it, her sinuses burned. She concentrated on her milk shake to hide emotions that embarrassed her.

Had her father felt that way about her, at least in the beginning? Had her first smile filled him with tenderness? Things had gone wrong, but she'd like to think he had loved her.

And Diaz… Why in heck did she turn to mush just because his eyes softened every time he mentioned his kids? Yeah, okay. It was a nice quality in a man. She was starting to think his ex-wife was an idiot. But she was not looking for a husband. Even if she had been, Juan Diaz wouldn't be on her list. So she really, really needed to stop with the knees-buckling, heart-swelling thing.

"Yeah, maybe someday," she mumbled.

He was looking at her in a way that made her shift on the hard plastic seat. "I'll bet you were a tomboy. I can see you. Baseball cap turned backward, sneakers, knees ripped out on your jeans. Not taking any crap from the boys."

He was right on, but she'd been like that because somehow, some way, she'd always known Daddy didn't really want a little girl. He wanted a little boy.

Until she'd turned sixteen and suddenly in his eyes she was supposed to be a girl—she sure as hell was never going to measure up as a son. Why wasn't she a beauty he could brag about to his friends? He'd have liked to make jokes about fighting off the boys, but it was painfully obvious to him and Ann both that no boys were interested. And she was still struggling to be that little girl in ripped jeans who didn't take any crap from the boys.

"Got it in one." She wadded up her garbage even though she hadn't finished her fries. "Can we go?"

Something flickered in Diaz's dark brown eyes, but he only nodded. "I'm done."

They were on the way to the hospital to talk to a woman whose husband had beaten the crap out of her the night before. Or so said the neighbors who had called 911 after hearing an escalating fight, crashes and screams. The woman hadn't been able to say anything; she'd lain unconscious on the floor, her face blood-smeared and distorted.

Ann and Diaz didn't do the average domestic disturbance call anymore. This one wasn't average. Gene Verger's first wife had been viciously beaten to death. Police had never been able to prove he had killed her. He'd claimed he'd found her when he got home from work.

When a 911 call with his address came in, it was like little red cherries all lining up. People who'd seen Marianne Verger's body had long memories.

His second wife looked grotesque. One eye was swollen shut; the other peered through a slit in purple flesh. One arm was in a cast, and the print of fingers was visible on her neck.

Ann took the lead. "Ms. Verger?"

The woman in the hospital bed gave the tiniest of nods, then winced. At least, Ann thought she had. With her face looking like a raw ribeye roast, reading expressions was a little difficult.

"We're hoping you can give us a statement about last night." Ann pulled up a chair.

Diaz stood near the foot of the bed, his notebook out. When the situation called for it, he was good at presenting himself as bland. Next best thing to invisible. This was one of those times.

Rochelle Verger studied him with what Ann took for suspicion, then turned her head on the pillow to scrutinize Ann.

"You're not wearing uniforms," she whispered, voice as damaged as her face and throat.

"No. I'm Detective Caldwell and this is my partner, Detective Diaz." Ann showed her badge.

She struggled to swallow before asking, in that hoarse whisper, "Why you?"

Ann chose honesty. "Because of your husband's history."

The woman didn't move for a long time. Finally, a tear seeped from her open eye.

"He's been arrested," Ann assured her. "He's behind bars."

"He... I fell. I always say I fell." More tears dribbled down her cheek even as her eye closed.

Ann touched Rochelle's lax hand. "He almost killed you."

She cried, her mouth opening as tears ran into it. Her hand turned in Ann's and clutched it in a painful, clawlike grip.

Never comfortable with emotional displays, Ann cleared her throat. "Hey. You're safe now. He won't get near you again." When that had no effect, she repeated, "You're safe. It's okay." Letting her hand be mauled, she kept murmuring the same things over and over. As if that would do any good.

At length the battered woman's grip loosened and the agonized contortion of her face relaxed. Ann reached for a tissue and said, "Um, do you want to blow your nose?"

The one eye peered at her again. The mouth twisted into what might have been a laugh. Rochelle Verger nodded and took the tissue.

She dabbed rather than blew, and even that must have been painful.

At last, in an exhausted, hoarse whisper, she said, "He killed her. He tells me he did every time he beats me. He says I'm lucky."

"Will you testify in court?"

The single eye fastened with heartrending intensity on Ann. "Do you promise he won't get off? That I'll be safe?"

At the foot of the bed, Diaz stirred.

Ann wanted, very badly, to promise anything. She wanted to twist Gene Verger's nuts until he screamed.

But that swollen, discolored face, tracked with tears, the desperate strength of the fingers that had probably bruised Ann's hand, stopped her.

"You know I can't promise. He should get several years for what he did to you. Whether he's convicted for murder depends partly on what he's told you."

The young woman who looked and sounded old started to whisper. Ann had to lean close to hear.

"He liked to talk about it. He liked to scare me. He told me everything."

Ann smiled at her. "Then you have the power to put him away for a lifetime. If you choose to use it."

The mouth twisted again, and this time Ann knew it was into an answering smile. In that raw whisper, she said, "I choose."

ANN HESITATED outside the bistro, then squared her shoulders and walked in. She bolstered herself with the thought that at least her eyebrows looked great.

"Ann!" Eva Pearce waved from a round table by the window. "Over here."

The hostess who had been about to waylay Ann smiled and gestured her ahead. Conscious of her plain navy slacks and blazer and solid, practical shoes in a way she wasn't usually, Ann crossed the small dining room, passing several tables of women who all seemed to have Eva Pearce's natural style.

"Thank you for coming." Eva smiled. "Gosh, I've been looking forward to this. We should have gotten together to commiserate years ago."

Some of the tension left Ann's shoulders. "You mean, to bitch?"

The blonde laughed. "Why didn't we? I so hated my father when I was about sixteen."

"I thought I loved mine then." The surprising admission just came out. Ann's mouth almost dropped open at the implication: that later, she hadn't loved him.

Or, at least, that she didn't want to love him.

Eva didn't seem surprised. "I had my phases, too. We never want to give up, do we?"

"I didn't want to even after Dad died," Ann admitted. "Isn't that pathetic?"

Eva blinked. "Okay, you have to explain that one."

Over glasses of wine and salads, Ann told her about the investigation that had been her father's obsession and which she'd taken over after his death. "I told myself I owed it to him. But really, I kept imagining myself standing at his grave telling him I'd arrested the son of a bitch." She shook her head. "As if...I don't know."

"You'd feel a ghostly pat on your back?"

Ann made a face. "Or some all-enveloping wave of pride. Heck, maybe a disembodied voice saying, 'You done good, girl.'"

Eva's laugh wasn't the expected ladylike tinkle. Instead, it was hearty and uninhibited. "Hey, you never know! Maybe death softened the old bastards up."

Ann snorted. "What are the odds of that?"

The other woman became pensive. "Do you ever wonder which direction they went?"

It was Ann's turn to give a startled laugh. "I actually hadn't thought about it. I haven't really gotten used to Dad being gone. I still have the sense he's looking over my shoulder."

"Why?" Eva shook her head. "Let me rephrase. What I mean is, do you feel like he'd want to linger? Are we really talking woo-woo here? Or do you have a hang-up?"

Ann heaved a sigh. "I have a hang-up." She had a sudden absurd image of herself standing up in front of a roomful of sympathetic strangers. *My name is Ann Caldwell and I have a problem.*

A dainty manicured hand with coral nails patted Ann's. "Tell Sister Eva all."

"This is supposed to be mutual," Ann protested.

"Oh, it will be. Believe me, I have hang-ups, too. But you first. You're more interesting."

Oh, yeah. That was her, Ann thought. Fascinating. Riveting.

"I seriously doubt it." She took a bite while she debated how much she really did want to confide in another woman. Sure, she'd casually known Eva since they were in kindergarten. But they'd never had a thing in common except their fathers, and they didn't now.

Too, she was only starting to understand what she'd felt for her father. Some people seemed to need to babble about their every passing twinge of guilt, lust, resentment or smugness. Ann had never had anybody to talk emotions out with. She knew, on some level, that she had to do some of that if she was going to have friends. But theoretical knowledge wasn't the same thing as breaking down in real life and pouring out her heart to someone she hadn't exchanged more than greetings with since they were in fifth grade.

But...she was here. Another woman had actually called her and suggested getting together. For once, Ann had looked forward to a day off, because she had plans that weren't solitary.

Now, *that* was pathetic.

"You had a mother," she said. "I didn't. I mean, not after she died."

Eva's delicate face hardened. "How true. You didn't have to watch your mother trembling with anxiety as she rushed to do your daddy's bidding because she was scared to death of him. Count your blessings.''

"Scared?'' Ann forgot her own preoccupation. "You mean…?''

"He hit her? Sure he did. Carefully,'' the other woman said, with something approaching hatred icing every word. "He wouldn't want anyone to see a bruise and ask questions.''

Remembering Rochelle Verger's damaged face, Ann felt the grip of rage. "Did he hurt you, too?''

"Once. That was the only thing that stiffened Mom's spine. She told him if he ever touched me again, she'd take me and leave. He scoffed, but I think he believed her, because he never did. We had horrendous fights when I got old enough to scream back at him, and a couple of times he lifted his hand, but he always thought better of it.''

"Wow.'' Food forgotten, Ann stared at Eva. "I never knew.''

"*I* was ashamed.'' Eva gazed with seeming blindness at her salad plate. "I never told anyone. My friends knew he and I fought, but I never told them that sometimes, when he got mad enough at me, he took it out on Mom.''

Shock whammed her like a steel door of which she hadn't stepped clear. "Oh, no! Eva…''

This new friend offered a twisted smile. "Pretty sick, huh?''

"You're making me glad he had plenty of time to know he was going to die.'' Seeing Eva wince, Ann closed her eyes. "That's a horrible thing to say about your father. I'm sorry.''

"No. Don't apologize. When I said I hated him most of the time, I meant it. Once I left home we worked out a civil relationship, but my teenage years were hell. I was so full of anger I couldn't restrain myself, and then the next morning I'd see Mom moving stiffly and I'd know." She shuddered. "I despised myself and him both. I was mad at her, too, for taking it. I will never understand…" Eva stopped. Let out a breath. "Mom won't even talk about it."

Ann bit her lip. "I almost envy you, being able to hate him like that. I've spent most of my life trying to figure out why nothing I ever did made my dad proud. Even when he did give a compliment, it was embedded with an insult. This time I'd done okay, unlike my usual, was always implied. I don't remember him ever, once, telling me I was great at something."

Or, God forbid, that she looked pretty. Sometimes she'd almost thought he was repulsed by her appearance. She had trouble remembering her mother, except in fleeting snapshots that might be illusions. But as a child she had pored over photograph albums, searching for some resemblance between herself and her delicate mother. Mostly she'd failed. Her eyes were her mother's, she supposed, and perhaps her height, but not her inconveniently large breasts or her sturdy figure. Not her thick eyebrows or dark hair or broad cheekbones. Compared to her mother, she was a gnome. A squat, homely creature that disappointed her father for good reason.

Or so she had thought as a child and as a teenager who could hardly bear to look at herself in a mirror.

Eva's face relaxed. "Maybe it isn't too late to learn to hate him. I'm convinced it's healthier."

"I can work at it." Ann took a swallow of wine. Despite herself, the cop that was so much a part of her was kicking in. "Do you think many people hated your father?"

Without hesitation, her lunch companion said, "Hordes. Armies. I don't really know, but I suspect. I used to wonder if he roughed up suspects, too. Why?"

Ann hadn't intended to share her suspicion with anyone but Diaz until she had to, but she couldn't think of any reason *not* to tell the truth.

"I've been wondering whether the accidents that killed our fathers were really accidents."

Eva stared at her with obvious shock. Ann had to explain, although she didn't tell Eva about Roarke's near miss and his abrupt switch from aggrieved victim to narrow-eyed secretiveness when he was questioned.

"Did you talk to my mother? She was home when Dad fell."

"Diaz did." Seeing Eva's blank look, Ann said, "Juan Diaz? My partner?"

Her face cleared. "Right. The guy who let me cry on his lovely broad shoulder."

So they weren't seeing each other. Ann had wondered. "I figured you'd hear from him." She shrugged as if she hadn't cared. "He seemed to enjoy having his arm around you."

Eva laughed. "Are you kidding? I probably terrified him. I saw him looking around before he spotted you. He wanted to be rescued."

That loosening in her chest was *not* relief, Ann told

herself. She didn't care whether Diaz was dating. Or who he dated. It was none of her business.

But for some reason, she *was* glad he wasn't seeing Eva. Like a child who didn't want to share, she liked the idea that this friend was hers, and hers alone.

She tuned in to realize that Eva was studying her frankly.

"I like your eyebrows. Did you go to someone?"

"You mean, you can do that to yourself?" Ann asked, appalled.

Eva laughed merrily. "It's not so bad when you're just doing touch ups. I keep mine from getting shaggy, and then go into the salon every once in a while for shaping."

"I'd be afraid to touch them myself. It hurt!"

Eva fluttered a hand, dismissing the pain. "The price of beauty. Don't you like the effect, though?"

"Yeah, I guess so." She'd spent a few days sneaking dubious peeks at herself in the mirror before concluding that she did look better. More feminine.

"I suppose you can't wear makeup on the job."

Ann shrugged. "I could as long as it was discreet. But I wouldn't want smudged mascara as the day went on, and most stuff would wear off." Nice excuse, considering her medicine cabinet hadn't been stocked with even the basics until her impulsive expedition last week.

"Were you working today?" Eva nodded toward Ann, presumably indicating her clothes.

A flush of embarrassment warmed her cheeks. "No-o. I was actually thinking of going shopping this afternoon." She hadn't been, but now that the idea had popped into her head, she thought she would. She didn't want to go home to her lonely apartment.

"Really?" Eva's face brightened. "Do you want company? I'm ashamed to admit how much I love to shop."

Ann's cheeks got hotter. "I'm...sort of a novice. I guess you can tell."

Of course, now Eva had to trip over herself apologizing for her assumption that Ann was wearing her plainclothes garb. "I sure know how to stick my foot in my mouth."

Humiliation made Ann's voice gruff. "I looked in my closet recently and realized everything in it is hideous. Maybe because of Dad, I...well, I've just never *tried*."

Eva got practical. "Can you afford a new wardrobe?"

Ann nodded. "I don't know what to buy." She heard her voice squeak and hated feeling so incompetent at something that came so naturally to other women.

Her new friend grinned at her. "Remember how much I loved playing with Barbie?"

Wary, Ann said, "Uh...yeah."

"You can be my Barbie." Eva gave that bawdy laugh. "I can see the whites of your eyes. Come on. We'll have fun. Trust me."

Excitement mingled with Ann's apprehension and embarrassment at needing help. This might be fun. Lots more fun than wandering helplessly through the department store by herself with no idea what might flatter her and no context for judgment even when she tried garments on.

"Okay," she surrendered. "If you're sure."

Eva lifted her hand for the waitress. "Oh, I'm sure."

ANN STAGGERED in her front door at six that evening, her arms so laden with bags she had trouble steering herself into the bedroom. She dropped them on the bed, then went back to her car for more.

She didn't dare let herself think about how much money she'd spent. Good heavens, she'd bought four pairs of shoes alone! She'd gone into some sort of frenzy. Every time Eva said, "Ooh. That looks fabulous!" Ann had given the same reckless response. "I'll take it."

Now she poked at bags, trying to remember what she had bought. Jeans, sweaters, V-necked T-shirts in paisley prints or embroidered or even decorated with beads. Dresses she couldn't imagine ever wearing, skirts and chinos and turtlenecks and even a bag full of fanciful socks from a store that sold nothing but. She seemed to remember a wool peacoat and a velvet "jean" jacket.

Maybe she was just tired, but Ann found herself staring at the pile and thinking, *I've gone out of my mind.*

Would she wear *any* of this?

And—oh, Lord—where would she *put* it?

Dinner. She'd have something to eat, and then maybe she could work up the energy to start cleaning out her drawers and the closet. She didn't have much choice now but to toss most of her existing wardrobe.

The phone rang just as she was popping open a cola for a quick energy fix. In the act of picking up the receiver, Ann indulged in a quick prayer. Please, please, not a summons to a homicide.

"Caldwell."

"Hey. It's Diaz."

Something skittered in her stomach, but she ignored it. "Tell me I don't have to go look at a dead body."

"What? Oh. No, that's not why I called."

"Uh…then?"

"You know our basketball league."

Ann sat down at her kitchen table. "Sure." She did vaguely know. No one had ever asked her to play on a team, even though the league was theoretically coed. The way gazes passed right above her head when teams were put together wasn't something she took personally. Even in high school P.E., she'd sucked at basketball. She was too short, and when a pass hit her in the chest it *hurt*.

"At a game last night, I heard the edges of a story that might have something to do with…" His voice got muffled, and Ann heard a giggle in the background. When he came back, he said, "You know. Pearce and your dad."

Her stomach knotted. "Yeah?"

"I guess it can wait. You're probably busy."

Oh, sure. Hot date, she thought. *Me and my closet.*

"I've been out all day. I'm not busy now. All I'm doing is poking around my kitchen looking for something to eat."

"You wanna come over for dinner?"

She held the phone away from her ear and stared at

it. Had he just asked her over to his place for dinner? As in… No. Jeez. Don't get ideas, she told herself. Cops went to barbecues at each other's houses. They went out for beer. They *socialized.*

"Your kids with you?" she asked.

"You heard that wicked giggle, huh?" A smile sounded in his voice. "Yeah. I've got 'em for the night. We were just putting together dinner. Chicken burritos."

Her stomach rumbled. Chicken burritos sounded better than whatever frozen something she'd have found in her kitchen.

"If you're sure you have enough."

"Hey, I invited you, didn't I?"

"I'm on my way," she said.

She was halfway to the front door when she caught sight of herself in the embossed tin-framed mirror she'd unwisely hung above a bookcase. After pulling sweaters and dresses over her head all afternoon, she looked like she had bedhead.

Detouring to the bedroom to brush her hair and restore it to its usual bun, she caught sight of the heap of bags on her bed and froze, a deer undecided which direction to spring to safety.

What better time to wear one of her new outfits? Diaz wouldn't know it was new. They'd never gotten together on days off before. If she picked something simple, he wouldn't think anything of it.

Simple. She fumbled through the first bag, discarding every possibility on sight. Nothing with a fringe of beads around the neckline. No to the airy linen skirt.

Ann grabbed the next bag, rooted through it and

tossed it aside. Where were the jeans? She found a pair, decided they looked too stiff and new without being washed first. Bags slipped to the floor as she searched, changed her mind, tossed clothes aside.

She finally settled on a pair of chocolate brown cords with a subtle boot cut and a cream-colored cotton turtleneck sweater. It was more, um, formfitting than she remembered, she realized uneasily a minute later as she eyed herself in the full-length mirror she usually ignored. Her waist looked tiny—she liked that. But the bosom she'd spent years doing her best to disguise stuck out like…like Dolly Parton's.

Ann almost chickened out, but in the back of her mind she remembered Eva's delight.

"Wow! Here you turn out to be the one with a figure like Barbie's, and I'm an A cup."

Eva hadn't sounded as if she thought Ann looked out of proportion or that she'd be embarrassing herself showing off a figure that was about as far from fashionably ethereal as a woman could get.

Finally, she went for broke, putting on a pair of boots with inch and a half heels and grabbing the ruby colored velvet jean jacket. Makeup, he'd notice. The rest of this, she was making too big a deal about. A sweater and cords were nothing. Everyday clothes for most women.

Faking confidence, she went out the door. Tonight was a good test. If she found out nobody else even noticed her new wardrobe, she could quit feeling shy about wearing it.

CHAPTER FIVE

DIAZ KNEW he was in trouble the minute he opened the door. If he were honest, he should have been worried earlier, when he caught himself singing while he stirred Mexican rice. He'd been pleased with himself, looking forward to Caldwell coming over.

The rumor he'd heard could have waited another day.

"Hey," he said, stupidly.

She breezed past him with no more than a smile over her shoulder. "Smells great."

He turned in slow motion, mouth open. Even the rear view of his plain, possibly chunky partner was enough to blow him away. Curvy ass nicely encased in pants that fit, legs longer than he'd have guessed, a dark gleam of sleek hair above wine-red velvet. And the front... He could hardly wait for her to turn around so he could test his eyesight. He couldn't have seen...

Yeah. Yeah, he had. Even in profile as he circled her he saw the kind of breasts men dreamed about.

Why in *hell* had she been hiding that kind of body for years?

"You look..." Incredible. Fabulous. Sexy. He was still groping for the right word, the one that would flatter instead of insult, that wouldn't qualify as sexual harassment, when he saw her cheeks flame.

"Different?" She nodded at him. "So do you."

He glanced down. Sure, he wore jeans, deck shoes without socks and a thin V-necked sweater with the sleeves shoved up.

"Yeah, but you're…" Diaz shook his head. He was making a fool of himself. And her uncomfortable. "You look really pretty," he finished, embarrassed at the inadequacy of words he'd have said to Elena when she wore a new dress.

Caldwell hunched her shoulders the way he'd seen her do a million times and mumbled, "Thanks."

"Can I hang up your jacket?"

She hesitated long enough he had the idea she didn't want to give it up. Finally, with the enthusiasm of a perp surrendering to a pat-down, she peeled it off, revealing a ribbed sweater that clung lovingly to every glorious curve.

He couldn't believe he'd been so blind.

And he wished like hell his eyes had never been opened. He'd never be able to look at her the same again.

"Your father was an idiot," he said.

She stared at him. "What?"

Why didn't he know when to keep his mouth shut? "Uh…I was thinking of what you told me that time. About him saying a cosmetology school wouldn't want you."

"Oh." She blushed again. "Thanks. I think. I mean, if you're saying…"

"That you'd be a good advertisement? Yeah, that's what I'm saying."

She pressed fingers to her cheeks. "I don't even have makeup on."

Tearing his gaze from her chest, he looked at her face and said, "You've got incredible eyes. You don't need it."

Dark lashes fluttered, veiling those vivid blue eyes. Her rosy cheeks kept him from being convinced by her light, amused tone. "No wonder I always hear women's voices in the background when I call on days off. You're smooth, Diaz."

Smooth? He felt incredibly clumsy. Afraid to say another word. Afraid to step too near her, for fear he'd touch her and not be able to stop.

"Wow." He shook his head. "I'd better check on dinner."

"Where are the kids?"

"In their bedroom." Diaz raised his voice. "Elena! Tony! Come meet Cald..." He cleared his throat. "Ann."

Oh, crap, he thought. He wasn't going to be able to think of her by her last name anymore, either, a nice distancing device. Something that put her in the buddy and colleague category. Made her one of the guys.

Tonight, no way was she one of the guys.

His kids burst out of the bedroom, Elena bumping Tony into the wall, him bumping her back. Diaz winced when framed photos hung in the hall trembled as if in an earthquake. Ann—Caldwell—was going to think they were hellions.

Flushed with triumph, his daughter reached them

first. Shaking his head, he put a hand on her shoulder
and turned her to face Ann. "This is Elena. And…"
with his other hand he found his son "…Tony."

"Hi. Um, your dad talks about you."

Elena fixed dark eyes on his guest. "What does he
say?"

Ann looked alarmed. "Just…that he misses you.
And, um—" she was obviously groping "—that
you're more like him and Tony is more like your
mom."

Elena gave a self-satisfied nod and a smirk at her
brother, who said, "At least I'm a *boy!* You're just a
girl."

Diaz tightened his grip on her shoulder when he felt
her tense to spring.

"I'm not!"

"Are!" Tony insisted, pleased with the effect he'd
had on his big sister.

"Not!"

Diaz rolled his eyes.

To his surprise, Ann bailed him out. "Elena's right.
She's not *just* anything."

"Huh?" Tony was distracted enough to look at her.

"What's *just* a girl mean?" She sounded as if she
really wanted to know. "I'm a girl, but I'm a cop like
your dad. So am I *just* a girl?"

Tony might be only seven, but he was smart enough
to know when he'd gotten himself in over his head.

He offered Ann a winning smile. "You're different."

"How so?"

"Um…" He shot his father a look of pleading.
"You're grown-up and…and she's not?"

"Trust me," Ann said. "She'll grow up, too. Yeah, she's a girl. You're a boy. So what? Neither of you are 'just.' Okay?"

"Okay," he mumbled.

Elena, of course, was glowing with pleasure at the squelching her brother had taken.

"It's very nice to meet you," she said, in her best prim and proper voice.

"I'm glad to meet you, too." Ann smiled at her. "And you, Tony."

Tony tilted his head back. "Is dinner ready? I'm hungry."

"Almost." Diaz released them. "Scoot. I'll call you when I put food on the table."

They crashed back down the hall and disappeared with a whoop.

Diaz gave Ann a rueful grin. "I know you're not used to kids. My two aren't always so combative."

"That's okay. They seemed like nice kids."

He doubted she was sincere.

"I shouldn't have said that," she added. "It wasn't any of my business."

Diaz lifted his brows. "About Elena 'just' being a girl? Why not? She needs to hear it, and so does he. Their mom is more..." He hesitated, finally choosing the tactful out. "Traditional, I guess. She didn't work until Tony started first grade, and she's a hairdresser. More into male/female roles. The kids tell me stuff, like Tony's job is to take the garbage out and only Elena has to set the table."

"And you don't approve?" Ann followed him to the kitchen.

"No. For one thing—" he lifted the lid of the kettle and sniffed the beans "—even men should be able to cook for themselves. And women should be able to change a tire or the oil in their car."

Ann crossed her arms and leaned against the cabinet. Her smile was soft and amused. "You're telling me you think every human being should be able to take care of him- or herself? Dang, Diaz. You're progressive."

"Don't make fun of me."

"Why not?" The smile metamorphosed into an open grin as she cocked a brow at the oven mitt he'd stuck his hand into. "You're so cute in the kitchen."

"You're going to ruin my reputation," he grumbled, pulling the warm tortillas from the oven.

He'd never seen her in a mood like this. She kept teasing him while she helped set the table and carry food out. He had trouble remembering she was his partner. Detective Caldwell was a sexy woman. Who'd have thunk it?

The kids bickered amiably over dinner, but also dragged Ann into conversations despite her awkwardness with them.

"Yeah, I've been up to Mt. St. Helens," she agreed in response to a question from Tony, who was currently fascinated by volcanoes and dinosaurs. "Haven't you?" She pinned an accusing look on Diaz. "You should take them. Up there, you can really imagine the power that it must have taken to rip half a mountain away."

"Dad says he heard it erupt. He said it was like somebody slamming something against the house."

"I don't remember hearing it, but I've heard other people say the same."

"Wouldn't it be cool if Mt. Rainier erupted?" Tony's awed expression gave away his fantasy of flaming lava and ash that blackened the sky and people running away screaming as if Godzilla stalked the streets.

"Actually, no." Ann sounded apologetic. Her eyes met Diaz's. "Lots of people would die. It's awfully close to Seattle and Tacoma."

He heaved a sigh. "I know, but I want to *see* a volcano erupt. *Kabooom!*" He flung up his arms to accompany the sound effects.

Elena smirked, as if she were immeasurably more mature than the little brat with whom she was forced to live.

"As I keep telling you—" Diaz removed Tony's elbow from his plate "—there are scientists who travel around the world to watch volcanoes erupt in places like the Hawaiian islands. If you stay interested, maybe you'll get a chance to do that."

Tony subsided with only a few rumbling sounds of lava spewing.

"Mommy permed my hair," Elena announced. "Do you like it?"

Diaz hated it, but had refrained from saying so.

Ann smiled politely. "It's nice."

"You could get a perm."

"I actually like mine straight. It goes more smoothly into a ponytail or a bun."

And it reflected the light with the rich gleam of a horse's dark coat. To him, a woman—or girl—with a perm looked like a cake overwhelmed with fussy frosting. He'd been speechless when he saw that his little girl's glossy black hair had been frizzed. But, damn it, what could he say to Cheri? *You can't alter her appearance without my agreement?* Yeah, that was going to fly.

"Is your hair really long?" Elena asked, scrutinizing Ann with a practiced eye. "Mom says if you have long hair you need to trim the tips and shape it."

Ann had that spooked look again. Something told Diaz she'd last trimmed the tips sometime before she'd joined the force.

"I'll remember that." Hastily, as if she really, really wanted to change the subject, Ann asked, "What do you want to do when you grow up? Do you want to be a hairdresser like your mom?"

Boy, did Diaz hope not. He had grander ambitions for both his kids. His generation—two of his sisters, his brother and he—had been the first in their family to go to college. He had hopes Elena and Tony would be professionals: doctors or professors or CEOs. He'd been sure from the minute each was born that they were smart enough.

"No." Elena shook her head. "I get bored watching Mom work. And she says she'll get varicose veins standing all day." Tiny, puzzled creases fleetingly appeared on her forehead, suggesting that she didn't know what a varicose vein was. "I like to read. A lot. Mom says if I don't get my head out of the books I'll be wearing glasses and need laser surgery on my eyeballs—" She ignored her brother's delight at the idea of slit eyeballs. "But I don't care. Since I like to read so much, I might be a teacher and help little kids read, or a librarian or…" She left the sentence hovering, having perhaps run out of notions of what a grown person could do for a living that would involve nothing but reading.

Ann pursed her lips. "Hmm. Maybe you'd like to be an editor. The person who decides what books will be published and then helps the author make them as good as possible."

"Or the author," Diaz suggested.

"You mean, like, *write* stories?" His daughter's back straightened and, in an instant, she had a queenly air. "I do make up stories. In my head," she explained. "When I'm trying to go to sleep."

"You might try writing some of them down." Diaz smiled at her. "Doesn't your teacher ever have you write stories?"

Elena shook her head. "Mrs. Reynolds did last year, but Mr. Oroyan says we shouldn't make up stuff. We need to learn *facts*. So we do reports."

Mr. Oroyan sounded dull as a stakeout to Diaz, but mild guilt stopped him from criticizing. He'd missed the November parent-teacher conference and therefore had never met Mr. Oroyan, who might, for all Diaz knew, be a passionate, committed teacher who just happened to favor history and science over fiction writing. Maybe he felt students had plenty of chances to indulge creativity in their day-to-day work.

"*I* get to write stories in class," Tony announced. "Yesterday, Miss Major let us write a different end for a book she read us. It was stupid."

Diaz's mouth twitched. "Let me guess. You made a volcano erupt and the sky go black."

Tony stopped midgulp, milk dribbling out of the corners of his mouth. "How did you know?"

"I figured it was that, or a T-Rex broke up the happy ending."

His son finished swallowing. "They were smooching. A T-Rex would have been fun, too."

Ann smothered a laugh. Amusement brimmed in her eyes and dimples flickered in her cheeks.

He set the kids to cleaning up and poured coffee for himself and her. As she accepted hers, Ann said, "The burrito was wonderful. I didn't know you were a cook."

He shrugged. "My mother taught me. My repertoire is limited, but I do a damn good job within it."

She laughed again. "I'd say something about modesty, but…"

"But you're way too awed by my cooking skills." He let her see his smugness.

"Of course that's it," she agreed, eyes sparkling above the rim of her coffee cup.

In the small living room of his apartment, she curled one foot under her at an end of the couch. He sat in his easy chair nearby. Not that there was a lot of choice; Cheri had kept most of the furniture after the divorce, and he'd never bothered to buy more than the necessities, and those at garage sales or import stores. Why waste money, he'd reasoned, with some vague idea that eventually he'd have a real home again. So far, he hadn't been stirred to think about anything like buying a house. The apartment was okay; he wasn't here that much anyway. It was mostly important when he had the kids. He wanted them to feel this was home as much as their mom's place was.

The living room looked a lot homier with a woman here. Maybe especially with a woman who was both familiar and not. Whose warning signals he could read, whose motives he couldn't. It was actually weird to look at her and see Caldwell, his prickly partner from the job, and Ann, a sexy woman, all at the same time.

To shut down his own unsettling awareness of her, Diaz said abruptly, "I know you didn't come just for dinner."

She immediately shrugged. "It's not like we socialize."

He'd been safer, in some way he didn't want to analyze, before he'd made the mistake of inviting her to dinner. But even though this stir in his groin scared the crap out of him, he wasn't sorry he'd asked her. He had liked seeing her laugh and enjoy food he'd made and talk to his kids like they were human beings.

"No reason we can't," he said.

"No reason we have to, either," she shot back.

That stung.

He shrugged, too, as if he didn't give a damn. "You can always say no."

Discordant as this silence was, bringing the causes into the open wasn't an option. He could just imagine her face if he said, *I wanted to see you tonight. That's why I called.*

He didn't even know if that was true. Or why it was true.

Irritably, he thought, *Get to the point.*

Nodding toward the kitchen, he said, "The kids won't pay attention to what we're talking about. Here's what I heard last night. Ellison—do you know him?"

Ann nodded.

"We were sitting in the bleachers waiting for the game ahead of ours to end, and I heard him talking behind me. He said something about what a shame it was that Pearce died, and how with the good ol' guys gone real justice was being knocked to her knees. I turned around and asked what he meant. I must have looked too eager, because first he mumbled something about all that legal crap in court and cops that were less experienced."

"Lawyers do get scum off."

"Sure they do. They also keep us honest."

"Maybe," she conceded.

Returning to the story, Diaz said, "I got into the spirit of it and grumbled with him. He opened up. Said some of those old guys had more guts than the rest of us. Said when a vic deserved what he had coming, they just turned away. Probably smiled."

Her voice rose. "He claims Pearce and my dad didn't write up assaults they thought were justified?"

"Claimed to know of one. Date rape, and the girl's father beat the shit out of the guy, who staggered out to the road bleeding and flagged them down. According to Ellison, Pearce told the bastard he was lucky the father was protecting his daughter and hadn't reported the rape. 'You're lucky to be alive,' is what he said, according to Ellison. 'If it had been my daughter, you'd be on your way to the morgue right now.'"

Ann sat in silence for a long moment, eyes dilated, hands clasping the coffee cup as if for warmth. At length, she said, "Eva says her father beat her mother." Her eyes abruptly came into glittering focus and alarm sharpened her voice. "I shouldn't have said that. It's confidential."

His mouth had curled in disgust, and he gave her a scathing look. "You really think I'd tell anyone?"

"I shouldn't have betrayed a confidence."

"It's relevant."

"No, it isn't. All it does is confirm what we already suspected—Leroy was an SOB."

"Maybe," Diaz suggested, "he thought a man's family was his property."

Her response was acid. "His to beat or not?"

"Something like that. But by God, no one else had any right to touch them. That might've been his idea of honor."

She shook her head, not in disagreement but as if she were repudiating the very idea that the bastard would've recognized "honor" if he'd encountered it.

"You're saying my father was with him. That the two of them drove away and left this guy bleeding on the sidewalk."

"No. Here's the interesting part." He paused. "Ellison mentioned Pearce and Roarke."

She didn't move, but her lips parted and he could see her thinking. Hard.

"So *I* said, 'Yeah, but Roarke isn't dead. Caldwell is.' And he grinned and told me the two of them weren't the only ones who had their own way of seeing that justice got done."

Ann set the coffee cup down with a click. "He's lying," she snapped.

Remembering Ellison's satisfied smile, Diaz didn't say anything. Sooner or later, every cop had to arrest someone he wanted to let walk, just like he had to let a bastard free even though he knew he'd kill again, or hurt another woman, or enlist some innocent kid to run crack for him. Maybe enough years on the force eroded your willpower. Maybe you started believing you knew more about justice than did the legislators who enacted laws or the judges who interpreted it. You might decide they wouldn't understand justice until they'd been behind the counter of a small store that had been held up fourteen times in less than a year. And maybe you didn't know it was time to retire when the line between law and Biblical justice smudged along with distinctions between the role of law enforcement and courts.

Ann glared at him. "I hate it when you don't argue!"

He met her eyes. "I was just thinking that either your theory is wrong, and what looked like accidents really were accidents, or you were right." He paused. "And that means there has to be a why."

Ann looked away. The sounds of running water and clatter of dishes from the kitchen were magnified. Diaz swallowed lukewarm coffee and waited while she thought it out.

"It couldn't have been this guy."

"The bloody one on the sidewalk? No. Not unless your dad somehow got involved, too."

"You're thinking they might have skirted the law regularly." She wasn't happy.

"I don't know," he said in honesty. "But if you once did what you secretly wanted to, and you enjoyed seeing this guy's broken teeth and rearranged nose, the temptation the next time might be greater. You know he's not going to call 911, he's already reported the crime to the police and they scared him, suggesting he was lucky still to be alive. Even if he didn't rape the girl, if it was consensual and now she's just scared to tell her daddy, he's thinking the cops aren't going to believe him. So he goes home, puts ice on his jaw and resolves to be one hell of a lot more careful who he has sex with the next time. Meantime, Pearce and Roarke are getting a glow. This time, the right person got punished. Some lawyer didn't get him off, while the father went to jail for doing what any father would do."

Ann stifled a sound.

Inexorable, Diaz continued. "They might even start looking for chances to make the right thing happen again. Could be they'd even consider taking a more active role next time. Say, beating the shit out of someone who deserves it, in their eyes."

She stared down at her own hands. In a stifled voice, she said, "That sounds like my father. He always thought he was right. Once, when we were arguing, I said, 'You aren't God,' and he laughed. 'Maybe not, but I'm betting when I get up there he pins another medal on my chest.'"

Making his voice gentle, Diaz said, "They were three of a kind. Your dad, Pearce and Roarke."

She thought of the crowd that often surrounded her larger-than-life father at the bar where he hung out. Since joining the force, she'd worked with many of them, and knew them to be honorable, people who'd gone into law enforcement for the right reasons. But his closer friends, all men, the ones who'd come to her house to play poker, drink beer and talk…

She lifted her head, face pinched. "There's others, you know. Not just those three. Dad had a circle. I'd hear them laughing about things that turned my stomach. I couldn't say anything, because…"

When she stopped, Diaz finished. "He'd say you didn't have the goods to be a cop. You were a sissy."

Her shoulders jerked. Both sat silent when the kids called, "We're done, Dad!" and raced down the hall to the bedroom.

Familiar rage filled him. Shame tangled with it. "Is that what you thought I was suggesting when we got assigned and I said I hoped you had your old man's goods?"

"Sure it is. You weren't asking whether I was smart. You wanted to know if I had his guts, his attitude."

He tried to remember what he'd been thinking and failed. The comment had been offhanded. A challenge. Tough-cop speak. You didn't say "welcome," you swaggered.

"Maybe it is what I was asking," Diaz admitted. "I believed then that your father was a good cop. I'd seen a few things I didn't like, but I thought that's because he was a different generation. Mostly, I thought he cared."

"I think he did," Caldwell's daughter said, low and

tired. "He was just willing to take a different route to what he saw as justice."

"We don't *know*," Diaz started to say, but she interrupted.

"Don't we? I wanted to think Dad's investigation of Lofgren was sloppy. He made mistakes. We all do. But there were too many. Obvious leads he ignored. Because he'd made up his mind." Her voice was hard now, angry. "Craig Lofgren killed his wife, and Dad was going to see him behind bars. I'm guessing he'd have manufactured evidence if he could have figured out how. He'd have sold his soul for a drop of Julie Lofgren's blood."

Diaz had lost respect for Sgt. Caldwell once he got deeply enough involved in the Lofgren case. Caldwell had been celebrated for his persistence. He was the cop who wouldn't give up. Wouldn't let the murdered wife be forgotten.

But somewhere along the way Diaz realized Ann's father hadn't given a damn about Julie Lofgren. All he'd cared about was vindicating his own investigation, his own dislike of Craig Lofgren. He'd seen it as a contest, one he was determined to win.

Diaz frowned at the inevitable, unavoidable thought: It had been mighty convenient for Lofgren to have the cop who was persecuting him die in an automobile accident.

But when he spoke it aloud, Ann shook her head.

"I thought of it then. Lofgren was in Mexico City."

"He could have hired someone."

"Sure, but then what about Leroy?"

Diaz frowned, trying to remember. "Who was with your dad on the Lofgren case?"

"Birkey." Her mouth twisted. "Who is, unfortunately, alive and well."

"You don't see him as a beloved uncle?"

"He used to corner me sometimes. When I was twelve, thirteen. Crowd just a little too close." She shivered, then reached for her coffee as if trying to hide the involuntary reaction. "I wanted to think I was imagining the way he looked at me."

Anger roughened his voice. "But you know you weren't."

"No." She was moving again, untucking her foot, readjusting her position, so that somehow she didn't have to meet his eyes. "I wasn't."

Diaz pictured her, young, motherless, trying to be tough to please a father who wouldn't appreciate her no matter what she did. She'd have worn baggy shirts to hide breasts that made men look at her in ways she didn't understand.

And he'd wondered about her prickles. He shook his head now. How else was she, vulnerable without her father's ready ear, pride and faith, to protect herself?

"You make me want to bury my fist in his nose."

Ann gave a short, sharp laugh. "Then you understand the temptation."

"To mete out your own kind of justice?" He grunted. "Of course I do. Don't you?"

She nodded, but her brows knitted as if she wasn't so sure. Diaz reminded himself she was younger, hadn't been in law enforcement for very many years.

Maybe she still had a crusading spirit. Maybe she hadn't yet had to make an arrest—or not make one—that left her feeling like something that ought to be scooped, put in a little bag and shoved in the nearest garbage can before the stink became unbearable.

"This means digging through old cases."

"We may not get anywhere," he warned. "We're talking twenty-five, thirty years worth. The relevant one might be recent, but it's also possible someone just got out of the pen with revenge on his mind."

"The whole idea may still be wacko," she reminded him. "Accidents do happen."

Diaz didn't have to hesitate to know what his gut feeling was. "Call me whatever you want. But I've got to tell you, 'accidental' as an explanation is satisfying me less and less."

He barely heard her murmur. "And here I'm wishing I *had* been satisfied with it."

"Why?"

She gave him a sad, crooked smile. "Because Dad's cronies were the closest thing to family I had. Investigating them doesn't feel right."

It went against the grain, but Diaz had to offer. "We can close the book right now if you want."

"You mean the can, don't you?" She stood. "But worms are already wriggling out. I think maybe it's too late."

Rising, too, he faced her. "The offer stands."

She tried to smile. "Thanks. I'll…think about it."

She stuck her head in the bedroom down the hall and said goodbye to the kids, told him again that dinner had been great and left.

Standing in his living room, feeling her absence, he wished he thought she had a single person besides him she could trust enough to talk about this with.

Hey, what was to say she altogether trusted even him? Why should she? It didn't sound like she'd ever been able to depend on anyone, at least since her mother died.

Prickly, Ann Caldwell might be, but she was also the loneliest person he'd ever known.

God help him, if his children hadn't been here, he might have followed her home and asked her to let him in, so that he could make sure she was never lonely again.

Swearing under his breath, he started down the hall to tell the kids to get ready for bed.

CHAPTER SIX

THE NEXT WEEK was notable mainly for a late season snowstorm that dumped six inches on the ground in Seattle and Tacoma and up to a foot in outlying areas. Major crimes plummeted to near-nonexistent, while traffic fatalities soared.

"It's supposed to be spring!" people kept complaining.

Diaz and Ann spent much of the week surreptitiously scanning old case files, since unplowed roads and black ice on the ones that were plowed limited their ability to pursue other investigations.

This morning the snow was nearly gone, but temperatures had dropped into the twenties overnight. Diaz was shivering despite gloves and a muffler when he locked his car in the garage and hurried toward the station. His breath hung in a frozen cloud before him. He felt sorry for the patrol officers dispersing to their units; the roads were solid ice.

"You hear the news?" one of them called to him.

"News?" He turned, chin buried in his wool muffler.

"Don Birkey was found dead this morning."

Stunned even though he'd known another death was possible, if not inevitable, Diaz asked for details.

Armed with what seemed to be common information, he went straight to Ann's desk, where she was reading off the computer monitor while she scrolled with her hand on the mouse. He paused for a moment, before she noticed him.

She looked tired, and he wondered how late she'd stayed the night before and how early she'd come in this morning. They hadn't gotten far this week, and she was impatient. He had to resist the desire to circle behind her and give her a shoulder massage.

Keeping his hands to himself was a hell of a lot smarter.

Diaz pulled off his gloves and made his voice brisk, as though he'd just walked in. "Hey."

Ann looked up with a start. "What? Oh. Jeez, my eyes are crossing." She rubbed both hands across her face.

He dropped into the chair beside her desk and unzipped his parka. "Find anything?"

The slump of her shoulders was dispirited. "Who knows?"

He couldn't think of a way to ease into it, although he didn't like telling her about the death of another of her father's old friends. "There's been another accident."

She stared at him. "Who?"

"Birkey."

The sound she made might have been a gasp or a sigh. "Is he…?"

"Dead? Yeah."

Her eyes closed momentarily. "He was a creep, but…"

When she trailed off again, Diaz said, "But you've known him all your life."

Her small, painful smile told him he was right. "I guess that's it." She shook her head as if to clear it. "What happened?"

"A neighbor found him. I guess his house is isolated."

She nodded. "It's more of a cabin. Right on the Green River. The houses are strung along the highway there. Some of them are just summer places, so they'd be empty right now."

"Well, so far as anyone can tell, he froze to death. It looks like he came home late and locked his keys in his car. He apparently broke a pane of glass with a rock, then took his coat off, maybe to pad his arm while he cleared the shards so he could climb in. Appears he slipped climbing on an icy wood pile, banged his head and froze to death right outside his own house."

Ann just waited, lips parted, face white.

"They're saying he was drunk," Diaz said baldly. "That's why the neighbor pulled into his drive this morning. They were at the same bar last night. Neighbor worried about Birkey's driving, but didn't stop him. Stewed all night, decided to reassure himself on the way to work by checking on him. Birkey probably passed out and just didn't wake up."

She processed that. Nodded. "He liked his booze. But…"

"You're thinking it wasn't a very reliable way to kill someone?"

He'd gotten good at reading her mind. She bit her lip and nodded again.

Diaz continued, "Birkey had a knot on his head. Either he passed out and knocked his head on the way down, they're saying, or he slipped and bumped his head. Nothing that would have killed him, but..."

"As cold as it was last night, he wouldn't have had to be unconscious very long."

"No."

She frowned. "What were the odds he'd do something stupid like lock his keys in the car last night of all nights?"

"Our guy seems to be patient. Who knows how long he's been watching Birkey?" He cleared his throat. "Of course, that's only one possibility."

With their gazes locked, Diaz could see in her eyes the thoughts crowding each other for a place in line.

"It could have been staged. Knock him over the head, drag him over..." She stopped. "There should have been enough snow that any other footprints would be visible."

"Don't know."

She nodded, accepting the gap in the scenario. "Break the window, lock his keys in the car, drive away." She paused, making a humming sound as she considered some more. "If they weren't careful, it's probably too late to look for tire prints."

"Once the neighbor drove in, then an ambulance, probably a squad car... Yeah. I'd say so."

Ann let out a ragged sigh.

"It sounds crazy."

"Yeah." He tossed his gloves onto her desk in a fit of frustration. "I know it does."

"But you believe he was murdered."

"Don't you?"

They were still staring at each other when Engen, balding and only months from retirement, wandered in, rapped his knuckles on the desk, said, "Lieutenant wants to see you," and wandered back out.

Ann's eyes widened in alarm. "Has he noticed what we're doing?"

"Maybe he thinks we aren't doing anything," Diaz reasoned. "Could be we're going to get our asses chewed because he thinks we're hanging around in the warm office playing solitaire on our computers."

She gave a choked laugh. "We might as well find out."

"Sure."

But neither of them moved for another thirty seconds or so. He was the one to finally groan and rise. He still had on his parka when Ann filed behind him into Lieutenant O'Brien's cubicle.

He scowled at them. "Shut the door."

Ann did so.

"Sit."

Diaz took off his parka and sat in one chair. After a brief hesitation, Ann sat beside him. Their shoulders brushed.

"You heard about Birkey?"

Both nodded.

"Damn fool."

Not sure what the appropriate response was, Diaz said nothing. Beside him, Ann, too, chose silence.

The lieutenant pinned her with a stare. "He was a friend of your father's, wasn't he?"

She nodded. "Yes, sir."

"Seems to me Pearce was, too."

Again she hesitated; again she nodded.

"I checked your computer last night, after you went home."

Diaz felt her stiffen.

"Care to tell me what in hell you're up to?"

"I, um, I..." She didn't once glance sidelong at Diaz. Her voice firmed. "You know I've always been interested in my father's cases."

Eyes narrow, gaze never leaving her, O'Brien took a toothpick from the cut glass bowl full of them he kept on his desk since he'd quit smoking. He put one end in his mouth where it stuck out like a single tusk.

"Half of what you were looking at weren't your father's."

Diaz couldn't tear his gaze from the toothpick, bobbing like a metronome. Beside him, he could feel Ann settling on a lie.

But it apparently stuck in her throat, because the silence drew on. He sneaked a glance to see her staring at that damn toothpick, too.

He thought they were in over their heads and it was time to be honest, but as he'd told her earlier, this one was her call. Her father, her hunch, her emotional investment. He was only the sidekick.

Into the silence, her words fell like small stones. "There've been too many accidents."

The toothpick paused, then went back to bobbing. "You started thinking this before Birkey died."

"My father, Pearce, Roarke." She ticked the names off her fingers.

His eyes flickered. "Roarke. The car fell on his head."

"Yes, sir. He told everyone who would listen that someone walked up to the car and started rocking it."

The lieutenant grunted. "Your dad's accident was pretty straightforward. Blood alcohol above the legal limit, he didn't make a bend in the road."

"He drove carefully when he'd been drinking," Ann argued. "And there was a furrow down the side of his truck that troubled the mechanic. No one listened."

That unnerving gaze swiveled to Diaz. "Your take?"

"Sir, I know it sounds…" He hesitated.

"Wacko," his partner said helpfully.

"A little crazy," he conceded. "But, like I told Caldwell, if these were genuine accidents, they should have been random, striking officers from recruits to detectives. Instead, the focus is narrow. These men were friends, they'd worked together over the years, they were all in the same age range, same seniority. So, no, sir. I don't think these have been accidents."

"You didn't go to Internal Affairs because…"

Ann spoke up. "Sir, it's headed by another friend of my father's. Merrill and he went way back. I believe he was at the bar the night my dad didn't make it home."

The eyes flickered again. The lieutenant's voice remained deadly polite. "And I suppose you put me in the same class?"

"Actually, no, sir." Ann was firm, unafraid. "You may have worked with him at one time, but the victims were all drinking buddies of Dad's. The kind of friends you share secrets with."

His voice became as icy as the pavement outside. "Then why in hell didn't you come to me?"

"Because...well..." She sucked in a breath. "We really thought the idea was nuts. Diaz was indulging me when we first started asking questions."

"But now Birkey's dead, too."

"Yes, sir."

Lieutenant O'Brien let out an explosive sigh and ran a hand across his close-cropped gray hair, the first sign of emotion beyond impatience with possibly renegade inferiors.

"No one else has connected the three deaths yet, but sooner or later someone will."

They both nodded.

"Do you believe it's internal?"

Ann and Diaz exchanged a glance. He shook his head. "No, sir. Not exactly."

"Innuendoes annoy me," the lieutenant remarked.

Diaz nodded. "Sir. Here's what we're thinking."

Taking turns, he and Ann described their speculations from the beginning, including the conversation on the bleachers at the basketball game, and their subsequent delving into old cases.

"The trouble is," Ann finished, "it's next to impossible to learn anything. There are no obvious flags. Or there are too many. I look at a case where they didn't pursue an allegation of rape. Why not? I look at another case where they arrested a suspect who was then convicted and given twenty years. Was there an angry spouse who sincerely believed her husband was innocent? Who knows?''

"Skip the arrests and convictions. If your suspicion is correct, these men were seeing that 'justice' was done in another way."

Diaz blinked. Was their superior officer giving them permission to investigate on the public's time?

Ann didn't seem to notice. ''But we may be making a big assumption,'' she pointed out. ''Every perp we put away is a potential enemy. And relatives hold grudges.''

O'Brien leaned forward and planted his elbows on the desk. ''That may be true for all of us, but we're looking at a cluster of particular victims here. Law enforcement officers who you have reason to believe may have become...if not vigilantes, certainly willing to turn a blind eye when their brand of justice called for it. Was there an organized group? How many officers belonged?'' Eyes piercing, he looked from Ann to Diaz and back again. ''How many more murders can we expect?''

''I'd expect Reggie to have another accident,'' Diaz said. ''It's pretty obvious our killer wanted these to appear to be accidents. Roarke couldn't have a second one too close to the first without someone wondering. But now it's been, what, five months since the car fell off the block. He's a logical next target.''

''Two deaths within a matter of weeks.'' The lieutenant shook his head. ''Maybe this guy doesn't care anymore whether we start an investigation or not.''

"Or maybe," Diaz suggested, "he just couldn't resist two irresistible opportunities."

Ann knew what he meant. The lieutenant raised his brows.

"What if you'd been watching Pearce," Diaz suggested. "Hoping for a good opportunity. It's a cold, gray day, so neighbors are staying indoors. But Leroy, he goes out, wires two tall ladders together—he did it in the driveway, by the way, where anybody could have seen what he was doing—then carries them back, leans 'em against the house and climbs up. If he falls, he won't just come down in the yard. No, he's above the canyon. Not much chance he'd survive that fall. If you were watching, and you wanted him to die, how could you resist? Quick stroll to the back yard, one push, you're back in your car by the time anyone hears the crash."

They were both staring at him.

"So you turn your attention to Birkey. Or maybe you've been watching him off and on, too. I don't know. But, see, you've found out right away that his house is isolated. You don't want to commit an obvious murder, so you're not sure how you can use that fact, but then this last brutal slap from winter strikes. Birkey, he doesn't go home in daylight, hustle into the house and lock the doors. Nah. He meets a couple of buddies at a bar and gets plastered. Staggers out late, weaves his way home, and you see the kiss of opportunity. Drunk people do stupid things, like lock their keys in their car. Right? So you maybe pass his car, and are waiting for him at home. Or you pull in right behind him, you say something like, 'Just noticed your

tire is almost flat' and he turns to look. You hit him.
Not too hard, just enough so that he drops. The rest is
easy enough to stage.''

The lieutenant turned his head, spit out his toothpick
into a wastebasket, and stuck another into his mouth.
He chomped it as he thought.

''How do these tie together? If we've got one killer,
with one grievance, then he feels wronged by more
than a pair of officers.''

''We're looking at incidents where more than two
were involved,'' Ann offered.

''Were they ever on a task force together?''

Ann faltered, ''I...don't know, sir.''

Diaz all but whacked himself in the head. Why
hadn't they thought of that?

''Your dad got tapped for a couple of serial killer
investigations. Sergei Belenky. Do you remember that
one?''

Who could forget? The Russian immigrant had tar-
geted teenage girls. He got five before one escaped
him.

The lieutenant frowned into space as he trawled his
memory. ''Birkey was involved in that mess when
Captain Danner killed his wife.''

The whole department's reputation had been damaged when Danner apparently beat his wife to death.
The family claimed in a lawsuit that Rosalie Danner
had called 911 several times claiming her husband was
abusing her, but no one took her seriously. Any more
than they had when, a couple of years before, she'd
gone to the hospital with broken ribs and a ruptured
spleen and told her doctor her husband was responsi-

ble. He'd called the cops, Danner denied her hysterical claim, which she withdrew shortly thereafter.

"Dad was one of the officers who interviewed her at the hospital." Ann's voice was tight, stripped of emotion. "I remember him saying she was drunk. Said she took a swing at him when he questioned her story."

"There was that other mess," the lieutenant said. "A couple years back. The aide—or was she an intern?—who claimed the county councilman raped her. Remember?"

Diaz was hazier on that one. He had been working undercover at the time, infiltrating a gang. His marriage had been going on the skids, in part because he was so seldom home, and when he was he'd changed. That was the longest he'd ever had to maintain another persona, and he'd known every day that he was walking a razor edge of danger. One slip, and somebody would find his gutted body under a freeway overpass. He'd been edgy, preoccupied, tired. He lived for the couple of days a week when he dared to go home, but when he got there he couldn't make an easy transition to father and husband. Going stir-crazy as a single parent of toddlers, Cheri wouldn't even try to understand. Anything outside his world of gang dealings and marital discord hadn't registered.

"Remind me," he said.

"She was young," the lieutenant said. "Twenty-one, twenty-two. Dated frequently, might have had an active sex life. That depends on who you believed. The councilman abased himself, admitted to an affair, his wife nobly and publicly forgave him. You know the drill. Big investigation, inconclusive result. Her father was on the news every night frothing at the mouth.''

Ann sounded thoughtful. ''He did make threats, as I recall.''

''Look into that one.''

Diaz rested his elbows on his thighs. ''Sir, are you authorizing us to continue our investigation?''

''I am.'' He leaned back in his chair and took the toothpick from his mouth. ''Quietly, for now. I've never heard even a whisper about Captain Merrill, but I also can't argue with your reasoning. We could trumpet this—we may want to, at some point—but for now I'd rather not alert the killer that we're suspicious about these deaths. I'll come up with a cover for you to ask questions about old cases. Let me think about it. In the meantime, get out to Birkey's. He's one of my men. Say I sent you to find out what happened.''

Somewhat dazed, Diaz and Ann retreated. He shrugged back into his parka and waited while she fetched hers, then led the way to their unmarked car.

In it, he started the ignition, then sat with it running while the engine warmed up. The steam of their breath clouded the windows, creating icy fronds on the frozen glass.

Staring straight ahead, Ann said, ''Well, that was unexpected.''

He gave a short laugh. ''That's one way to put it.''

''I really *didn't* think he might be involved in anything Dad and his cronies were up to. Did you?''

''I considered and dismissed the idea. The lieutenant is too insistent on procedures and detailed reports. I've never gotten even a hint from him that it might be okay to let regulations slide. Plus, I remember getting a feeling a couple of times that he didn't much like your father.''

Her head turned sharply.

"Sorry." He shrugged. "There wasn't any reason to say anything until now."

Ann grappled with what he'd told her, nodded at last with visible reluctance.

"Now what?" she asked, after a long silence.

"Now we go stick our noses in where they don't belong."

She remembered how to get to Birkey's and directed Diaz. The farther out of town they got, the more snow had fallen. By the time they reached the cabin, he was having to concentrate hard on driving the snow-packed roads.

Ann didn't have to tell him where to stop. Emergency vehicles clogged the narrow driveway that cut into forested land that blocked any view of the house or river. Diaz pulled—carefully—to the side of the highway and left his flashers on.

Getting out, he tugged on his gloves. Shaking his head as they crunched along the snowy shoulder, Diaz said, "Tire tracks are history."

Ann didn't have to reply. The medical examiner's van blocked in a fire truck, an ambulance, two squad cars and an unmarked police car. Birkey's SUV and a pickup truck were parked closest to the cabin. Damn near a whole precinct had turned out at news of another tragedy befalling one of their own. Diaz felt ghoulish by his very presence.

A patrolman nodded and let them pass when they

showed their badges. The house, when it came into view, looked like a summer place: small, ramshackle, apparently built piecemeal. Diaz could tell that what had once been a screened-in porch had been enclosed and it looked like a couple of additions had been added with cement blocks and posts beneath. Moss crept over the cedar shake roof, and the dark shingled exterior needed a new stain job. Diaz could see right away why responding officers had assumed Birkey had fallen; the cabin was built high off the ground, perhaps because of frequent high river levels. He wouldn't have been able to reach even a front window from the small stoop.

Apparently reading his mind, Ann said, "There is a deck out in back, but those windows would be into the main living area. He might have decided to break the window to an unused bedroom that could be shut off."

Larry Maslow, who Diaz and Ann both knew, turned from a huddle of officials at the sound of their footsteps crunching on snow. "What in hell are you two doing here?"

"O'Brien wanted a report." Diaz shrugged. "Up close and personal."

"Besides..." Ann shoved her hands in the pockets of her parka and stared past Maslow at the packed trail in the snow that led around the corner of the cabin. "Birkey was a friend of my dad's."

"Yeah, you must have known him forever." Maslow jerked his head in the direction she was looking. "We haven't moved the body yet. You sure you want to see him?"

''I guess I do.'' She managed to sound a little broken up about the death. ''Do you mind?''

''Nah. Go right ahead.'' Dismissing them, he rejoined the cluster of firefighters, EMTs and cops that were either conferring or gossiping, their collective breaths rising like a mushroom cloud from the huddle.

Diaz followed Ann around the corner, where a dark figure sprawled on the trampled snow. A stack of firewood that extended the length of the house had caved in just beneath a window, so that split pieces of alder lay strewn around the body.

Okay, logical, Diaz thought. Birkey decides to climb the stack of firewood to reach the window. It collapses, he strikes his head, freezes to death. As an accident, it was believable. Stupid, but nowhere near as stupid as Leroy Pearce's stunt with the ladders.

The medical examiner was packing up. Shaking his head as he passed Diaz and Ann, he said, ''You two get off on this stuff? Can't stay away?''

Hunched in his parka and concentrating on getting his gloves on without dropping his bag, he didn't wait for an answer. The couple of cops standing nearby looked cold and morose. Ann and Diaz approached, careful from habit to step in other footprints.

''Either of you the first here?'' Ann asked.

''Yeah, I was,'' one of them said.

''Can you tell me what you saw?'' she asked. ''He was a friend of my dad's.''

Young, rawboned and carrottopped, Officer Levenkron shivered and stamped his feet. ''Pretty much what you see. We haven't moved him.''

''I understand a neighbor called.''

He nodded. "Right. Guy's still here. He's inside. He was waiting for me out front, led me around here. He's real broke up about it. Says he should have driven Detective Birkey home last night."

"What did he do this morning, follow Birkey's footprints?"

"Nah, there wouldn't have been any. There sure weren't when I got here. The thing is, here along the house there was already a trail trampled in the snow. I figure the detective had been coming out for firewood regularly since the snowstorm."

She nodded encouragement.

"I figured my first obligation was to be sure the victim, er, Detective Birkey, was really dead."

"That's true," Ann agreed.

"And he was. I mean, he's *stiff.*"

"I can see that." Although she hadn't, in fact, taken a long look at all, Diaz had noticed. She'd glanced, then pretended to be examining their surroundings.

"Anyway, this neighbor said when he didn't get any answer to his knock, he walked around the house just to peer in windows." He gazed at the body. "He wouldn't have felt anything, would he?"

"Except for the bump on his head?" Diaz shook his head. "Doesn't look like he ever stirred."

Birkey's gray head lay inches from a piece of firewood upon which blood was frozen. He could have knocked himself out when his head connected with it. It could just as easily have been used as a weapon.

Glancing at Diaz, Ann nodded toward the river. "Want to walk around that way?"

"Sure." Why not? Appeared everyone else had done so.

They followed a track that circled the body before disappearing around the cabin. There, a blue plastic toboggan lay next to steps leading to the deck. The bed of the toboggan was battered and littered with bark and splinters. Birkey had used it to haul firewood.

They went up the steps onto the small deck, where rusted metal showed under a heap of snow. Diaz took a closer look. A barbecue kettle, he decided.

The view from up here was nice: deep green forest, silent and snowy, and not twenty feet from the edge of the deck, the river gurgling between frozen banks. Only one other roof could be glimpsed on the other side of the river, and that would probably disappear when the vine maples were leafed out in late spring and summer.

The cheap aluminum sliding door behind them opened, and Maslow stuck his fleshy face out. "You want to warm up?"

They went in, although Diaz felt himself cringing at the glimpse, uninvited by its owner, into another cop's life. He hadn't liked Birkey, but the other man still deserved more dignity than he'd been left with, his body sprawled obscenely out in the snow and a bunch of near-strangers standing in his living room, looking at the empty beer cans and crumpled bags that had held Doritos and barbecue potato chips.

Or maybe he didn't deserve any dignity, Diaz thought, remembering Ann's story about how Birkey had cornered her.

"Did he have kids?" Maslow asked.

Ann shook her head. "He was married, but he and his wife got a divorce back when I was, oh, nine or ten. I don't know if they stayed in touch. I don't really remember her."

Maslow shook his head. "Damn stupid way to go."

Three cops had died—and one had narrowly escaped death—doing something stupid. Their killer was taking advantage of his victims' own carelessness. Diaz wondered if he even saw it as murder, or thought of himself as merely helping them along a little.

If there was a killer at all.

"This is Mark Comack," Maslow was saying. "He's the neighbor who found Detective Birkey."

Comack was maybe forty, with the look of a beefy high school linebacker going to fat now. His dark hair was shaggy and he wore a beard that he kept fingering.

"If I hadn't waited... Followed him home..."

"You thought he was too drunk to drive?" Ann asked.

He moved uneasily, shrugging and ducking his head at the same time. "It wasn't like he was staggering. You know. I just thought maybe he'd had a couple more than usual."

"Getting loud, was he?" Maslow said, with a knowing grin that offended Diaz.

Comack frowned. "Nah. He was kind of quiet, actually. Broody. He'd been like that lately. He almost seemed..." He stopped.

"Seemed?" Ann asked.

He did the twitching, shrugging thing again, as if his body was apologizing for his words. "Scared." Expression startled, as if he hadn't known what he was going to say, he shook his head. "No, not that. Worried, I guess. I thought maybe he was having heart trouble or something like that he didn't want to talk about. You know?"

Maslow raised his brows at Ann and Diaz.

"I never heard anything like that," she said.

"Hell, maybe he had a premonition," Comack said gloomily.

"A couple of his friends have died this past year." She glanced at Maslow. "My dad and Pearce."

He nodded, his face clearing. "That does make you feel mortal."

The neighbor looked relieved, too, as if she'd provided a satisfactory explanation for the fear he'd sensed but had a hard time putting into words.

Ann's gaze met Diaz's, held for a long moment. They both knew what the other was thinking.

Yeah, a man would start feeling mortal. Especially if he started wondering whether those friends had been murdered. If he had an idea why they might have been but couldn't tell anyone, he'd get to feeling an itch between his shoulder blades. A habit of listening at night for creaks that weren't natural.

Knowing your name might be next on a killer's list would make anybody broody. Real careful, too, if he was smart. Unfortunately, Birkey had done something stupid instead: he'd tried to drown those worries in booze.

Thereby guaranteeing his death.

CHAPTER SEVEN

ANN STARED OUT the side window as Diaz drove. She didn't feel like talking.

Today had been...weird.

Don Birkey dead. Not long ago she'd said it was too bad he wasn't. She felt bad, remembering that. She hoped nobody up there had been listening. Seeing Birkey lying there, skin blue, frost white on his lips and open, staring eyes, had really bothered her. She was used to seeing bodies, but not ones belonging to people she'd known when alive.

Shutting her mind to that image, she made herself move on. More weird. Lieutenant O'Brien listening as if what she and Diaz said made sense, then okaying a continuing investigation. *Did* any of it make sense? Ann swung between certainty and doubt just about every hour, on the hour.

Diaz saying he'd had the impression the lieutenant hadn't liked her father. *Everybody* had liked Dad! Everybody except, sometimes, her. And she hadn't even admitted that to herself until recently. Then, she'd known only that he made her feel inadequate. She hadn't even resented his belittling. Instead, she'd scrambled to find the magic accomplishment that would change his disappointment in her into pride.

She pictured her father, walking down the hall, grinning, slapping backs, other cops drawn to him just to say a few words. He'd never been alone; others trailed him, fetched coffee for him, sat on the corner of his desk, asked his opinion, his advice, his blessing.

He was bigger than life, her father.

She turned her head to look at her partner. "Did *you* like my father?"

He glanced at her, surprise flickering in his eyes before he concentrated on the road again. "I thought he was a good cop."

"That's not what I asked you."

Her arms were crossed over her chest, and she realized she was still cold. Deep down chilled, despite the heat pouring from the vents.

"He was entertaining." Diaz still spoke with restraint. "But I thought he was arrogant. He didn't respect the dead or the people he dealt with. We all say insensitive things sometimes. But most of us don't cross a line. He could be cruel."

She'd always defended her father. Ann waited for the flare of indignation, because Juan Diaz had dared to criticize the man who had filled her world.

It didn't come.

Yes, Sgt. Michael Caldwell had been capable of enormous cruelty. He'd slice her deep with a few devastating words, then be astounded and irritated if she showed distress.

"For God's sake! Toughen up," was his favorite advice. That *he* might have said something wrong or hurtful was never an issue; she was soft because she'd flinched. If he'd thought about it at all, he would have insisted he was doing her a favor helping her create emotional callouses.

Life, she thought, had been a giant, continuing game of chicken for him, and he'd always won.

Until…

The word jumped into her mind, and her back straightened. Until that night, when someone had somehow challenged him, and he wouldn't back down. Wouldn't brake, pull to the shoulder, shake his head at the idiocy of other drivers. Not her father. Hot-tempered even when he was sober, he'd have decided to show the punk who had guts.

"That's how he was murdered," she marveled aloud. "It was that simple."

Diaz turned his head to stare at her until he suddenly swore and wrenched the wheel. Muttering an expletive, he said, "How in hell did you get to that?" Then, not waiting for an answer, "How was he murdered?"

"If you'd watched him drive, you'd know. He didn't speed for fun, but he didn't like punks—that's what he always called them—cutting ahead of him. He hated being passed, even when it was legal. I've seen him speed up just to keep them from going by. Or edge his car over during a traffic slow-down to make sure someone else couldn't use the shoulder to exit."

Diaz grunted with interest. "You're thinking a 'punk' tried to pass him that night."

"You could rile him first. Crowd his bumper. Maybe flash your high beams a couple of times. Boy, did that piss him off." She almost smiled remembering, understanding the beautiful simplicity of it. In a cosmic sense, the *justice* of it. Using his weakness, in a way she'd never mastered.

"Get him steamed, so when you move over into the other lane, he speeds up."

"Right. You go faster, he goes faster. He's darting looks at you, not remembering that sharp curve in the road ahead. After all, he'd had a couple of beers." She could see it: the narrow, dark country road with a faded yellow line down the middle illuminated only by headlights, two vehicles racing side by side, her father's sneer. He'd have been exulting because he was winning—until the moment his headlights caught the wall of trees ahead and he remembered that near right-angle bend. Then he might have braked, figured he could still make the turn.

"That's when the other driver bumped him. Just a scrape, but enough to leave him fighting for control. And he wasn't wearing a seat belt."

"Idiot." Diaz shot a glance at her. "Sorry."

"A cop who doesn't wear a seat belt." She shook her head. "What else can you call him?"

"Have you talked to the mechanic?"

"Yeah, he's got some paint samples for us. Charcoal-gray. He says the furrow along the side is high enough that the other vehicle had to be another pickup or an SUV. Something like that. Not a sedan."

"You sending the paint sample for analysis?"

"I haven't because I didn't want to raise questions." She pursed her lips. "Should I now?"

Diaz tapped his fingers on the wheel. "If we can figure out a way to do it without saying where those samples came from."

Ann nodded.

They were creeping along in a line of cars, Diaz keeping a safe distance between his bumper and the Honda in front of him. When a light turned red ahead, cars fishtailed on the ice as they braked.

With some drivers, she might have been tense, her foot working the floorboard. Diaz drove with such relaxed competence, she'd quit glancing over her shoulder before lane changes. In fact, they'd fallen into a pattern in which he drove most days. She hadn't even thought to resent it.

She hated it when this happened, when she suddenly started thinking about *him*. Feeling him beside her.

Ann sneaked a look at him, the fan of tiny lines beside his eyes, furrows carved beneath nose and mouth, creases becoming permanent on his forehead as middle age neared. Mexican heritage showed in wide, blunt cheekbones that reminded her of statues she'd seen of Olmec or Aztec gods.

His skin was darker than hers, his eyes a deep brown. A bit over six feet, he was broad and strong, with big square hands and shoulders bulky enough to intimidate most perps. Besides playing basketball, she knew he ran and worked out with weights to stay fit. It showed.

Damn it, she thought. *Why him? Why now?* She imagined how appalled he'd be if he guessed that sometimes just looking at him made her belly heat or her heart skip like a kid trying to miss a crack in the sidewalk. It was getting worse, harder to dismiss now that she had to admit she liked him.

Liked him? She turned her head to stare out the side

window so he couldn't see her expression. Weirdly, he was the closest thing to a best friend she had right now. She'd told him stuff she'd never admitted to anyone else. She could *talk* to him. Say almost anything and know he wouldn't ridicule her, that he'd give her a chance.

Like this thing with her father. She had taken a couple of days to marshall her arguments so she didn't sound too crazy. Even then…well, if someone had presented her with the theory, she'd have called it crackpot. But Diaz had taken her seriously, which made her go mushy inside.

Ann wished she just *liked* Diaz. She wished the liking and gratitude weren't getting tangled up in trust, which was way more complicated. Better yet, she wished she didn't have a serious case of lust. She'd had crushes before, but even the one guy she'd slept with in college hadn't caused heat between her legs just seeing the way his mouth tilted or his hand flexed on the steering wheel. She had it so bad, she'd considered going to one of Diaz's basketball games just to see him with his shirt off.

This itchy feeling made it hard to say casually, "You busy tonight?"

"Huh?" He glanced her way.

Oh, good. Asking once had been hard enough. Ann cleared her throat and went again for that "Hey, I don't really care" tone. "You busy tonight?"

He gave her a friendly leer. "Finally noticed my manly charm, did you."

A rude snort came more naturally. "You know,

Diaz, you'd better give it up. If you weren't hot ten years ago, you ain't ever gonna be.''

"Who says I wasn't?" he demanded with a show of indignation. "Women went into mourning on my wedding day."

Being able to laugh felt good. "Well, here's news. I wasn't one of them. Ten years ago, *I* thought you were an old guy. Kinda lumped you with my dad."

He groaned and clapped a hand to his chest. "Jeez! You know how to wound a guy."

"I'm a cop. They teach us that at the academy."

This grin was amiable. "If you're not asking me out, what do you have in mind?"

"I'm supposed to have dinner at the Roarke's. I wangled an invitation from Mary. She thinks I'm starving on my own cooking." At his sidelong assessment, Ann bared her teeth. "Not a word!"

Diaz just laughed. "You're going to chat up Reggie, huh?"

"That's the idea. Not about his accident. Just get him talking about his career."

"Say, task forces he might have served on?"

"Subject might arise."

"Are you suggesting I come?"

Be dense, why don't you? She shrugged. "If you're interested."

His tone suggested skepticism. "You're just going to show up with me in tow."

"Mary told me to bring a friend."

Ann didn't tell him how hard she'd worked for that invitation. How she'd giggled—giggled!—when Mary asked if she was seeing anyone. She'd played coy until

Mary said, "Now, you bring your young man to dinner with you."

Diaz gave her a second assessing look, his dark eyes inscrutable. "You know how Reggie will take it."

"He might be suspicious," Ann admitted.

"Or think we've got something going."

"Yeah, you're right." She frowned, as if she hadn't thought of the possibility. "Dumb idea. I just thought you'd be interested in hearing him reminisce."

"Actually, I would. Which means we *want* him to think we're seeing each other on the side, so he doesn't get suspicious and clam up."

God. Her palms were sweating. "You want me to blush when you help me take off my coat?"

"Hey, wouldn't hurt." Diaz sounded cheerful. "Do you know how?"

"To blush?" Damn it, her cheeks were heating right now. "Hell, no! I'll just titter behind my hand."

The creases in his cheeks deepened as he smiled. "Oh, this is going to be fun."

Her heart was pounding as hard as if she were seventeen and waiting for a boy to agree to go to Homecoming with her.

"So, you want to come?"

"Hell, yes. What time?"

"Six."

"I'll go home and change and pick you up at 5:45."

She shrugged while her blood sang. "Sure."

OKAY, IT WASN'T A DATE. But it felt like one.

Ann changed clothes four times, going from the simplest of her new garments to the most daring and back again. Turning this way and that in front of the full-length mirror, she tried to remember why she'd bought a shirt that swooped so low in front she looked like one of those yodeling barmaids with her bodice cinched so tight her boobs spilled over the top. Only, Ann didn't have to cinch. Hers were eager to spill from her brand-new periwinkle-blue satin bra, only a distant cousin to her usual stern maiden-white cotton harnesses.

Okay, skip that shirt until she got a whole hell of a lot braver. If ever. She pulled it over her head and tossed it onto the bed, reaching for a sweater that looked safe before remembering she'd worn it to Diaz's house that other night for dinner.

Muttering under her breath, Ann rooted through drawers. She found a white sweater, knit with an open, airy weave, and tried it over a long-sleeved powder-blue T-shirt that fit tighter than her own skin. Of course, that meant ditching the first pants—black—in favor of a pair of bleached jeans. Her bed was disappearing under the heap.

She studied herself dubiously. The effect wasn't as modest as she would have thought. The sweater had a tendency to…well, not cling, but *drape* in a way that had had Eva rhapsodizing but made Ann want to hunch her shoulders and hope no one noticed. On the other hand… Damn it, she wasn't going to hide under ugly blazers her whole life!

She used some of her vast stock of makeup. Just enough to enhance her eyes and add a little color without, she hoped, being noticeable. She was getting better at this, she decided, studying the result. She brushed her hair and reached for her usual band to pull it into a ponytail, then hesitated. What if she just left it down?

Panic rippled down her spine. She was going to look like she was dressing up for Diaz. She'd probably make him uncomfortable. Reggie would make jokes about her down at the station, making her sound pathetic. Desperate.

She was actually shaking, there in front of the mirror. *Breathe!* she ordered herself. In through the nose, out through the mouth. *Slow. Don't hyperventilate.*

Why would Diaz think she was dressing up for him? By most women's standards, what she had on was ordinary. If she hadn't spent her life as a fashion retard, she wouldn't be questioning her choice. It was past time she started shocking people a little anyway! Unless she wanted to go from living like an old maid to being one, she needed to shake up everyone's view of her.

Starting with her own.

Buoyed by the defiant mood, she ran the brush through her hair again, gave her head a shake, and turned away from the mirror without letting herself take a last anxious look.

The doorbell rang before she could chicken out again. Ann grabbed a purse—also new—and stuffed a few necessities in it. She couldn't help marveling that they *were* necessities—she'd never needed to take a hairbrush or lipstick anywhere with her. Still bemused, she opened the front door.

It was Diaz, of course. Ohmygod, was all she could think as her mouth worked like a guppy's. In a leather blazer, white shirt and jeans, he looked good. No, great. Fabulous. No, sexy.

Could a mind stutter?

And she couldn't seem to squeeze a single word out of a throat that had closed as surely as if a noose tightened around it.

His voice was quiet. "You look beautiful."

Swallow. Speak. She could do it.

And she couldn't, didn't dare, take him seriously. The preservation of their working relationship was at stake. She had to sound amused.

"Practicing? You're good. Reggie'll buy it."

Diaz shook his head. "Caldwell, you don't know how to take a compliment."

"I—" Oh, blast it, her voice squeaked. Before she could think, she blurted, "I haven't had…" Humiliation hit her like a blast from a fire hose, shutting her up. Thank God. She'd been about to admit to more than she wanted anyone to know. Especially Diaz.

"Anybody to encourage you to smile sweetly and say, 'Thank you'?" He reached out and fingered a strand of her hair, sending a wave of heat through her. "Let's try it again. Repeat after me: 'Thank you, Juan.'"

She *needed* a blast from that fire hose. The colder the better.

His knuckles brushed her jaw.

"Thank you," she whispered. "Juan."

She'd never said his name before. He'd never asked her to.

"Soft," he commented, letting his hand drop. Without, she prayed, noticing her burning cheeks. "Ready to go?"

"I need to grab a coat."

The charcoal wool peacoat was new, too. She'd felt elegant in it when she'd tried it on in the store.

Ann was reaching her hand for the first sleeve when she felt Diaz behind her. He held the coat while she slipped into it. She bent her head and pulled her hair out, letting it tumble free. Still standing behind her, Diaz straightened the collar and smoothed the wool over her shoulders.

"Got your keys?" he asked, apparently so used to helping women with their coats that he thought nothing of their nearness.

Wordless, Ann picked up her purse and held it up.

"Good." He stepped out. "Lock up."

"I'm a big girl." Goodie for her, she almost sounded normal.

"I hope you're careful," he said. "Living alone."

"Diaz." Now that he was a few feet away, she was starting to *feel* normal. "I'm a cop. Remember? I keep a gun next to my bed. The neighbors all know I'm a cop."

"You're also a woman."

"Gee, you noticed," she snapped. "I'm moved."

"Caldwell, you need reminding that you're a woman." His hand touched the small of her back as if she also needed steering to the parking lot. Even through the heavy coat, she felt it. And wished, oh she wished... For things she couldn't have.

"Who says?" she muttered, like a sulky child.

"I say." He held open the passenger door and grinned at her astonishment. "I can be a gentleman."

She couldn't think of a comeback to save her life. She climbed in, let him close the door, and waited while he circled the car and got in behind the wheel. She felt discombobulated. Was he flirting with her?

Would she recognize it if he was? Heaven help her, what if she tried to flirt back and embarrassed him? Or *didn't* flirt back, leaving him thinking she didn't want...well, whatever she wanted?

"Mary a good cook?" Diaz asked, starting the car.

Grateful for the mundane subject, Ann said, "Yeah, if you like casseroles, ham and baked potatoes. That kind of thing. Her pies are to die for. If you're really, really nice, she'll send a few pieces home with you."

"I can be nice."

She felt his glance. Had no idea whether he'd meant that to have a double meaning.

Conversation was a struggle. It seemed as if everything he said could be taken two ways, and she was too big a coward to do anything but pretend she heard only the surface meaning.

Or maybe that's all that existed, and the rest was in her mind. Who knew?

In a different mood, she'd have enjoyed the expression on Reggie Roarke's face when he opened his front door in response to the bell and saw her in her new clothes—and makeup!—and then a moment later her escort. Of course, he'd killed her pleasure the minute he said, "Can't get a date, Caldwell?"

Appearing behind him, his wife tried to shush him, but too late.

Ann was opening her mouth for a snide comeback when Diaz laid an arm across her shoulders.

"Who says she can't?"

Reggie's jaw just about hit his chest, although he recovered quickly. "You're working together."

"Sure." Diaz squeezed her shoulder and released her, smiling at Mary. "It's worked out great."

"But...if you two..."

A face as weathered as Diaz's shouldn't be able to achieve a look of bland surprise. "If us two what?"

Now Ann was having fun.

Reggie's eyes narrowed. "You just said..."

"Oh, leave the kids alone." Mary swatted his arm. "You haven't even let them through the door. Ann, I'm so glad you could come. You look especially pretty today. And Juan, what a nice surprise!"

"Nobody's called me a kid in years." He kissed her cheek as he stepped in. "I hope it's okay. Ann told me what a great cook you are."

Ann. Her heart gave a bump. Diaz had called her Ann, not Caldwell. Had he done it deliberately, or slipped? Was that how he thought of her?

"Of course it's okay!" Mary beamed. "I love to feed people."

"You sound like my mother," Diaz said.

That's what Ann imagined mothers were like. Most mothers.

Talking happily, asking questions, Mary ushered them into the living room and insisted on getting them something to drink. While she bustled, Reggie sat in his recliner.

Ann settled for her usual soda and Diaz accepted a

beer. She did notice that he took only a couple of sips before setting it down, while Reggie drained his and called to his wife for another one.

Ann stood. "Can I help you?"

"Dinner'll be on the table any minute." Mary waved her back to her seat. "You three just talk."

"Talk" consisted of a critical recap of the Seahawks season and an analysis of the Mariners chances for making the playoffs this coming year.

"Took a vacation and went down to training camp last year." Reggie took a long swallow. "That Fernandez kid was batting about eight hundred. Then he pulled that hamstring. If he's good to go this year..."

Diaz commented, and they were off again.

Ann sat with a pleasant, interested smile fixed in place and wondered why so many people found baseball fascinating. Or maybe it *was* fascinating to a discerning individual. Heaven knew she was in the minority.

Funny, when she'd tried so hard to please her father, that she hadn't managed even to fake an interest in any of his hobbies or leisure activities. If the engine of her car clunked, she didn't whip open the hood. She took the car to the shop, nodded intelligently when the mechanic handed her odd bits of metal that'd had to be replaced and paid the bill. Poker was fun, but she was too rash. Her father barred her from games. Football was okay, if she was at a gathering and everybody else was cheering, but she couldn't have said what a cornerback did. She couldn't work up even minimal enthusiasm for baseball. As far as she could see, hours went by in games without much of anything happening.

When Mary caroled from the doorway, "Come to the table, everyone," Ann rose with relief.

"I hope you all like ham," Mary worried as she shooed them into the dining room. "I thought something simple would be nice today."

"It looks wonderful," Diaz assured her. "Where do you want us?"

Mary pointed out places at the table. He put his hand on the small of Ann's back again, as if she couldn't take a few steps without guidance. Then, to her stupefaction, he pulled out her chair for her.

Ann gaped at it, then at him. His back to the Roarkes, he winked. Rolling her eyes, she sat and let him help her scoot the chair in.

"For Pete's sake!" Reggie grumbled. "We're not in some fancy restaurant."

"I figure," Diaz was careful not to look at her, "a little practice never hurts."

Mary patted his hand when he sat down. "What a gentleman." Ignoring her husband's continuing grumbles, she lifted a bowl of potato salad and handed it to Ann. "Everybody can dish up for themselves. Save room for Dutch apple pie."

Diaz inclined his head. "With pleasure, ma'am."

Inevitably, conversation turned to Birkey.

"What a sad way to go." Mary passed a bowl of broccoli to Diaz. "All by himself. If he'd been married, it never would have happened."

Her husband sneered. "His wife couldn't take the

pressure of being married to a cop. I stood up at his wedding, you know. Didn't like her even then.''

"Really?" Ann didn't have to pretend surprise or interest. "You were his best man?"

"We went through the academy together."

"Why didn't you like his wife?" Ann asked. "I barely remember her."

He shrugged. "You could tell she was flighty. She was always wanting to take trips."

"Rhonda was a travel agent," his wife said. "Remember? We booked that week in Waikiki through her."

"Yeah, yeah, that's right. But planning other people's trips wasn't good enough for her. Every couple of months she started dreaming up some other vacation, and she couldn't believe Birkey couldn't get away if he really wanted."

"They weren't a very good match," Mary agreed. "Rhonda must have been thirteen, fourteen, years younger than Don. Don't you think?" she appealed to Reggie.

"At least." He snorted. "Idiot thought starting with a young one meant he'd have the upper hand."

Or else, Ann thought with distaste, he just plain liked them young. The younger the better.

Inspiration struck. "Personally," she said, "I had the impression he didn't like women at all."

Reggie reared back as if she'd flung a tarantula on the table. "You thought he was a fag?"

She almost laughed at his horror if not his use of a word she disliked. "No, no! I didn't mean it that way. I just meant that he didn't seem to respect women. He always thought the worst of them. In fact..." She frowned as if pursuing a faint memory. "Wasn't he one of the officers who blew off Captain Danner's wife?" She glanced at Diaz as if for support. "You remember that one? There was a lot of talk."

Reggie crushed his empty beer can in one hand and glowered at her. "Yeah, and some of the talk says he never did lay a hand on her."

"He was convicted."

"Your dad and I always thought..." He stopped abruptly, turning his ill-tempered stare on his wife. "Mary, can't you see that I need another beer? Diaz, what about you? You must need one by now."

Diaz held up a hand. "No, I'll have coffee though, if you have it."

"Coming right up," Mary said as cheerfully as if her husband wasn't an SOB.

The minute she bustled toward the kitchen, Reggie said, "I didn't want Mary to hear me say this, but Mike and I always thought the bitch framed him. The way she set him up, no one would believe she killed herself."

Ann blinked. "You're claiming the whole thing was a setup? She'd call 911 every time she got a bruise?"

"Rosalie liked her booze. Did you know that? Hell, yeah, she got a lot of bruises! Probably passed out halfway up the stairs!" He leaned forward. "I can tell you this. She'd have had a couple of DUIs if she hadn't been Danner's wife." He grunted. "She got her breaks from cops, all right."

Diaz cleared his throat. "If he never laid a hand on her, why'd she hate him?"

"Who the hell knows!" Reggie made a sweeping gesture. "She was crazy. That's all."

"You knew her?" Ann asked.

"Hell, I was part of that investigation!" He raised his voice. "Damn it, Mary, you watching a TV show out there?"

Shaking her head, Mary appeared with a tray. "He's no more patient than a two-year-old," she said indulgently. "Ann, you want coffee, too, don't you?"

"Please." She started to rise. "Let me get…"

But Diaz had already taken the tray from the older woman and set it down on the table. Not seeming to notice, Reggie grabbed his beer and popped the top, lifting it for a long swallow.

"Okay," Ann said. "So maybe the Danner case wasn't a fair example. But I've heard other stories. That county councilman. I heard Birkey talking about the intern who said she was raped," she fabricated. "He was telling anyone who'd listen that she was a slut."

Reggie made a disgusted sound. "Oh, hell! You know she screwed…" He caught his wife's gaze and harrumphed. "She slept with him until someone found out. Then she cried rape. Oldest story in the book." He nodded and kept nodding.

Ann wondered how many beers he'd had today.

As if by chance, his wife said, "Now, I know you're ready for your coffee, too, Reggie. You can't drink beer with pie."

To Ann's surprise, he didn't argue. Perhaps Mary wasn't the doormat she appeared. Maybe she drew some lines, and he knew better than to stumble over them.

He sat in brooding silence while his wife went back to the kitchen for the pie. She served it still warm from the oven, cinnamon and tart apples and crumbled brown sugar and oatmeal topped with vanilla ice cream. While they ate, she was firm in steering conversation away from police business and Birkey's death, asking Diaz about his children and Ann about whether she'd considered finding a nicer place to live.

"I know you didn't want to keep your father's house, but Reggie pointed out your apartment complex when we went by one day, and it seemed...well..." She hesitated, apparently at a loss for words.

"Crummy?" Diaz suggested.

Ann glared at him. "It's not crummy."

"I wouldn't go that far," Mary said tactfully. "But if you bought one of those new town houses toward Covington—do you know the ones I mean?—you'd be able to use that beautiful swimming pool, and I hear there's a walking trail and a playground and..."

Ann killed that dream, pointing out that she had no use for a playground. What she didn't say was that she wouldn't be caught dead lounging around one of those kidney-shaped pools with all the Yuppie singles in an upscale apartment complex. Especially if she had to do that lounging in a bathing suit.

She couldn't see any way to bring the conversation back to a relevant subject. *Hey, anyone want to talk about serial killers?* didn't seem like a workable gambit. Diaz must have agreed, because he didn't argue when she made their excuses shortly thereafter.

Mary hugged Ann on the doorstep, something that always made her uncomfortable. Tonight, just for a second, it felt almost natural. Even nice.

The night was dark and cold, but edging above freezing; the snow in the street was turning to slush. Diaz held open the car door for her again. Forestalling any protest, he said, "They might be watching."

She shook her head and got in. Once he'd started the car, he turned up the heat and briefly flicked on the windshield wipers.

"Interesting," he said after a minute.

"More like depressing."

"Yeah, respect for the police force would plummet if John Q. Public heard our Reggie once he's had a couple of beers."

Ann made a face. "A couple?"

"A couple of six-packs?"

"More like."

Diaz put the car in gear, checked over his shoulder although the street was dark and deserted, and pulled out.

"Well, now we know Birkey and Roarke were on a couple of task forces together."

"And my father was involved in both those cases."

She felt his glance.

After a minute, he said, "Then they're a good place to start. Especially if Leroy was in on one but not the other."

Ann gave a jerky nod.

Stomach churning, she wished she'd never mentioned her suspicion to Diaz, never started any of this. Right now, she was thinking maybe all those old-time cops who had endowed themselves with God-like powers had gotten what they deserved. Maybe, if the killer wasn't done, she and Diaz should let him finish.

The next instant, repulsion welled in her, and she knew the horrifying truth: she was just like her father.

CHAPTER EIGHT

DIAZ DROVE with one eye on Ann. He didn't like her
silence, her fixed gaze. Wet snow thrown up from the
wheels of a truck in front of them blurred the windshield, and he turned on the wiper blades, but she
didn't seem to see them.

"Something's bothering you," he said.

He hated to think the sound she made was a laugh.

"Plenty of things are bothering me."

"What?"

"Lemme see." Her voice was filled with irony.
"Where to start. Okay, here's a good place. I'm bothered that I didn't know."

"That they were misogynists?"

"Why wrap it up in a fancy word? They hated
women. *I* am a woman."

He picked carefully for a response. If he said something wrong, she might explode. Without touching her,
he felt her quivering tension.

"Despising women in general doesn't mean…"

His effort was wasted. She was consumed by her
need to know where her fault lay.

"I heard them say stuff, but I never put it all together. I thought they were the best. I grew up with

this sense of awe and fear and pride all muddled up. When I joined the force, I wanted to *be* them.''

''We all thought they were good cops.''

''You didn't live with one of them.''

''Ann...we're programmed to respect our parents. Maybe you more than most because your mother was gone.''

''No wonder he never remarried.'' Bitterness corroded every word.

Diaz knew he had to keep her talking. He was afraid to let her sink into a murky well of remembrance.

''Did he see women?''

''You mean, screw them? Yeah, probably. Sometimes he went out at night and came home in a really good mood but not smelling like beer. I wonder if he went to prostitutes?'' She shuddered. ''I don't want to think about it.''

''Then don't. He's gone.''

''How can I not? I am who I am because of him.''

''No, damn it!'' Diaz slapped the wheel. ''There've been other people in your life, too. Your mother...''

''Do you know how she died?'' She turned in the seat to face him. ''She killed herself. Did you know that?''

He swore. ''No.''

''I don't remember her that well. She was pretty and sad. That's mostly what I remember. Dad was angry. He didn't want to talk about her. I could feel his contempt for her so I signed on to the conspiracy of silence.'' Grief swelled. ''She wasn't worth talking about. I wasn't going to be like my mother. I'd be strong, like him. I wouldn't wonder..." Her voice broke. "I wouldn't wonder why she left me."

He turned into the parking lot of her apartment complex. "Ann..."

"*Am* I like him?"

He parked, set the emergency brake and turned to meet eyes dark with desperation. The lighting was good enough that he could see her face well.

"No. You're not like him."

"Do you know what I thought tonight?"

He shook his head.

"I thought maybe he deserved what he got. Maybe they all did. And I thought maybe we should let whoever it is finish." She made a hiccuping sound of distress. "That makes me like them. Wanting to let something *I* call justice have its way, even if a judge or jury would say it's wrong."

"Ann, we all think things like that. What separates you from your father is that you're repulsed because, for a minute, you were tempted. If you weren't tempted at all, you'd be a saint."

"Oh, God." She scrubbed at her eyes. "I'm going to cry. I never cry."

He had heartburn. He hoped like hell it was heartburn and not something more dangerous.

Diaz unbuckled first his seat belt and then hers. "Damn it, Caldwell, come here."

She sniffed. "I gotta go. Don't listen to me. Forget I said all this crap, okay? It was just..."

Pulling her into his arms was like trying to cuddle a cat that didn't want to make his acquaintance. All

JANICE KAY JOHNSON 147

bony angles and stiff resistance, she strained away even as tears welled in her eyes.

"What are you doing?" she said in a panic. "I can't..."

"Can't what? Cry on my shoulder? Why not?"

"Because...because..." Just like that, she crumbled. Tears spilled and ran down her cheeks. She stared at him as they ran, her mouth forming an astonished, anguished O. And then she collapsed, burying her face against his chest and clutching his shirt.

Diaz held her tight and laid his cheek against the top of her head as she sobbed. His own eyes burned as he felt the sobs wrack her body. She was lost in remembered pain, crying like the child who probably hadn't been allowed to grieve. He didn't even know what she was crying about: her mother, her father, her illusions, her terror about who she might be.

He only knew that she had let herself go because she trusted him, and that he wanted her to keep trusting him in ways that had nothing to do with backing up a fellow officer.

Oh, yeah. He was in deep.

The sobs became shuddering hiccups and then rasping breath as she lay against him. He gently nuzzled her hair. It smelled good. Not flowery, more like kitchen herbs. Rosemary, maybe, with a dash of mint.

She yanked backward so fast she smashed her head against his jaw and he bit his tongue. The salty taste of blood filled his mouth.

Now he did have tears in his eyes. "Damn it, Ann!"

"I—" She clapped a hand over her mouth. "Oh, God. I hurt you!"

"Damn straight you hurt me!" He swallowed and grimaced. "What'd you think, I was going to rape you?"

"No, I..." She moaned and closed her eyes. "I need to blow my nose."

He touched his tongue and winced. Then his jaw and winced again. "Try the glove compartment."

He kept a box of tissues there for Tony's tears. Elena didn't cry; she was too stubborn.

Ann thrust a tissue at him before blowing her nose. She didn't try to be delicate. Hell, after what he'd seen of her face, mascara running and eyes swollen near shut, delicacy was a moot point.

Diaz spit blood on the tissue and wiped his mouth.

"I'm so sorry." She sounded weepy again.

"I'll survive." His ego felt worse than his mouth. So much for her deep sense of trust in him.

"I just can't believe I did that."

"Whacked me?"

"Cried."

Diaz shook his head. "People do."

"I don't." She blew her nose again, a defiant honk.

With incredulity, he asked, "You didn't cry when your father died?"

She sniffed and shook her head. "I was...shocked. I never saw his body. It didn't seem real. The only time—" She stopped.

"The only time?"

Head bent, Ann gave an awkward shrug. "The funeral was hard." Her voice was still thick, watery. "Everyone was staring at me, and I was mad because he'd been careless and left me, too. After Mom... He was all I had left! He knew that!'' She squeezed her arms to herself, as if she were cold. "But I'm a cop. I was there in uniform, my captain standing next to me. I couldn't cry. I kept trying to think about other things. Like how I'd finish Dad's work. Be worthy of him.'' Her bitter laugh was choked off. "Funny, huh?''

"One of my sisters died of breast cancer a couple of years ago,'' Diaz said. "I cried. We all did. It's normal, Ann. Nobody would have thought less of you if you'd cried at your father's funeral.''

She shook her head in automatic denial. "I'm a woman. I can't—''

"That's a tired excuse,'' he said with a spurt of irritation. "You and I both know your gender doesn't have anything to do with it. Your father told you it was weak to cry, and you're still taking his word as gospel.''

Her back went ramrod straight. "You don't know…!''

"Know what?''

"What I think! Or feel!''

Keeping his voice as gentle as if she were one of his kids, Diaz said, "Then tell me.''

She stared at him from puffy, smudged eyes, then abruptly turned her head away. A breath shook her shoulders. "I'm not normal.''

"Yeah,'' he said with a tinge of humor. "I know.''

She sniffed again, a sad sound. "I always looked at families like yours and wondered what it was like, having…oh, I don't know. Birthday parties and hugs and noisy, cheerful arguments. Stuff everybody else takes for granted.''

His chest felt hollow as he imagined her, a big-eyed girl who couldn't take hugs for granted. Trying not to sound stunned by the realization, he asked, ''Was this the first time anybody has held you when you cried?''

She still hadn't looked at him, but after a moment her head bobbed. ''Since Mom died.''

Killed herself and deserted her daughter is what Ann meant. ''God.''

''Well.'' She straightened her shoulders. ''Like you said, it's past. I'm a big girl now. It's just… I wanted you to know why I freaked. Can we forget this ever happened?''

His eyes narrowed. ''That you ever cried, do you mean?''

She bent to grope for her purse on the car floor. ''I'd appreciate it.''

''No, I don't want to forget it.'' Red-hot anger lay in his belly like a glowing coal. ''You know what? I thought you needed to cry. I was idiot enough to think you cried on me because you trusted me.''

One hand on the door handle, she went still. She was silent so long, the coals burned to ashes. He'd blown it. Let hurt feelings damage a relationship that was starting to mean too much to him.

''I do,'' she whispered. Took a shaky breath. ''I think I do.''

The next instant, she opened the door and scrambled out, tossing over her shoulder, ''Thank you. I'm sorry. I mean… Oh, damn it. I'll see you tomorrow.''

He was out of the car as fast as if someone had just

shot at her. Across the hood, he said, "I'm walking you to your door."

"Oh, for Pete's sake!" In her exasperation, she sounded almost like herself. Her body language as she stomped away reassured him more.

Diaz was right behind her anyway.

They passed a couple of apartments. The first window was curtained, the blue flicker of a television visible in the dimly lit interior. In the second window, the silhouette of a couple in a clinch was clearly outlined. Ann's step checked briefly before she marched on.

At her door, she fumbled in her purse, finally coming up with keys. Watching her unlock, Diaz had the sense of a clock ticking. She was going to close that door in his face any second. He could ask to come in for a cup of coffee, but he knew that wouldn't be smart.

As she got her door open, he said, "I like you, Caldwell. Tears and all."

"Damn it, Diaz!" She glared at him. "Why do you say things like that? Can't you just let me…"

"Sulk?"

Her chin rose another notch. "Be strong."

He couldn't help himself. He lifted a hand and caressed her face. A light stroke, not enough to commit himself, but enough to set her to quivering with alarm.

"You are strong." His voice was husky. His tongue was swollen, he told himself. He wasn't about to do something really, really stupid.

She closed her eyes momentarily. "Diaz, you're turning me to mush. Go away."

Despite the ache beneath his breastbone, he grinned. "Yes, ma'am."

"I don't think I'm a ma'am."

"Yes, sir! Or should I say 'miss'?"

"Oh, jeez." She went inside and started to close the door. When it was no more than an inch ajar, Ann said, "I like you, too," and closed it in his face, just as he'd foreseen.

But he was smiling when he went back to his car.

ANN LOCKED the door, dropped her purse and went straight to the bathroom. The sight of her face in the mirror made her whimper.

He'd *seen* her like this!

Still staring at herself in horror, she turned on the water and let it run until it was hot. Then she bent over and splashed it over her face. Only then did she get out cold cream and carefully wipe off the tracked mascara.

She didn't look a lot better without it. Her skin was blotchy and her eyes swollen. Ann groaned.

Hair braided and teeth brushed, she stripped off her new clothes and put on a pair of flannel pajamas. It wasn't really bedtime, but she was so exhausted she could hardly make herself turn off lights and check the locks.

Crying had drained her. It did, literally, make you weak, she was discovering. Knees shaky, collapse into bed weak.

Humiliated, too. As she curled up on her side and pulled the covers to her chin, she tried to imagine what Diaz thought about tonight's display.

A funny feeling crept over her, warming her chest. Maybe he really did think her breakdown was normal. Maybe, if he'd been hit by tragedy and cried, he'd expect her to take it in stride. Was that what friends did?

She'd have told anybody she *had* friends. Not many—she wasn't very good at girly gossiping and she was always surprised when someone did want to spend time with her—but she'd made a few in high school and later. Now she suspected none were really friends. More acquaintances. Nice to see, but not people she thought about between visits.

She'd never cried in front of any of them. Had never told another soul that her mother had killed herself.

Actually, she couldn't believe she'd done either, and with Diaz. A partner she'd spent months believing she didn't like. A cop.

A man.

A ripple of reaction ran from her scalp down to her toes. She turned out her lamp, squeezed her eyes shut and remembered what his arms had felt like around her.

Good. Strong. Safe. She tried not to cringe at the memory of burrowing against him, of soaking his shirt with her tears, of whacking her head against his jaw.

She just let herself remember the urgent beat of his heart, his warmth and his strength. And finally, she thought about the way he'd grazed his fingertips over her cheek with a look in his eyes she could only call tender.

Afraid of the hunger that swelled in her until her chest ached, she curled tighter. Was she so needy that she'd gone from spending her days hoping for a nod of approval from her father to longing for a smile from another man?

But this was different. She knew that much. Smiles wouldn't be enough. She wanted his touch. She wanted to see hunger in his eyes. Desire for her alone.

Ann pressed a cheek that was inexplicably wet into her pillow. This time the tears only seeped from beneath closed lids. She'd never dare call him in the evening again. How would she survive when she heard a woman laugh in the background?

She slept poorly and looked almost as bad to her bleary gaze in the morning as she had the night before. For the first time, she applied makeup before going to work, but as a form of defense rather than out of vanity. It was effective enough that she looked much as usual by the time she was ready to go out the door, Ann decided.

Diaz was already at his desk when she walked in. He was so intent on his computer monitor, he barely nodded at her. Either that, or he was doing a good job of pretending. Either way, she told herself she was grateful.

She paused beside him. "Find something good?" Ann was proud of her tone of casual interest.

"Hmmm?" He seemed to wrench his attention from the screen to her. "Oh. Yeah. Here, let me print it." A moment later, he handed her a page from the printer.

Skimming, she saw a list of calls Rosalie Danner had made to the police. Officers responding: Leroy Pearce and Reggie Roarke the first time, Birkey and her father at the hospital, Roarke and Pearce again, and finally another pair of officers.

Forgetting her discomfiture about last night, she said, "There they are. All four of them."

"Along with Stillman and a Norm Douglas. Do you know him?"

"Yeah, he was a funny-looking guy. I'll bet you'd remember him. He'd been a boxer, I remember Dad saying. He had a mangled nose and cauliflower ears and squinty little eyes."

Rubbing a hand on his jaw, Diaz nodded. "Yeah, yeah. Real quiet."

"Lacked personality," she agreed. "Maybe boxing killed too many brain cells."

His gaze sharpened. "You said 'was.' He *was* a funny-looking guy."

"He died...I don't know, maybe two years ago. Must have been right after Danner was arrested." She tried to think. "Maybe even before. You don't remember—?"

"Did he have an accident?" Diaz asked.

"No, a heart attack." She shook her head before he could even open his mouth. "No, really. Rumor has it that he and his wife were having sex and he just grunted and collapsed on top of her."

Diaz raised an eyebrow.

She scowled. "Yeah, okay, that was probably his usual sexual technique."

Diaz's mouth twitched. "This time, he didn't just say he'd died and gone to heaven. He really did."

She sloshed cold water on his humor. "Odds are, he went the other way."

He bent his head in acknowledgment. "True."

"Anyway, unless someone paid his wife to, uh…"

"Work him up to a fever pitch?"

She'd been thinking of a saying that had to do with bunnies, but she nodded. "Seems unlikely, don't you think?"

Diaz leaned back in his chair, fingers laced behind his head. "Even if someone did, there are worse ways to go."

She just shook her head in mock disgust. Imagining Diaz naked and in bed with a woman—say, with her—was not an option this morning.

Fortunately, Diaz moved on. "Stillman doesn't fit the profile of the others. He's by the book."

She nodded agreement. "Wasn't he the one who actually arrested Captain Danner?"

"Presumably he didn't buy the framed-by-suicide theory."

"We should talk to him." Ann tried to remember what she'd heard about Earl Stillman, who couldn't be far from retirement. "Isn't he north end now?"

"Yeah, I saw him at Pearce's funeral."

"Oh, God," she said with a sinking feeling. "Birkey's funeral."

"These days, you've got to get that dress uniform dry-cleaned right away," he agreed. "You never know when you're going to need it."

"Stillman could be next on this list."

"Unless he's spared because he made the arrest."

Her momentary fire sputtered. "If they took turns responding to Mrs. Danner's calls, it's because they were patrolling the same area. There may be a dozen similar, lower profile, instances.''

''I can't argue.'' Diaz shuffled through papers on his desk. ''My gut feeling, though, is that this killer isn't your average Joe. Most people wouldn't remember the names of the particular officers who responded to calls. They might have a generalized anger at the department, but wouldn't even know how to go about tracking down the individuals they think hurt them. Maybe the anger wouldn't *be* aimed at individual cops. They'd figure we're all corrupt.''

''That makes sense.'' Ann perched on the corner of his desk, ignoring a scuffle in the hall and the stream of invectives that went with it. A body slammed against the wall, the glass inset in the open door quivered, and a moment later a flushed cop shoved his struggling, cuffed suspect past their line of sight.

Diaz paid no more attention than she had. ''When bad things happen to people with education and some money, it *becomes* high profile. That's what makes news. The scary stuff that can happen even to people like us. So I'm thinking we can skip most of the calls where charges weren't filed, even if they should have been. Where nobody but family knew the police had done wrong. Even if, later, tragedy happened. We want the cases that were in the news, the ones that brought public criticism of the sheriff's department.''

''The ones where that criticism was met with supposed internal investigations that ended with statements claiming officers were justified in their decisions, yada yada.''

He nodded as if she were a bright student. "Exactly."

She thought about it. "Okay. I tend to agree."

"Then I propose that, for the moment, we focus on three cases—Rosalie Danner's murder, the alleged rape committed by our esteemed county councilman and Sergei Belenky, who killed girls from well-to-do families."

"There was a lot of anger," she remembered. "Even reporters thought we should have caught him sooner."

"Right. And all four of our guys were on that task force."

"Along with close to a dozen other officers."

Diaz rocked his chair back. "Who's to say our killer doesn't have a long list?"

She made a face. "There's an ugly thought."

"Oh, yeah." He nodded a response to a wave from La Vorie, who'd been out sick with this year's most vicious strain of flu. Attention back on Ann, Diaz began, "What say we…"

His phone rang.

"Lemme just get this…" He grabbed it. "Diaz." When his voice changed and he said, "What's up, Cheri?" Ann eased off his desk. He'd forgotten her existence anyway; furrows formed between his brows and tension lines creased his cheeks.

She wished her desk was farther away and she didn't have to hear his side of the conversation, but his voice followed her.

"No. I haven't forgotten I'm supposed to have the kids this weekend. I promised Tony we'd—" Pause.

"You know I couldn't help that. He understood I had to work."

Involuntarily, Ann looked back at Diaz, whose voice became muffled as he bent his head and kneaded his forehead. Then she heard, "Elena told you what?" He growled with impatience. "You want me to keep them in a vacuum when they're with me? They can't meet my friends?" He listened for a minute. "You know what, Cheri? If I have a woman in my life who's important to me, I want her to meet my kids, and I want them to meet her." His face hardened at whatever his ex-wife said next. "Yeah, I'll have her over again this weekend. Live with it." And he slammed down the phone.

Ann ducked her head and pretended to be searching in her drawer for an illusive something.

If I have a woman in my life who's important to me... So he was seeing someone. Last night had been just kindness. She was such an idiot to have imagined anything else.

"Do I seem irresponsible to you?"

She glanced up as if in surprise. "Irresponsible?"

Anger roughened his voice. "Do I forget my every commitment?"

"Uh...no."

"Cheri and I lived together for ten years. If anybody should know how much I love Tony and Elena, it's her. But she's always sure I'm going to slough them off. Break every promise to them and their hearts while I'm at it."

"I take it you've had to cancel visits."

"Sure I have." He rotated his head as though his

neck ached. "I make it up to them. They understand. Heck, I'm okay with it when they switch weekends on me because of a friend's birthday party or whatever. Cheri's the one who's pissed if she has to change her plans. I don't even blame her for that. She needs a break. But she knows I can't clock out when something's come down." He swore. "You have any aspirin?"

"Ibuprofen."

"I'll take it."

She finally had something to look for in her drawer. "Want coffee to wash it down?"

"Thanks."

When she returned with two cups and the bottle of ibuprofen, he was still massaging his neck. After swallowing the pills, he shook his head. "The minute I hear her voice, my muscles knot up." He gave her a hopeful look. "I don't suppose you're really good with those hands."

About to go back to her desk, she stopped. "You want a massage?" Her hands, on him?

His shoulders hunched. "Forget I asked. It's probably sexual harassment or something. Thanks for this." He lifted his cup of coffee.

Ann turned around, set hers down on his desk and marched behind him. "Don't spill," she advised, and went to work on the taut muscles of his neck and shoulders.

He groaned and let his head drop forward. Muscles rippled under her hands and he gave a few moans of appreciation as she kneaded.

"I take it you're seeing someone?" Heaven help

her, the question just popped out, without her knowing she was going to ask. The only thing she could say for her pride was that she'd managed to sound only casually interested.

"Mmm?" He rolled a shoulder forward to enable her to grind the heel of her hand into tense muscles. "Oh. Elena told her you were over for dinner."

She could quit this massage any time, Ann thought. She just didn't want to.

"Why didn't you tell her it was just me?"

He went rigid under her hands. "*Just* you?"

She lightly chopped at the thick muscles that ran from neck to shoulders. "You know what I mean."

"You're a woman. You were over for dinner. What difference does it make to her how I know you?"

"But I wasn't there because…"

"Yeah, you were." His voice had deepened.

Ann stilled. "What?"

"I lied. I wanted you to meet my kids."

Gaping at the back of his head, she said, "But… We're not…"

"No." He turned, eyes meeting hers. "But we could be. If we want to take that step."

Just like that, she felt…tipsy. Hot and cold. Light-headed. Giddy, but uncomfortably aware that she might do or say something she'd regret.

There was a reason she rarely drank.

"That step."

A flicker of some emotion narrowed his eyes for an instant. "You're telling me it hasn't occurred to you?"

"It." Now she sounded stupid.

"The idea of us."

"I thought…we were getting to be friends."

His expression closed. "Sure we are. Maybe we should leave it at that."

Of course they should leave it at that. They were partners. They wouldn't be able to keep working together if they had any kind of romantic or sexual relationship.

Right this second, she didn't care.

No! she cried inside. *No, I don't want to leave it at that.*

But she had no idea how to say that without sounding desperate. "I just…had no idea."

"Then we will leave it there." He stood. "What do you say we go track down Stillman?"

"Um…sure. Let me grab…" She gestured toward her desk and backed away. "And, uh, I've got to go to…"

"Yeah, maybe I'll do that, too."

A moment later, safe in the refuge of the otherwise empty women's restroom, Ann planted her hands on the counter and let her head bow.

He'd wanted her. At least a little bit. And now he'd never say another word about it, because she was socially retarded, and a coward besides.

Such a coward, she realized, as pain cramped in her chest, that she would never say another word about it, either.

After a moment, she turned on the water and washed her hands, then dried them and walked out.

CHAPTER NINE

THEY CAUGHT Stillman at his desk writing a report. Not sure if she'd recognize him, Ann did right away. Medium-height, he had the wiry build of a runner. He kept curly, graying hair cropped close.

"Danner?" he said in surprise after they introduced themselves and explained why they were there. "What in hell…?" His face became expressionless. "You internal affairs?"

"No," Ann said. "We're pursuing a case that might connect. I'd rather hear what you remember before we explain, if you don't mind."

His chair squeaked. He considered them. "Rosalie Danner has been dead for a couple of years. Captain Danner's trial was over—what?—a year ago. You're not suggesting her murder was committed by somebody else?"

"No. Actually, we're not."

Without moving or saying a word, he went on point like a setter. She felt it.

"All right," he said. "I'll give you some slack. What do you want to learn that you can't get out of the reports?"

Diaz nodded at Ann to take the lead.

"I know the first time you went to the Danner res-

idence you didn't file charges," she said. "Were you
aware then that Mrs. Danner had accused her husband
of abuse at least a couple of other times?"

"I was," he said readily. "There'd been talk."

"And what did you find there?"

"A noisy quarrel. On the previous occasions, Mrs.
Danner had called 911 herself or made an allegation
to doctors treating her at the hospital." He sounded as
formal as if he were on the stand. Chances were, he
was still wary about their interest. "In this instance, a
neighbor heard raised voices, crashes, a scream, and
made the call. Captain Danner answered the door and
told us somewhat curtly that our presence wasn't required. We asked to speak to his wife."

"That must have been awkward," Diaz commented.

He grunted. "Damn awkward." Picking up the narrative again, he said, "Mrs. Danner came to the door.
She was staggering and smelled of alcohol. She had a
bruise on her jaw, but it appeared to be an old one.
She claimed her husband had just knocked her to the
floor, but when she pulled her shirt off her shoulder to
show us where he'd struck her, there was no mark. We
asked if she felt she needed to go to the hospital, and
she said no. They kept breaking into argument right in
front of us. He was clearly furious, with her and about
the fact that we were there. In the end they agreed they
needed to cool down, and we drove her to her sister's
house in Kent."

"Considering how things turned out, do you regret
not arresting Captain Danner that evening?"

He was shaking his head before she finished. "I
couldn't have. There was no basis for charging him."

"I'm assuming that, after her murder, you read the reports on the earlier calls."

He dipped his head. "I did."

"What was your reaction?"

For the first time, Stillman hesitated. After a minute he said carefully, "These things are always messy. You know that. Honestly...I wondered why an arrest hadn't been made. However, I also have to say that Rosalie Danner's drinking problem muddied the waters. Her injuries could conceivably have been caused by falls taken when she was drunk, as her husband claimed."

"After the autopsy?"

"I was appalled by the extent of her injuries. Not only those sustained the day of her murder, but those that were partially healed." His jaw tightened. "The report left no doubt that she'd been abused for several years, at least. Her collarbone alone had been broken half a dozen times. Did you know that?"

Ann shook her head. She was dealing with the knowledge that her father had seen this woman in the hospital when her arm had just been broken and he'd refused to take her seriously. Because her husband was a fellow police officer? Because she was a drunk? Or just because she was a woman?

"That's the story. She worked up the guts to call us a few times and faced disbelief. Apparently she was too afraid to leave him. Too dependent, maybe. Who knows? But she's dead, and he's in jail."

"Did her family attend the trial?"

"Her sister did faithfully. She wanted the jury to

see her sitting there. She smiled when she heard the verdict. Then she cried.''

''Was she angry at the officers who hadn't believed Mrs. Danner?''

Again he hesitated. ''I think she felt too guilty herself to blame anyone else.''

''Because she didn't believe Rosalie, either,'' Ann said slowly.

''Oh, Ms. Rendell—that's the sister—hated Danner. Quit socializing with them as a couple, because she detested him so much. But she got frustrated because Rosalie wouldn't do anything about the boozing, wouldn't go to a shelter, and because of her inaction Ms. Rendell was never sure how much of her rantings to believe.''

''Have you stayed in touch with her?''

''I called her once, a few months after the trial. She said she was okay. That she liked to think Rosalie was at peace, after years of abuse and inner torment. She'd been to the cemetery just the Sunday before and left daffodils. Rosalie loved them, she said.''

They were all silent for a moment. Ann had visited her father's grave every few weeks at first, but she hadn't been in months. She had never visited her mother's. She knew where she was buried only because of paperwork she'd found when cleaning out her father's house.

Maybe, she thought, she'd take some daffodils to her mother's grave.

''You've been very helpful,'' she said, but didn't get any further.

''Whoa.'' Stillman's voice had the crack of command. "You're not going anywhere until you tell me what this has been about."

Again, Diaz and Ann exchanged a glance. On the way, ignoring the undercurrents between them, they'd discussed how much they should tell Stillman, but not reached a conclusion. Both of them knew him, but not well. Now Diaz gave a barely perceptible inclination of his head again, letting her know that he was leaving the decision to her.

The other cop just waited.

Ann went with her gut feeling. "You're aware that Officers Birkey, Caldwell and Pearce have all died in the past eight months."

"I was at the funerals and I intend to be at Birkey's." His expression changed; he knew what was coming.

"We're investigating the possibility that they did not in fact die in accidents, but were murdered."

A hiss of air was followed by a long silence. Finally, "Explain," he ordered.

She kept the narrative brief, and was frank about the fact that they were poking around in the dark.

"You know that story about the blind men who each touched part of the elephant? That's us. We may be touching the part we think we are, but we may find out we're patting down a tree trunk."

His mouth twitched at her analogy. "Even assuming you're right and there's a killer out there, what made you zero in on the Danner case?"

"It's only one of several that are at the top of our list."

She let Diaz explain his reasoning, and Stillman nodded.

"You've got to start somewhere. But in this case..." He shook his head. "I don't think it's the one. Who's your killer? Marie Rendell? She's a nice woman. Fifty, fifty-five, I'd say. A little plump. Nicely groomed. Divorced some years ago, seems on good terms with her two kids. They're both on the east coast. She said once she thought with Rosalie gone she'd move back there to be near her grandkids."

"What about one of her children?"

He shook his head again. "Her son came out for the funeral, and the daughter was at the trial in the beginning and then for the verdict, but they made it plain they were there for their mother, not their aunt. I got the feeling both of them preferred to have nothing to do with her when she was alive. The son once said, 'Do you know how many Christmases she ruined by getting drunk?'"

"No other relatives?"

"The Danners had no children. Thank God," he added. "Rosalie and Marie's parents were dead. Danner's defense, as you may recall, tried to claim Rosalie might have had a lover who got angry, but we found no evidence whatsoever that she had been unfaithful. To the contrary. This was a classic situation—she had no friends, no job, no life. The sister said that Danner didn't like his wife going out, always wanted to know where she was, who she saw, what they said. What friends she had dwindled. Her sister was more stubborn. She refused to go away. She encouraged Rosalie to leave, even though she said he'd sworn to kill her if she did.''

''What a life,'' Diaz said.

They all sat quiet for a moment, imagining the emptiness, understanding the need for anesthesia. Rosalie Danner had had two choices: run and keep running, or stay and dull the pain.

They thanked Stillman and left, Ann brooding.

She saw parallels between herself and Rosalie that disturbed her. Oh, her father hadn't physically abused her. He probably wouldn't have given a damn if she'd moved out one day and never come back. But she had lived, like Rosalie, with the powerful need just once to do something right in the eyes of the only person that mattered. She had let life pass her by because she was too focused on someday, somehow, winning her father's approval. She hadn't quite known what she was doing until it was too late; until she had no idea how to go back and learn the skills to make friends, attract men, enrich her free time with the kind of hobbies most people had.

She pictured Rosalie, standing in her quiet, elegant, spotless house one day, probably years ago, listening to the phone not ringing, perhaps in pain because she hadn't been able to go to the doctor for that broken rib or collarbone. In that one instant, she knew what she had lost in tiny, scarcely noticeable increments. Facing a terrifying choice, she decided to pour herself a drink even though it was only ten in the morning. Why not? What else did she have to do?

Ann had felt discontented with her life even before her father died, but it had never occurred to her to blame him or a relationship she now saw had been one-sided. Having been deserted by her mother, she'd felt such terrifying need. The best parent in the world would have had a hard time filling that need. But he hadn't tried.

Her father hadn't loved her, not really, or he couldn't have been so cutting, couldn't have found humor in her distress. She could never please him, not because she'd failed, but because he didn't need or want anything she could give. She was a daughter. A disappointment.

Or perhaps, he simply wasn't capable of real love. Maybe he wouldn't have done any better with a son.

Opening the car door, she said, "What a son of a bitch."

Diaz stopped on the other side of the car and looked at her across the roof. "Danner?"

"My father. Danner, too."

After a moment, he nodded. He didn't say, *How in hell did your father get into this?* He understood, she thought.

She got in, and Diaz followed suit. He put the key in the ignition but didn't start the engine.

"You want to talk about it?"

"Not really," Ann decided. She'd wept enough last night. What's more, she was starting to feel awfully self-centered. All paths seemed to lead back to her.

"Okay." He still didn't reach to start the car.

"Last night," she said. "Um…thanks."

"You're welcome."

The silence suddenly pulsed with what they weren't

saying. One hell of a lot was swirling under the surface of their workday conversation.

The weird sensation would go away, she'd told herself. Talking with Diaz would start feeling natural again. They'd both forget, for long stretches, what he'd suggested.

But she didn't want to forget. Wasn't that what she'd done all her life? Let opportunities slip past? Once upon a time, she'd believed they would come again. She had to show her father she was serious about the academy; she could go out with the others later, once they graduated. Okay, once they weren't recruits. But by that time, they'd quit asking her. She was fine with that, because she was busy proving herself. Being the best—that was what mattered. Sgt. Caldwell would see that she was a chip off the old block. He was the center of her world, because he was all she had.

Later never did come. Now…now she was adrift. What did matter? Ann wasn't so sure anymore.

But she knew that she was letting another chance to *live* slip by. This time just out of habit and cowardice.

"What you said this morning…" It came out in a rush.

Diaz sounded very reserved. "I told you we could forget it."

"Is…is that what you want? Are you sorry you said anything?"

She wasn't quite brave enough to look at him. He was silent so long, she realized she wasn't breathing as she waited. Her lungs ached to snatch a breath.

"I'm sorry if I've made you uncomfortable."

"I'm not exactly uncomfortable." Yeah, she was. "I just... You've been thinking that...about *me?*" Her voice squeaked at the end.

"Why not you?"

Her cheeks must be flaming. She was glad they were in the cocoon of their unit. "I guess I tend not to think of myself as..."

"Desirable?" He frowned. "You must have..." Shock edged his voice. "Haven't you?"

"Of course I have," she said too hastily. "But it's been...a while. And you and I...I mean, we work together. I try not to think..."

"Yeah." His mouth twisted. "I've been trying not to think, too. But I've been failing."

She squeezed her hands together and stepped into the line of fire. "I have, too."

"Ann." He gave a sharp laugh. "I don't know what to say."

"You don't have to say anything." Pedaling backward seemed like the smart thing to do. "I mean, maybe this isn't such a good idea. We couldn't keep working together. And, jeez, when it belly flops, we'll still have to see each other around." She ignored his scowl. "But earlier...I was chicken. And I just wanted you to know that, uh..."

"You'd consider having dinner with me if we didn't work together."

Her heart sank. She'd chickened out after all; reasoned herself out of any chance of romance with Diaz.

"Something like that," she muttered.

"You sure know how to make a guy feel good." He grinned at her. "Here's news, Caldwell. I'm not letting you off the hook that easy. Now that you've admitted you have the hots for me, we're going to do something about it.''

Warmth curled in her stomach. ''But…what if…''

''We belly flop?'' He was definitely laughing at her. ''Beats sitting on the edge of the pool dangling our feet and not having the guts to get in. Don't you think?''

Suddenly dizzy with…relief—yeah, that was it— Ann grinned back at him. ''Is that what we've been doing? Getting out feet wet?''

''Seems that way.'' He held out a hand. ''What do you say? Ready to climb up on the high dive?''

Panic warred with elation. ''Can we just paddle around first?''

''Yeah.'' His eyes caressed her. ''What say we start with dinner tonight?''

She shrugged as if men asked her out all the time. ''Why not?''

''I guess,'' he said, in a voice that was a little gravelly, ''it wouldn't look good if two cops started making out right in front of a police station.''

''Probably not.'' She wished he could kiss her right now. Instead, she was going to spend the rest of the day getting nervous. By tonight, she'd be so scared she'd probably slug him if he touched her.

Diaz smiled as he reached for the key in the ignition. ''This should be interesting.''

HE HADN'T DATED much since his divorce. At first, he'd been the walking wounded. In his family, marriage was for good. Remarriage happened, after a suitable period of mourning, if something tragic befell your husband or wife. If you weren't getting along... well, you screamed at each other for fifty years or so. You didn't walk away. You didn't shuttle kids between homes.

Only, the choice hadn't been his. He and Cheri hadn't screamed much at each other; she'd just gotten bitter and her tongue sharp. In bed, what he saw mostly was her back after she'd rolled away when she felt his weight on the edge of the mattress. They hadn't made love in six months when she announced one day that she'd packed his clothes.

According to Cheri, it was all his fault. Maybe she was right. He'd turned a sunny, fun-loving, sometimes tender woman into an edgy, angry one. On good days, Diaz told himself she'd known what he did for a living when they got married. They'd talked about the high rate of divorce among cops, the long hours, the stress of undercover work and the toll it took on a man to see horrific deaths and mindless cruelty day in and day out. On bad days, he thought he should have quit. Was the job more important than the woman he'd told himself he loved? Than being part of his children's lives seven days a week instead of just one or two?

He'd gone so far as to look for another job, but the alternatives were so bleak he'd always backed away. He'd find something else, he would tell himself. He couldn't sell insurance, for God's sake. Or drive around apartment complexes and warehouses in a little pickup with an insignia on the door and feel important because he could still carry a gun even though his main job was to call 911 if he saw anything suspicious.

In the end, he faced the fact that he was a cop. He'd always wanted to be one, and he'd been one too long to change. He told Cheri, she nodded and, while he was at work the next day, packed his things.

So he had to live with guilt. Yeah, she'd left him, not the other way around, but he'd made a choice and laid it out on the table like four aces. *Beat that.*

He knew she bitched to the kids every day. She had no choice but to work full-time now, standing on her feet eight hours a day styling old ladies' hair. Married to him, she'd claimed she wanted to go back to work, but now that she had to, she insisted that she was exhausted all the time. She was desperate for him to take the kids two days a week, so she could have a little fun. His apartment was only a mile from their house, which made it easy for them to catch a different school bus, or for him to pick them up and drop them off. As bitter as she sounded, there were days he dreamed that she might let them live with him, but when he'd said something once, she snapped, "You weren't home enough to be a father when we were married. You're sure as hell not home enough now for them to depend on. I'm scared when they're with you that you'll pull some case and decide they'll be fine by themselves."

Not so scared that she didn't send them with alacrity, of course. The gut-wrenching part was that he knew she was right. Right now, they went to day care after school, but at least Cheri's hours were regular. His weren't. Diaz tried to make sure his days off coincided with their weekly stay. But there was no way he could switch to a nine to five Monday through Friday schedule. And what would he do with Tony and

Elena on weekends if they lived with him? More day care? His mother would take them when he worked, he knew, but she was already caring for his sister Delora's two now that she'd taken a job as a bookkeeper to make ends meet. She'd raised her own kids; she shouldn't have to raise all her grandkids, too.

After his gigantic failure as a husband and father, Diaz didn't see himself marrying again. Tony and Elena had to be his priority.

So when he'd surfaced from the grief, he'd stuck to casual relationships: a few dates, sex but no sleepovers, no hurt feelings at the end. Sex felt necessary, like a meal grabbed when he'd been working for ten hours straight and knew he should be hungry. But he'd been viewing the necessity with increasing distaste. Damn it, he was too old for the dancing around needed to give him physical release! He wanted to sleep with a woman in his arms, not get up and fumble around for his clothes, then drive home. The last time he'd done the dance, he'd found out later that the woman had lied to him and was married. He'd felt dirty then.

He hadn't taken a woman out for six months now. And counting. Diaz hoped he wasn't thinking below his belt now. He'd noticed his partner had breasts— nice ones. And his dick was going, *Hey, yeah, go for it, man.*

Ann Caldwell would be easy to hurt. Her mother's suicide and then that son of a bitch of a father of hers had wounded her so badly, Diaz could see her fear and self-doubt and even self-loathing as clearly as if they were old, yellow bruises beneath her white, white skin. He didn't want to add to those bruises.

Razor in hand, he stared at himself in the mirror. Shaving cream clung like Santa's moustache to his upper lip. Uh-huh. Here he was shaving, so he could get nice and close to her tonight without giving her whisker burn. Thinking about sucking on her lower lip, seeing her sharp blue eyes get soft, even dreamy, was enough to make him hard.

He uttered an imprecation. Just how *was* he going to avoid hurting Ann? He couldn't cancel now without hurting her, and he couldn't make love to her without hurting her eventually.

Maybe, if he was real lucky, she'd hurt him instead.

He finished shaving, slapped on aftershave and went to get dressed. Perhaps it was selfish, but he didn't want to cancel.

Half an hour later, he rang her doorbell. She answered it so quickly he knew she'd been ready and waiting.

"Hey," he said.

"Long time no see." It didn't come out as flip as she'd probably hoped. She was nervous and it showed. Her eyes shied from his, her color was high and she was trying to hold her head up and her shoulders hunched at the same time.

She wore a red sweater that clung to her ample breasts and tiny waist. Black, drapey pants did nice things to her hips, while heels had added a few inches to her stature.

Down, boy.

"You look incredibly sexy," he said. "So sexy, I'm going to say we should go to dinner."

"I'm not…"

He shook his head. "Bat your eyes and say, 'What makes you think I was going to ask you in?'"

She stared at him. "I don't know how to bat my eyes."

Voice husky, he asked, "Were you going to ask me in?"

She forgot to hunch her shoulders. Neck long, chin tilted, she said, "Hell, no."

But he was pleased to see how pink her cheeks were as she grabbed her coat from the closet and her little black purse from the hall table.

They'd agreed before parting this afternoon that they would go out for seafood. They were both familiar with a little place on the Tacoma waterfront. Afterward, maybe a movie. They had to work tomorrow, so the evening couldn't be a late one.

Paddle around, he'd reminded himself. She needed swim lessons before she dove in.

What in hell am I doing here? he asked himself again, as Ann locked her apartment door, then turned to bump into him. He shouldn't have started this. She wasn't experienced, and she wasn't casual. He was violating his most basic tenets.

But, God, he wanted her.

She tipped her head back. "Um... Are we going anywhere?"

He kissed her. A brush of mouths, a quick nip at her full lower lip, and his heart pounded against his rib cage. He heard the lurch in her breathing.

He started to bend his head again.

Paddle.

"Yeah," he said, gruffly. "Are you hungry?"

JANICE KAY JOHNSON

"I think so." She sounded uncertain, her voice reedy.

He gripped her arm and turned her toward the car, marching them both along the walkway before he started kissing her again and didn't stop.

She must have been shaken, too, because she didn't protest.

On the drive, Ann talked about work. Her way of making conversation. They'd agreed after talking to Stillman that the Danner case wasn't their answer. They'd begun reading up on Sergei Belenky. He was the Russian immigrant who'd murdered five girls, all between the ages of fifteen and seventeen, before one escaped and was able to identify him. He'd admitted eventually to raping several other teenagers before escalating to murder. There were interviews to pore over, a transcript of the trial, newspaper clippings, even videotapes from King 5 news and other local stations. Public hysteria had been fanned by rallies where police competence was questioned and families were advised to keep their teenage girls under lock and key. Police spokesmen protested in vain that they couldn't be everywhere. One girl was snatched from a high school parking lot. Belenky later admitted he'd been hiding in her unlocked car. Another left a movie in a multiplex to use the bathroom and never came back. No one saw her hustled out a side exit. A third got mad at her boyfriend, refused to let him drive her home and had already vanished by the time he decided to go after her.

Ann was making points he wouldn't remember tomorrow. He didn't want to think about the job, because that reminded him that she was his partner. Partners went out for a casual drink; they took their wives or husbands or girlfriends to barbecues at each others' houses. They didn't date. They didn't become lovers.

She shut up again when he parked. After a brief moment of silence, she said, "I hope we don't run into someone we know."

"So, we stopped for dinner." He shrugged.

"I'm wearing makeup. Nobody would believe we 'stopped' for dinner."

"We don't hold hands at the table."

After a minute, she nodded. "Okay."

Maybe, if they called it off now, she wouldn't be hurt. Maybe she'd be relieved.

Refusing to examine his own mood, Diaz stopped before he opened the restaurant door.

"I've got to ask." With enormous effort, he maintained an even, nonjudgmental tone. Hey, the job gave him lots of practice. "If you have cold feet and want to call this off, just say so. I'll take you home."

She went still, her gaze on diners glimpsed through the tall windows. He'd gotten adept at reading her face in profile from the hours they spent driving from crime scene to interviews to the station. This time, he didn't have a clue.

His breathing didn't resume until she shrugged.

"Your call. I'm okay with it."

Relief hit him harder than the street the last time he'd tackled a perp.

"We're here. Let's eat." He opened the door and they went in, like any other couple.

CHAPTER TEN

LOW-HANGING LAMPS bathed each table and booth with a golden glow. The hostess seated Diaz and Ann by the window. Through the glass, Ann could see lights on ships and the black skeletons of cranes through the window, and at the same time the reflection of herself sitting, Diaz doing the same on the other side of the table.

A moment ago, she'd stood outside looking in, seeing the couples at these tables intent on each other. Now she was here, half of a couple. Someone outside might be looking in right now, as she opened the menu.

Colors seemed rich, like she remembered in Renaissance paintings she'd seen long ago at the Seattle Art Museum. China gleamed, glassware caught light, faces around them weren't pasty, but were instead ivory and coffee and every hue in between.

Diaz ordered wine, a luscious deep ruby when she watched it swirl into her glass. Ann felt surreal, as if she'd wandered into one of those paintings.

She was on the other side of the glass, where couples laughed softly, clinked wineglasses as they made promises, murmured in velvet voices, left finally arm in arm.

She gave her head a small shake. This was ridiculous! She'd eaten here before, for Pete's sake!

With friends. With her father. In a booth at the back, where bigger groups were more boisterous. She'd tried not to see the couples at the front.

"What are you thinking about?" Diaz asked.

"I...nothing." She shook her head again, dispelling the peculiar sense of disorientation. "I was overcome by the weirdness."

His eyes were dark, the solid planes of his face somehow less familiar. "Of us?"

"I don't know. I guess I've never been here on a date." *You guess,* she mocked herself.

"I haven't either," he said, to her surprise. "Cheri doesn't like seafood. And I haven't dated that much, since my divorce."

"I hear women's voices sometimes when I call you."

He shrugged. "My sisters, my mom. We're a close family."

"Really?" Relief out of proportion to the news that he didn't have a string of beautiful women swept over her. At the same time, she became conscious of a wistful desire to know more about a big family that chose to spend time together. "You're actually friends?"

"Yeah." He smiled at her expression. "We are. Maybe growing up with so many of us, we had to depend on each other, not just our parents. The big kids changed the little ones' diapers, helped with homework..." His shoulders moved again. "Teased, bullied and protected."

The waiter arrived to take their orders. When he left,

Ann guessed, "You're one of the big kids in your family."

"What makes you say that? No." He held up a hand. "Don't tell me. It's my commanding presence."

"'Bossy' was the word that came to mind."

They bickered amiably about her assessment before he admitted she was right. "I have...had," he corrected himself, "one older sister. Carla—Carlotta—is the one who died of breast cancer. She was tiny, but fierce. Only Mom could overrule her. Then comes me, Delora, Maria, Lucia and Manuel. Not so many of us."

She laughed in astonishment. "You're kidding, right?"

"About what?"

"I can hardly imagine having one sister or brother, never mind..." She counted mentally. "Five."

"My parents are Catholic. Plenty of their friends have seven or eight kids. Mom miscarried a few times. We have some gaps."

"Gaps."

"My aunt Rosa and Uncle Paco have nine kids and... I've lost track. Fourteen grandkids already, I think. No, Lola just had a baby. Fifteen."

"My God. What do you do about Christmas?"

He laughed. "We don't exchange with cousins, if that's what you're asking. Even in our immediate family, we draw names. We'd go broke if we felt obligated to buy for all the nieces and nephews. And think how spoiled they'd be."

"I had..." She stopped. "Never mind."

Voice gentle, he prompted, "Had what?"

She shrugged as if it didn't matter. "Four or five

presents at Christmas. Mom's parents always sent a box—I remember how excited I was when that box came.'' It was part of Christmas, the arrival on the doorstep via UPS of a good-size carton, always sealed with so much packing tape it took scissors and determination to separate the flaps. Inside would be wrapped gifts, a tin of homemade cookies already crumbling, candy canes and, for her, one of those Advent calendars that had a chocolate for each day until December 25. "Dad's parents lived in California," she continued. "They just sent money. It went into a fund I really did appreciate when I started college, but when you're eight years old, it's not so exciting."

"And your parents?"

She was silent for a moment, recalling the emotional seesaw that had been the holidays when she was young. "Mom loved Christmas, but it made her sad, too. One day she'd sparkle, and the next she'd cry." She drew a breath. "After she was gone, Dad tried, but it wasn't the same. He'd buy a couple of presents, put up outside lights…" Because everyone else on the block had done it, she'd always believed, not because of the excitement on his daughter's face. "…I'd beg until we got a tree. But it was never the same."

Diaz murmured something she realized was in Spanish. Their salads arrived just afterward, and not until the waiter had left them alone again did she ask, "What'd you say? A minute ago?"

"Pobre pequeña niña," he repeated. "You poor little one."

So that she wouldn't cry, Ann said, "I've never heard you do that before. Speak in Spanish, I mean."

"We all grew up bilingual. It's been handy on the job. I guess you and I just haven't run into a situation where I needed it."

"Do you think in English?" she asked out of curiosity.

"I switch back and forth. Whatever I'm speaking." His brows drew together. "What did you do this Christmas?"

This holiday, the first without her father, had been the loneliest of her life. But she wasn't about to tell Diaz that. So she shrugged. "I have friends."

His eyes narrowed and she could tell he didn't buy it.

Not giving him time to probe, she asked, "Do you get the kids for some of the time?"

"Cheri's family always opens presents Christmas Eve, mine Christmas morning. So that's how we divide it."

"You miss them, don't you?"

The expression on his face was bleak. "Every day. I'd have stuck out the marriage for their sakes, but..." It was his turn to shrug.

She was having to readjust her entire image of this man. The few times she'd called him on their days off or in the evening and heard women's voices and laughter, he hadn't been partying. He'd been with family. What she'd heard was his sisters teasing him, maybe. She had a big-screen flash, bright and noisy: babies on hips, gossip, news, shared memories. His mother giving him an affectionate hug as she passed, kids shrieking in the next room.

Ann bit her lip. "I'm sorry."

Unaware she was apologizing for her misconceptions as well as his loss, Diaz spread his hands. "What can you do?"

They ate and talked about things they'd never touched on before. Diaz admitted to pride in his daughter, who had recently tested as gifted and been put in a special class. He worried aloud because she missed her friends, and because Tony might get frustrated trying to live up to his sister's accomplishments. Ann told him about selling her father's house and having to sort through his possessions.

"He hadn't planned for death. You know? It's not as if he'd had a heart condition or something like that. So I came across stuff he probably would have thrown away rather than let me see."

Gaze warm, intent, Diaz asked, "About your mother?"

"Yeah, some of it. I didn't have that many pictures of her, but I found a whole carton of them up in his closet. And some letters she'd written before they married. She apparently hesitated about marrying Dad and went back East for a while. I read a couple, but they were so intimate." She shook herself. "I couldn't make myself shred them or have some kind of bonfire. I just...put them away with the photos and the papers about her death and stuff like that."

He nodded. "We stored some of Carla's things. Mom was too emotional to make decisions. Someday."

"She wasn't married?"

He shook his head. "She was the smart one of our generation. Carla was a doctor. Can you believe that?"

He seemed to marvel at the very idea: his sister, the doctor. "Nobody in our family had even gone to college, but Carlotta, she always got straight A's, and teachers always said, 'Your Carla can do anything she sets her mind to.'"

"Were you jealous?"

In surprise, Diaz said, "Jealous? Why would I be? I was an okay student, but I always knew what I wanted to be."

Ann smiled at him. "Then why do you assume Tony will be?"

"Because I have to worry about something?" He shook his head. "I don't know. You're right. I should tell him about my big sister and how smart she was and how the whole family celebrated when she got accepted to medical school."

"Yeah, you should."

The whole family celebrated. Her father couldn't even say, "I was proud of you today," but the Diaz family celebrated the accomplishments of their children. When she imagined such a thing, the toasts and the hugs and the laughter, it had the quality of a childhood fantasy. Everything perfect, every face shining with joy, no petty jealousy, no shrugs—*So, what's the big deal?*—no undercurrents. A make-believe world.

"Had your sister put off marriage because of medical school, or just not met anybody?" she asked, to keep Diaz talking as much as out of curiosity.

"I think maybe she met somebody and got her heart broken. She never said much, but there was something in her eyes."

When he fell silent, Ann asked, "What do your other sisters and brother do?"

"Mmm. Lucia is a nurse practitioner. She wanted to be a doctor, too, but she couldn't get into medical school. She claims now she's happier the way things turned out." His mouth tipped up at one corner. "'Except for the money,' she always adds. 'A couple more years of school, and they make $100,000 more? Where's the fairness in that?'"

Ann smiled, too. "Whoever said life had to be fair?"

"You're right." He grinned. "Let's see. Manuel is a cop, too. Works for SPD. He's only been on the job a couple of years, and he's already been shot." Diaz shook his head. "Scared the crap out of all of us."

"What happened?"

"Just one of those things. Pulled someone over because his taillight was out. Turned out the guy had a trunkful of meth. He waited until Manuel was ten, fifteen feet away and opened fire. Got him in the shoulder, but Manuel dove behind the guy's car and he took off. They got him right away. And Manuel..." The humor and liking in his laugh lit Diaz's face. "He ate it up. Wounded in action. Women fluttered around." He made a careless sound. "They flutter anyway. My little brother is good-looking."

Ann was sure that was an opening she should use to flirt. But by the time she'd run through possibilities, he was talking about Delora, who had worked at Boeing for a few years but had quit when her third child was born. Lately she'd gone back to work part-time.

"Two still in diapers." He shook his head. "She and José are good churchgoers. They'll probably have eight."

"And your other sister? Maria?" Had she gotten the name right?

"Maria is the rebel. She's a social worker who spends her summers in migrant worker camps. We used to tease her because she was so sure she could save the world. But she's actually trying. She took after Carla."

"She's fierce, too."

"Yeah." Diaz sounded bemused and proud again.

When the waiter offered them refills on coffee, they decided to skip the movie. They kept talking—about movies, cop shows on TV, favorite espresso stands and impersonal apartments that defied attempts to give them character.

When waiters started clearing tables and putting up chairs, Diaz said, "I think they're trying to get rid of us."

With regret, she agreed, "Unless we're planning to sleepwalk tomorrow, it's time we left anyway."

The waterfront was dark at this hour, the streets deserted. Diaz unlocked Ann's side of the car first, then opened it for her. Nobody had ever opened doors for her, pulled out chairs, treated her like a woman. Thinking back, she realized the guy she'd slept with in college had lacked social graces. His lovemaking hadn't been what you'd call polished, either. She'd always wondered what it would be like to be in bed with a man who knew what he was doing. Of course, men like that probably chose women who knew what they were doing, too.

She hated the fact that now she was wondering about Diaz. Could you ever *quit* wondering, once you started? Maybe it would be better if she just found out. If he turned out to be clumsy in bed, too, thinking about himself and what he wanted, she could get over this gigantic crush she seemed to have on him.

He got in and slammed his door. Reaching for the seat belt, he asked, "So, are you really thinking about buying a house?"

Grateful for the mundane subject, Ann made a face. "I don't know. Yeah, some days. I slow down sometimes when I pass one for sale. Or I look at the Sunday classifieds. But I haven't actually called a real estate agent or anything like that. They'd ask what I want, and I don't know."

He backed out of the parking spot. "Oh, come on. You must have started a list. Do you want a big yard?"

"Not a big one," she said without hesitation. "But big enough for…" Whoa. A swing set? Had she almost said that? Had that clock started ticking without her noticing? She didn't even like children! Weakly, she finished, "For some flowers. You know. Roses. My mother grew roses."

"Really?"

"Hybrid teas. With big fragrant blooms. She liked to have bouquets." Ann stared ahead through the dark windshield, remembering. "After she died, Dad ignored them. When I was twelve or thirteen, I noticed they were half-dead and scraggly and the flowers weren't that big anymore. So I made Dad take me to a nursery and they gave me a pamphlet on roses and I bought some fertilizer. Mom had a green thumb, but I kept her roses limping along, at least.'' Her only attempt, she realized now, to keep her mother's memory alive, to maintain some kind of connection. Then, she would have lied even to herself and said she just liked flowers. Now she remembered closing her eyes, inhaling the powerful, sweet scent and feeling an ache that was both joy and grief.

"Okay," Diaz said. "Room for a few flower beds. How about bedrooms? How many?"

"I want to say three, but that's just because houses are supposed to have three bedrooms." She laughed a little. "I really only need one, I guess."

"A town house?"

Ann shook her head. "No, I want a real house. In a neighborhood."

"Hey, we're getting somewhere." He sounded pleased, not as if he was laughing at her. "New house?"

She hesitated. "Yeah…maybe. I don't know. I guess I don't care. I don't want to have to work on a house."

"Okay. Not an old one. Big kitchen?"

"I microwave," she admitted.

Diaz nodded. "I actually like to cook, but I only do it when Elena and Tony are with me. The rest of the time, I eat out or buy frozen dinners."

"I can do basic stuff. Dad liked baked potatoes and roasts. I had to do the cooking when I was growing up. I guess that's why I don't like to do it now," she realized. "Cooking for him, I couldn't try new recipes.

We had this rotation. Meat loaf, roast, ham, hamburgers, spaghetti, which had to taste just like Mom's, and fried chicken. Then I'd start over.''

"Him and Reggie."

"Yeah, I can just imagine Reggie if Mary put a new casserole in front of him.'' She mimicked him. Or maybe it was her father's irritation she remembered as if she'd heard his voice ten minutes ago. "'What the hell is this? Goddamn it, I can afford to put real meat on the table!'''

Diaz laughed. "Yeah, he must be a real pleasure."

Ann half turned in her seat. "Why don't you buy a house?''

"I'm not sure I can afford to. Child support takes a big chunk of my paycheck. And I try to help when there's extras. Like, Elena wants to go to summer camp this year. Maybe the Girl Scout one over on Hood Canal.''

"That sounds fun.'' Ann had known girls who went. She had envied them. She'd hated summers, when she had to hang around the house every day. She'd watched endless videos and read. She hadn't been allowed to go more than a block from home, so she'd ridden her bike around and around and around that block, until she knew every crack in the sidewalk, every bump where a tree root tunneled under, every little kid who waved when she went by. She'd been old enough to take care of herself, but she didn't like it.

"Tony's talking big about going to camp, too, but I'm not so sure he's ready. Even Elena may chicken out. I told you she's...tentative.''

"Maybe because she thinks too much," Ann suggested. With too much time on her hands, she'd done that. Imagined every pitfall along with every glorious possibility, whether either were ever realized or not.

"That's probably it." He was quiet for a moment. "Anyway, right now I want to stay nearby, so they can take the school bus to my place and exchanging them isn't a big deal. My apartment is okay."

"Mine is, too. It just doesn't feel like home."

"Ditto."

He turned into her parking lot and she fell silent, heart thudding in her chest. Was she supposed to invite him in? She wanted him to kiss her, but the idea scared her, too. She hadn't made out with a guy in a really long time, and she'd never felt that natural at it in the first place.

Ann drew a tremulous breath. They shouldn't have started this, considering they worked together. It would ruin everything. She *liked* having him as a partner. What if she said now, *This was stupid. Let's forget we ever*...

Now. She had to say it *now*. He'd already parked and was putting the car into park.

"You've gotten quiet."

This was stupid were not the words that popped out.

"I'm just tired, I guess." Sure you are, she jeered at herself.

"Then I'll say good-night."

She gave a jerky nod.

"Don't look so terrified."

Ann swallowed. "I...can't help it."

A muscle jerked along his jaw. "Maybe this wasn't a good idea."

He was going to go. Say, *This was stupid, let's forget it.* Wasn't that what she wanted?

No. What she wanted—what she ached for—was him to kiss her. She was being a coward again, sabotaging any chance for a relationship.

"No." She squeezed her hands together until her nails bit into her flesh. "I'm just, uh, not that experienced. I mean, I don't date very often. Woman cop and all that."

He reached out and touched her cheek, smoothed hair back over her ear. "We've got something good, you know. We're risking it for something better that might not happen."

Ann nodded again.

The broad pad of his thumb caressed her lower lip. Voice low and rough, he asked, "Is it worth taking the chance?"

Her lips parted and she shocked herself by touching his thumb with her tongue.

He groaned.

"Yes," she whispered.

"Yeah." He plunged his fingers into her hair. "It's too late, isn't it?"

She murmured some kind of agreement just before his mouth closed over hers.

Thoughts blurred, and she wallowed in sensation instead. His warm, seeking lips, the scrape of his jaw against hers, the nip of his teeth and stroke of his tongue. His fingers moved restlessly, kneading her head and nape, tugging her hair to adjust the angle of her mouth. She gripped his shirt with one hand while she laid her other against his neck. She felt the vibration of his groans, the strength of tendons and muscles.

This was easier than she'd ever imagined it could be. Kissing didn't seem to require planning or experience; all she had to do was meet his tongue with hers, suck gently on his lip after he had on hers, let out odd little sounds when he kissed her neck and ear and nuzzled her cheek and throat.

Okay, the emergency brake dug into her thigh and she'd forgotten to take off her seat belt, which flattened one breast and made breathing hard when she strained against it. But who needed to breathe?

Her hand sneaked up to stroke his hair and he turned from her mouth to press a hot kiss into her palm. Oh, this felt so good! She wanted...

He nipped her lip suddenly, hard, and lifted his head. His breath rasped. "I think," he said, in a voice that didn't sound like his, "that I really had better say good-night now."

She blinked at him. He wanted to stop?

Then humiliation rushed her cheeks and burned her eyes. Probably she hadn't been doing anything right. Why else would he be unbuckling her seat belt and all but lifting her away from him?

"I'm sorry," she said incoherently. "I...I don't know what I was..."

With a growl, he gripped her shoulders and turned her toward him again. "What the hell are you sorry for?"

She gaped at him.

"Caldwell, if I don't stop now, I'm going to be on

my knees between your legs. I figure that's not the way we should do it the first time.''

"You want me?'' It came out as a timid squeak.

He kissed her again, with hard, hungry passion. When he lifted his head, they were both breathing hard.

"Yeah. I want you.''

She ached between her legs. She wanted him there, even if it was in his car in the parking lot. The image she had of him kneeling, of her legs wrapped around his waist, was vivid and erotic. It snapped her out of her daze.

"Oh.''

He laughed. Or tried, anyway. "We're going to paddle, remember?''

"Paddle?'' She felt stupid.

"Instead of diving in?''

Memory stirred. Dumb idea. Diving in seemed lots smarter right now. All right, maybe not smarter, but definitely more gratifying.

"I want you, too,'' she said.

His fingers bit into her upper arms. "Maybe you shouldn't have told me that.''

A giggle, absurdly carefree, bubbled from somewhere in her chest and rose to pop out like a hiccup. "Just think. Tomorrow morning we're going to have to pretend we never said any of these things. Or did any of them.''

His face sobered and he let her go, sitting back in his seat. "Yeah. You know, we're going to have to admit to our sins eventually. Unless we want to sneak around for the rest of our lives.''

She filed away "the rest of our lives" part to think about later. "One of us will have to transfer."

"I know."

"Will we get to choose who goes?"

"Probably not." Pause. "Maybe. Would that be any easier?"

Why hadn't she thought all this through? She'd wanted, badly, to step into her father's shoes. But Diaz had seniority, experience, the right to send her back to patrol or to the Pawnshop Unit or maybe, if she was lucky, something exciting like Vice, where she'd probably end up in a skirt that didn't cover her butt, standing on a street corner trying to look like she knew how to summon men. Wouldn't that be the ultimate humiliation, to pretend to be a hooker and have no one try to pick her up?

"I...don't know," she said.

"You look like this hadn't occurred to you."

"I'm not that dumb! Of course it did. But this has happened fast. I hadn't gotten past us having to face each other in the morning."

"Yeah." His voice was flat. "Let's leave it at that for now, shall we? See where this goes."

Biting her lip, Ann nodded. She still had that achy feeling low in her belly, but panic also fluttered in her chest. She *was* that dumb. She should have thought all this through. She'd worked hard to get where she was, and now she was supposed to give it up for a man. That was how it always worked, wasn't it? Diaz had as much as told her himself that his marriage had ended over his job. Ann knew he'd been involved in drug investigations, which meant lots of undercover work. Maybe all his wife had wanted was for him to quit that in favor of something more regular, like Fraud.

The illogic of her resentment occurred to her—*she* didn't want to leave Homicide & Assault, while he should have been okay with monitoring pawnshops so he could save his marriage. But that was something she'd think about later, too.

"Thank you for dinner," she said by rote. "I did have fun."

Sounding gruff, he said, "I did, too." He reached for his door handle. "I'll walk you up."

She knew arguing wouldn't stop him, so she only nodded. They met at the front of the car and he walked beside her to her unit. Neither said anything until she'd unlocked her door.

Then, "We'll work something out," he said, and kissed her. Quick, hard, hungry.

In a daze again, she watched him walk away.

She was supposed to think tonight. And all she wanted was to call him back. To say, "I don't care what happens."

But she did care. It was her life—who she was. She didn't know if she could be anyone else, like a girl-friend or a lover. Or a wife.

Wife made Ann think of her mother, frying bacon and eggs for her husband and daughter's breakfast while tears ran down her cheeks. Or Mary, ignoring her husband's abuse while serving him hand and foot.

Chest squeezed as if she were having an asthma attack, Ann backed inside, shut the door and turned the dead bolt. Her hand was shaking, she saw with detached surprise.

Then she turned to face her empty apartment and the possibility that she wasn't capable of any other kind of life.

CHAPTER ELEVEN

THE HOUSE was standard-issue split-level in a development of them, all with cheap siding, small squares of lawn and bikes lying on their sides in the driveways.

Diaz had come alone. He and Ann had agreed that morning to divide up the names. The suggestion had been hers, making him wonder if she felt so uncomfortable with him she'd come up with the excuse to get herself away from him.

The door was opened almost immediately after he rang. The man who had answered studied Diaz with penetrating, almost angry eyes.

"Mr. Loew?"

"You're the police officer who called?"

"I am."

His jaws knotted. After a moment, Arthur Loew stepped back. "The wife's waiting upstairs."

"Thank you."

Diaz followed the other man up the half-dozen stairs that led to the main floor of the house. The kitchen lay ahead, to the left was a hall that undoubtedly led to bedrooms and bathrooms, and to the right was a long, combined dining room/living room. Diaz took in the decor with one glance: imitation early American dining set, plaid sofa and a pair of recliners, gas fireplace with a mantel crowded with framed photos.

Mrs. Loew rose from the couch when the two men appeared. Maybe in her early forties, she looked sixty. Grief did that to people. She hadn't bothered to color the gray in her brown hair, or to use makeup to cover the dark circles beneath her eyes.

"Can I get you a cup of coffee?"

Some people would be happier with the chance to bustle in the kitchen, make conversation, create a level of comfort. Diaz sensed that she would make the effort, but it would exhaust her, as everything probably did.

"Thanks, but I'm fine."

She nodded and sat. Her husband sat beside her on the couch. Both looked at Diaz, the wife with dull eyes and the husband with hostile ones. Neither said, "Please, have a seat."

Diaz chose a recliner facing them and sat anyway, opening his notebook on his lap.

"I'm sorry to bring back bad memories, and I'm grateful for your willingness to talk to me."

"Why are you here?" Arthur Loew asked.

"We're doing some follow-up on how the investigation of your daughter's killer was handled. I understand that you felt at the time that the police hadn't done enough."

"You can say that again!" Loew snapped. "How the hell could he waltz right out of a public place with our Carrie?"

"Arthur," his wife said. Her voice was…flat. Wiped

clean of intonation. "You know they couldn't be everywhere."

"Were you in court when he was sentenced?" Arthur Loew asked. "Did you see him weep and beg for mercy? He couldn't help himself, he said. It was like a dream when he hurt those girls." He leaned forward, eyes burning. "Was he dreaming when he stalked them for weeks beforehand? He should have gotten the death penalty. I wanted to see him die."

"Arthur."

He looked at her, and his shoulders sagged. With quiet anguish, he said, "I want to blame somebody. But I know…" he choked. "I know that evil is hard to stop."

Hating the necessity of asking a single other question, Diaz did it anyway. "Do you remember the deputies who spoke to you at the time?"

Arthur Loew turned an uncomprehending gaze on Diaz. "I don't remember anything except that Carrie was missing. We kept waiting for the phone to ring…" He swallowed. "We thought she'd run into a friend, done the kind of dumb thing kids do. We thought she'd call."

Tears silently ran down his wife's cheeks.

"I'm sorry," Loew said. "You might have been one of those deputies, and I wouldn't remember your face."

"You have a son."

"Jared just turned fourteen. He's growing up in a house of mourning. We try, but…"

Mrs. Loew wiped her cheeks.

"It takes time," Diaz said, despising the platitude.

What was "it"? Fading memory, so that they had to look at photos to remember their daughter's face? He'd seen enough tragedy to know that time did heal most wounds, but not all. Some festered, some merely ached. Some were quiet until the season of loss came around. He imagined losing Elena the way these people had lost their child, and he knew he would never recover.

Mrs. Loew seemed to drag herself from some far away place. "We try," she said, in that colorless voice. "We took Jared out of school this fall and went to Kauai for a month. His teachers were good about it. I think...all of us were better there. I could sleep, a little."

"You didn't go over Christmas break, then?" Diaz asked, as if casually, closing his notebook.

She shook her head. "We couldn't even face Thanksgiving in this house. We had to do something."

"We went for the whole month of November," Loew said. "Back home, we're right where we left off. Getting away was so good for us, I've put in for a transfer. We need to start over."

"We'll take Carrie with us." His wife's gaze strayed to the mantel, where Diaz realized a silver box among the photos must hold the murdered girl's ashes.

"You were lucky to be able to get off work for a month," Diaz commented to Loew.

"They've been good, too. My boss understands."

"So you didn't have to commute back and forth?"

"I'm an insurance adjuster. One of dozens in my office. I'm not that important."

Satisfied—Roarke's "accident" had happened November 10—Diaz rose. "I think you're wise to move. Fresh surroundings and people who don't always think of the tragedy when they see you might allow you to heal in a way you can't here."

"That's what we think." Loew laid his hand over his wife's, just for an instant, but she lifted her gaze to his and tried to smile. Then he stood, too. "Did we answer your questions?"

"Yes. Thank you."

Diaz shook Arthur Loew's hand at the door and walked out into a day that felt like spring despite last remnants of snow. Diaz had actually seen an open daffodil on the drive here.

Getting into his car, he wondered how Ann was doing—whether she'd faced grief as palpable as he had in that ordinary split-level house.

For a moment, he closed his eyes. God, he didn't want to go to the next interview. He kneaded his forehead, trying to ease the pain that squeezed his scalp. It didn't help.

After a moment, he started the car and pulled away from the curb. He had a half-hour drive ahead, and no Caldwell to bounce ideas off. None of his thoughts were welcome.

He kept seeing the faces of the Loews, the bleak knowledge that they had failed their daughter in the most fundamental way: they hadn't been able to protect her from a monster. He imagined the pictures they must see every night when they tried to sleep, the way they must beg God for a second chance that couldn't be granted.

Then there was Ann. The way she'd responded to

his kisses, with astonishment and delight. The memory of her hair, heavy and sleek as it slipped through his fingers, the ample pillow of her breasts pressed to his chest, the taste of her mouth, all made him shift uncomfortably. One kiss, and he'd been ready to beg. Diaz wasn't used to feeling desperate.

She was different than women he'd known. More difficult. She was a cop, and a good one—gutsy, bold, able to come at things from a new angle. She was tough, too, until you peeled away a layer or two and found raw emotions and vulnerability that scared the crap out of him even as it activated a protective instinct as strong as he felt toward his kids. Every minute with her, he had to be aware how easily he could hurt her.

They'd passed a point of no return, even though they hadn't made love. But he had a feeling she hadn't figured that out yet. Last night, she'd understood that they would have to make sacrifices to have a relationship, and she'd panicked. She wasn't used to making little adjustments to accommodate someone else, never mind big ones. After losing her mother, the only person she had ever really tried to please was her father— and she'd failed. Diaz thought she had begun to realize that she wasn't to blame for either her mother's depression or her father's rejection of her, which was healthy. This was probably a piss-poor time for him to be asking her to make room in her life for him.

He was back where he started, knowing he should end this before it really began, and knowing also that he wasn't going to. He couldn't go back to the days when she was a good partner he could put out of his mind the minute their shift ended. He thought about her damn near all the time. He wondered what she was doing, who she was doing it with. Whether she was bored, lonely. What his mother would think of her, and her of his mother. How she'd be with his kids, day in and day out. Whether she'd put the cap back on the toothpaste, steal the covers at night, burrow against him or roll away to sleep.

He was picturing her moving in with him after one date. He hadn't touched her breasts, he hadn't seen her naked, he didn't know what her favorite foods were, but he knew he wanted to live with her.

He also knew the idea had never occurred to her. He was moving too fast. Way too fast. But how the hell was he supposed to slow down, when he could barely get through a day without her at his side?

WITH A FERVOR that embarrassed her, Ann wished Diaz was here. He'd know what to do. She could handle violent drunks twice her size, freeze idiots with a few chilly words and interrogate scumbag lawyers who thought they could outsmart mere cops. But a grieving mother was not her forte.

When the woman started to cry, Ann had no idea what to say. Her awkwardly expressed sympathy was unlikely to help. Diaz was so much better in this kind of situation. Ann took the back seat where emotional women or children were involved, unless they had reason to be terrified of men.

The first parents she had interviewed this morning had been bad enough. This was way worse. So far, she'd pretended she hadn't noticed the tears welling in eyes fixed on hers with the desperation of a helpless drowning victim. Doggedly, she asked, "Is your ex-husband in the area?"

Fern Abbott sniffed and shook her head. "He... hadn't seen Jennie since she was three. I haven't heard from him in so long, I didn't even bother to let him know she's dead."

"When your daughter initially disappeared, was he a suspect?"

"The police asked me about him, but I told them he wouldn't abduct her. Why would he, when he didn't even send birthday cards?"

"Did they locate him?"

Thank heavens, Ms. Abbott was too incurious to wonder why Ann was asking about the ex. She shook her head again.

"They found Jennie's body. The..." Her voice hitched. "That's when they started to think she'd been killed by the same man who murdered the other girls."

"Did you attend the trial, Ms. Abbott?"

She dashed away tears, her voice hardening. "Every day. I took a leave of absence from my job. I wanted the jury to see me and know what he'd done. I wanted *him* to see me."

No, she had no other family in the area, no live-in lover. Jennie had not had a boyfriend. Fern Abbott herself didn't seem to blame the police.

"It might have been different if he'd attacked girls in the same neighborhood. But with him moving around the way he did, and different police departments investigating each murder, I'm surprised they were all tied together as soon as they were. I was grateful for the call when he was arrested, so I didn't just find out listening to the radio or something.''

"You've been very helpful, Ms. Abbott." Ann closed her notebook. "I'm terribly sorry I had to bother you."

That hopeless gaze stopped Ann, halfway to her feet. "Do you have a child?"

She shook her head, almost wishing she could say, *Yes. Yes, I understand.* After a brief hesitation, she sat down again. "I'm not married."

The gaze lost intensity and seemed to turn inward even as Fern Abbott's voice dismissed this woman police officer. "Then you don't know. You can't know."

"No. I don't."

"She was my only child." She seemed almost to be speaking to herself.

"I'm so sorry."

Ms. Abbott shook her head with finality. "You don't know. I'm not sure why I get up in the morning. Someday...I just won't."

A ripple of alarm raised goose bumps on Ann's arms. "I hope you have support. Friends, or members of your church, or..."

"They say it'll get better, but it won't."

"It...may." Ann hated sounding timid. She cleared her throat. "I lost my father last year. He was my only family. I felt lost. But it is getting better."

"Your child is different." With enormous dignity, she rose to her feet. "I hope I told you what you needed to know." The pause felt significant. "Whatever that is."

"Yes, I..."

But the tall, slender black woman with close-cropped hair was walking away, toward the front door. She wanted Ann to leave.

Ann mumbled more thanks and complied. The door brushed her back when it closed behind her.

Fern Abbott was unlikely to have gone to the window to watch Ann walk to her car. She had probably forgotten the visitor had ever been there. Nonetheless, Ann went down the walkway and got in her car as if eyes followed her.

When—if—they found a murderer, it would be somebody like this woman who thought no one understood, no one cared. Somebody driven by a loss so profound, the only emotions left were rage and grief.

Somebody, Ann thought, with nothing more to lose.

She should have started the car but didn't. She felt this huge pressure in her chest. So good was she at ignoring emotions she didn't want to feel, it took her a moment to realize she was filled with anger and a sense of loss so powerful, she knew they'd lived in her for years. Since the moment her father met her at the door after school and said, "Your mom's dead."

Why hadn't her mother loved her the way Fern Abbott had loved her daughter? Had her mother even *thought* about what she'd be doing to her young daughter?

The grown-up, the cop, knew intellectually how depression swamped people, turning them inward. Det. Caldwell knew that someone profoundly depressed enough to kill herself was incapable of thinking about other people.

But the child inside grieved nonetheless.

Her rage and grief had barely quieted when her cell phone rang.

She punched Send. "Caldwell."

"Hey," Diaz said. "Is this a bad time?"

"No, I'm sitting in my car." *So sad I'm unable to move.*

"Yeah, me, too. You want to meet for lunch and compare notes?"

Once again, he was her lifeline. "Yes. Please."

After finding out where he was, she suggested a pizza parlor midway.

He was waiting on the sidewalk by the door of the pizza place when she got out of her car. The first thing she said to him was, "This sucks."

His smile was wry. "You had a good morning, too. I can tell."

He didn't touch her on the way in, although he held the door open for her. Inside, they briefly discussed what to order, then filled plates at the salad bar. Self-conscious after loading hers with macaroni and potato salad as well as a green one buried in croutons and grated cheese, she noticed how spare his choices were: spinach, vegetables, fat-free Italian dressing and a sprinkling of sunflower seeds.

He must have caught her sidelong glance, because he said, "Cholesterol."

"Cholesterol?"

He grimaced. "Had my annual checkup the other day. I got a lecture about the bad versus the good kinds of cholesterol. My ratio is off. I figured it was the pie à la mode."

"But...you're only..."

"Thirty-seven." He set his tray on a table and slid in on one side of the booth. Without discussion, they'd chosen one under a window, well away from the scattering of other diners. "My father died at forty-eight. His second heart attack. My mother nags, too." He looked without enthusiasm at his salad. "I thought I'd try to eat better."

"Oh."

He nodded at her plate. "You ever get your cholesterol checked?"

"I don't know. I guess so." Damn it, she was hungry, and now she felt guilty about her heaped plate. "My doctor hasn't said anything."

"Count your blessings." He picked up his fork.

"I have a family history of depression instead," she felt compelled to point out.

"Do you? Besides your mother?"

She'd start with the green salad. Maybe by then the edge would be off her hunger and their number would have been called. "Does it take more than one parent to make a history?"

"Medically speaking, yeah. I think so."

"I don't really know. Mom was an only child, too. Her parents seemed okay, but I didn't know them that well. My grandmother was Italian, and she complained a lot about the food in this country. That's mostly what I remember about her."

"And your grandfather?" Diaz ate with apparent enjoyment.

"He was quiet. If anyone asked a question, he'd look at her. Maybe he'd forgotten how to talk."

"Or *he* was depressed."

Ann paused with the fork halfway to her mouth to consider the possibility. "I don't know. He seemed happy enough. She was the one who was super critical. She scared me. She'd frown at me as if something was always lacking."

"I take it they're dead?"

"Actually, no. But I haven't seen them since Mom's funeral. They still send me a check for my birthday and Christmas. The same amount as when I was sixteen." It always gave her a pang. The year after her mother's suicide, they'd sent a box with gifts like always, but after that they started giving her money instead. Maybe because her mother wasn't around to tell them what to buy her. She added, "My grandmother always writes a few sentences on the card. You know. 'My arthritis is acting up but otherwise we're fine. Your grandfather insisted on remodeling the kitchen this year. Hope all is well with you.' That kind of thing."

Diaz stared at her like she was crazy. "You have family, and you don't bother to visit them?"

"They don't visit me."

He scowled at her. "Have you ever asked them?"

"I hardly remember them!"

"Has it ever occurred to you that your father might have discouraged visits? Or even that they disliked him?"

Weirdly enough, it hadn't. She'd assumed, with the utter lack of confidence of a child who'd never fit in anywhere, whose mother had abandoned her in the most final way possible, that they were only marginally interested in her.

Diaz saw the answer on her face and shook his head. "Did you tell them your dad died?"

"I wrote a note on my Christmas card," Ann mumbled.

"And?"

"My grandmother sent a note back saying they were very sorry to hear the news and asked if I was all right."

"And?"

"And what?" she snapped.

"You didn't write back? Call? Nothing?"

Feeling mulish, she glowered at him. "Why would I?"

"Because family is important? And you don't have any?"

She squirmed. "I guess I could write them."

"Why don't you call?"

"What would I *say?*"

He muttered something in Spanish that she took for incredulity or disgust. "'Hi. I wondered how you are. I'm sorry we didn't stay in closer touch after Mom died.'"

"Why should *I* have to say that? Why not them? They're the—" She braked.

"The adults?" He raised a brow.

"Well," Ann said sulkily, "they *were* the adults."

Shaking his head at her again, he asked, "Where do they live?"

"Arkansas. Mom grew up in St. Louis, and they retired to a small house on a lake in the Ozarks. I guess it's cheap there or something."

"Beautiful, too, I hear." Diaz pushed aside his salad plate and stood. "That's our number."

Ann ate a few bites of potato salad while he was gone. To heck with cholesterol.

She guessed she could call. After all, she was their only family, too, and they were getting old. Calculating, she decided they were probably in their seventies. Not that old.

How had they felt when their only child killed herself? Had life become meaningless, or did it make a difference if you at least had one other person? She could still see her grandmother wailing at the funeral service, and her grandfather clumsily putting his arm around her.

She couldn't remember much about that visit. They must have stayed for a little while after the funeral, but those days ran together in her mind. She had lain on her bed and stared at the branch of the maple tree she could see from her window, feeling so empty inside, she knew now she should have had counseling. When her father banged on her door and yelled, "For God's sake, what are you doing in there?" Ann would wheel her bike from the garage and ride around the block. Around and around, pedaling so hard her thighs burned.

She had a flash of memory. She hadn't slowed down enough to turn at the corner. Her bike had skidded off the curb and she'd flown through the air. She had hurtled straight into the fender of a passing car. She remembered a flare of satisfaction instead of fear. Because... Ann didn't know. Because she thought she was going to die? Because her father would be sorry now? Because she'd get some attention if she was hurt? She had no idea.

Diaz returned with the pizza and a couple of plates. He looked at her oddly, but when she reached for the knife and dished up a slice of pizza, he didn't say anything.

Not until they'd eaten in silence for several minutes did Ann finally break it. She wanted to root herself again in the here and now. "Find any possibles this morning?"

He shook his head and put down a half-eaten slice. "I eliminated the families of two of Belenky's victims. I felt like scum making them relive something so horrific when the odds were minuscule to start with that any one of them is our killer."

"Me, too."

"You cross everybody off your list?"

"Oh." Dispirited, she tore a piece of crust into shreds. "I guess one mother is a remote possibility. Fern Abbott. Her daughter was the one who was nabbed at the high school. Belenky was hiding in her unlocked car."

"Right." Diaz nodded.

"The dad was out of the picture. There are no male relatives, no boyfriend. Mom didn't have a live-in. But the murders could have been committed by a woman. Birkey's is the only one that's a question mark, because his body might have been moved."

Gaze on her face, Diaz listened.

"Abbott is a tall woman. Slender but she looked strong. She's devastated. She kept saying, 'You can't know what it's like.' Jennie was her only child. She was pretty frank that she doesn't have much to live for.''

''And you're wondering if revenge is the little she does have.''

''Something like that.'' Ann looked down at the pile of crumbs that had been pizza crust. ''The thing is, she claimed not to be angry at the police. She knew the first murders were committed in different jurisdictions. When I mentioned the names of the deputies who'd dealt with her and asked if she felt they had been responsive to her concerns, she kept shaking her head and saying, 'I'm sorry. I don't remember any of them. I know police officers were here, but…they didn't matter. The only thing that mattered was Jennie.''' Ann couldn't suppress a shiver.

''Yeah, I got that, too,'' Diaz said.

''I'll check her out. Work schedule and so on. Maybe we can eliminate her that way. But she got me thinking.''

''Always dangerous.''

''Thanks.''

His grin was lopsided, and she could tell it had required an effort. He was feeling bummed, too.

''Go on. Shoot,'' Diaz said.

''First, the timing is okay if, say, Fern Abbott lost her daughter and decided to start killing because she thinks we should have caught Belenky sooner. But the girl's killer *was* ultimately arrested, tried and convicted, so she had that much satisfaction.''

''You think we should be looking for someone who didn't get that satisfaction.''

''Maybe.'' She shoved her plate away and planted

her elbows on the table. "Other cases we've looked at don't work timing-wise. That county councilman, for example. I mean, that happened—what?—three years ago? Why would the enraged dad or brother or boyfriend wait over two years to start killing?"

"That's a good question."

"And second, is rape as a crime adequate to throw this hypothetical father off the deep end? I mean, *he* wasn't raped. And he hasn't lost his only beloved child, the way Fern Abbott did. Yeah, sure, she got hurt, and that pisses him off, but a killing rage...that's something different."

"Another good point. Damn." Diaz gave a tired sigh. "Maybe we've gone at this wrong."

"Maybe we're just plain wrong. Maybe Dad and a bunch of his buddies really did have separate and unrelated accidents."

"I don't know." Diaz scrubbed a hand over his face. "I need a nap."

"Me, too," she admitted, even though she wasn't sure she wanted him to know that she'd tossed and turned rather than slept last night.

He tried a friendly leer. "What say we take one at your place?"

"In your dreams."

She was glad they'd met for lunch. This morning, she hadn't known what to say to him. But once they got to working, things became easier. More like they'd always been. This was what she stood to lose if they went any further than they had last night.

A great working relationship, a voice in her head pointed out. *Nice, sure. But jeez, girl, get your prior-*

ities straight. Imagine going home to him every night.
Talking about your day, cooking dinner together, un-
dressing each other. Remember those kisses.

Ann was about to argue with herself, but had the
self-control to refrain. *Later,* she told herself.

Having been absorbed in his own thoughts, Diaz
said, "Let's go back to the basics. Your father's the
first victim we're aware of."

She didn't bother to agree. She was just the audi-
ence.

"So why then? Why him? Chance, or was he tar-
geted first?"

"You're right." She stared into space. "His murder
wasn't like Pearce's. He didn't present an irresistible
opportunity. The other driver took some risks. Somebody might have seen him bumping Dad's pickup.
Heck, Dad had a cop's instincts behind the wheel,
whether he'd had a few drinks or not. He might have
rammed this guy off the road."

"So let's go back to the computer and take another
look. What had they been working on in the immediate
past? Was there anything all of them had been involved in together, besides the Belenky task force, in
the three or four months before your father died?"

"You're saying we drop the earlier possibilities?"

"No." Steady, dark, his eyes met hers. "I'm saying
we look at those, too, and do some research. If somebody didn't start killing cops then, why later? Did
something happen that we don't know about? Like,
what if this enraged father did get some satisfaction
when his daughter slash wife's killer went to prison,
but then, on appeal, the conviction got thrown out?

Maybe our deputies fouled up the chain of evidence and are responsible. Maybe a decision was made not to go for another trial.''

''That's more the prosecutor's decision...''

''But does our guy know that?'' Diaz's voice crackled now, his eyes were sharp, intelligent, awake. ''He just knows they could have prevented the crime if they'd *really* done their job. And now he has no satisfaction. Who else can he blame?''

''The murderer?''

''Maybe he took care of him, too.''

''Wouldn't we have heard if something like this happened?'' she said doubtfully.

''Could be we were wrong and it wasn't a high-profile case. Maybe it was just a lot of little screwups that added up to something bad for someone.''

Her back straightened. ''Or maybe something else happened. Say, it wasn't a murder at all. But maybe the wife who'd been raped suffered so much depression she eventually left her husband.''

''Or maybe,'' Diaz said softly, ''she killed herself.''

They stared at each other.

Heart drumming, she said, ''There weren't that many cases where all four deputies worked together. Or had contact with the victim.''

''No. There weren't.''

''And where the perp either didn't get convicted, or got off.''

He was ahead of her. His eyes gleamed.

''Maybe,'' she said, ''we'd better find out if that nice girl who claimed the county councilman raped her is still alive and well.''

CHAPTER TWELVE

ANN STARED at the computer screen. There it was. If they'd looked sooner...

"Diaz."

At his own desk, he turned his head. "Huh?"

"Deidre Moskowitz is dead."

With a muttered imprecation, her partner came to look over her shoulder. "You're sure that's her? What was she doing in Rhode Island?"

"She was a graduate student at Brown." Seeing that he was reading the obit, she added, "Not, you notice, in political science. She was in psych."

He was still reading. "Apparently self-inflicted." He grunted. "Father urges thorough investigation."

"Let's find out if her body was returned to Washington state for burial."

They came up with a small obit in a Renton local paper, giving details of funeral plans. Nothing in the *Seattle Times* or the *P.I.*

Diaz had pulled up a chair and straddled it so he could breathe down her neck as she scrolled. "Family must not have sent information to them."

"The question is, why not? Wouldn't you think they'd have wanted to raise a stink?"

"Yeah, you would."

She kept staring at the date of death. "Six weeks before Dad died."

"Plenty of time for anger to fester after the funeral."

She'd found the father's address. "Now? Or shall we wait for morning?"

He glanced at his watch. "Tony and Elena took the bus to my house. A neighbor is keeping an eye on them. I don't want to be late."

He was still so close, she didn't dare turn her head. "Oh. Sure."

"Want to come to dinner?"

"You don't have to ask me."

Diaz growled under his breath, gripped her chin and turned her face to his. "I want you to come or I wouldn't have asked."

"Oh," was the most intelligent response she could make.

"Is that a yes?" he asked in a soft rumble.

Fascinated by the details of a face seen up close, she nodded dumbly. He needed to shave already; the faintest trace of stubble darkened his chin. His lashes were long, thick, a woman's envy. And his eyes...

Behind her, their lieutenant said, "Am I interrupting something?"

Momentarily, Diaz's fingers tightened on her chin, then relaxed as he let her go. "We just discovered something interesting."

"I could tell." A razor-sharp gaze left Diaz's face and paused on Ann's. "I'll talk to you in my office."

Ann didn't move a muscle until she heard the footsteps recede. Then she slumped. "Oh, jeez."

"I'm sorry. This is my fault." Diaz shoved his chair back and stood. "I'll tell him I was coming on to you. This isn't your fault."

"Don't be ridiculous." She stood, too, and scowled at him. "Of course it is."

"Ann, I know what it means to you to work in this unit. Only one of us has to take the fall."

"We could lie."

They stared at each other.

He nodded finally. "It's been done."

Her sinuses burned. "Crap," she said, and turned to march toward O'Brien's office.

Diaz was right behind her.

The lieutenant was waiting behind his desk. "Sit."

Ann obeyed. Beside her, Diaz sat, too, for once not swinging the chair around to straddle it. His solid presence was the only reassurance she had.

"What in the hell were the two of you thinking?" Tone blistering, O'Brien raked them with cold eyes.

"Sir—" she began.

Diaz overrode her. Talking to her instead of to the lieutenant, he said, "No. Damn it, Caldwell, I touched you. Not the other way around."

The cold gaze drilled her. "Was his touch welcome?"

Ann swallowed. "I...yes. Sir."

"Was this the beginning?"

Fear squeezed her chest and tap-danced down her spine. She could salvage everything she'd worked so hard for if she lied now. Diaz would back her.

But she heard herself say, "No, sir. We had dinner last night."

Beside her, Diaz said, "We've socialized. Like any other partners. Until just recently."

"You intended to sneak around."

"No, sir." Her throat was dry. Her mouth felt gritty. "One of us would have asked for a transfer. We hadn't gotten that far."

"Lieutenant." Diaz sat square-shouldered, hands seemingly relaxed on his thighs. "We're getting somewhere on the cop-killer. Let us nail him before you write us up."

O'Brien narrowed his eyes. After a moment, he reached for one of his toothpicks and stuck it in his mouth, where it bobbed as the silence filled the room like rising water.

Ann struggled to retain her dignity and wait while withstanding the thoughtful gaze that seemed to read her mind.

"What do you have?" he asked at last.

Ann remembered to breathe. Diaz jerked enough to poke her with his elbow. She jumped.

"Oh! I mean…sir. We just found out that Deidre Moskowitz committed suicide. She was the young woman who claimed the county councilman raped her. The timing of all this bothered us." She explained their reasoning.

"She died six weeks before your father's death," the lieutenant repeated.

"That appears significant to us."

"You've been looking elsewhere."

"And eliminating possibilities," she confirmed.

"Have you talked to any members of Ms. Moskowitz's family yet?"

"No. We planned to try to set up an appointment for morning."

"Hmm." He turned his head and spit out the mangled toothpick. In the quiet, they all heard it strike the side of the metal wastebasket. "I should send you both back to patrol. At opposite ends of the county."

Neither said anything.

He leaned forward, elbows braced on the desktop. His eyes had become fierce. "Can you two keep your goddamn hands off each other? Can I trust you?"

The room had become a vacuum again, air scant. Ann was very conscious of Diaz's upper arm brushing hers.

"Yes, sir."

Tone wooden, Diaz agreed. "You can trust us."

"Two weeks. Then at least one of you is out of here." He looked from her face to her partner's. "I'll be watching."

"Sir." Ann scrambled to escape. Diaz already had the door open.

At her desk, she sank into her chair and closed her eyes. If her father had still been alive and heard about this, he'd have ripped her limb from limb, if only verbally. She heard words in her head: disgrace, humiliation, failure. All in his voice.

What had she been *thinking?* How had getting her eyebrows plucked and buying a new wardrobe mushroomed into making out with her partner and even flirting with him at her desk in front of the entire unit?

"Hey."

She opened her eyes in alarm at the sound of Diaz's voice.

He stood beside her desk. "Don't worry. It's not that bad. Remember when Fisher and Ryman got married? I'm betting they didn't keep their hands off each other before the announcement."

She hardly heard him. "My father would have killed me."

He snorted. "Your father, as you've discovered, didn't exactly set an ethical standard to aspire to."

"I don't want to go back to patrol!" she all but wailed.

"You won't have to." He sat on the corner of her desk, as if they hadn't just been warned to quit fraternizing. "He's not that ticked, you know. He wouldn't be giving us so much rope if he was."

Ann finally identified the misery bubbling inside her. "I've never been reprimanded. I hated feeling like…like…"

Diaz's gaze was keen. "A kid whose father is raking her over the coals?"

"Yes!" she burst out, then looked around quickly to see whether anyone was listening. "Maybe your parents understood if you screwed up. Mine didn't."

He shook his head. "So you've never let yourself fail."

She fired back, "I want to be good at what I do. Is that so bad?"

"You know it's not." Diaz suddenly looked tired. "Is falling in love on your list of major screwups?"

Stunned, she stared at him. Falling in love? Was that what she'd been doing? More to the point, was *he* saying that he was in love with *her*?

"Diaz…"

"Forget it." He stood, face a mask. "I'll see you in the morning."

"Wait!"

But he didn't stop. He grabbed his coat from the rack and walked out.

She almost went after him, but stopped herself. What would she say? *I don't know if I'm in love with you?*

How could you be sure? Ann knew few people with successful marriages, and none well enough to feel comfortable asking them something like that, especially since she'd have to explain about her relationship with Diaz.

After a minute, she logged off her computer and left, too. She wished she were on the way to his apartment for dinner. Instead, she had to stop at the grocery store to stock up on frozen meals, none of which looked enticing.

At home, she couldn't make up her mind which to stick in the microwave. Finally, on impulse, she called Eva Pearce.

After identifying herself, she said, "Are you busy? I can call another time…"

"No, I'm thinking about putting dinner on." Eva gave a gusty sigh. "Cooking for yourself is no fun."

"You want to go out and eat?"

"I have a better idea. Why don't you come over here? I do like to cook when I have somebody besides myself to appreciate my efforts. Are you picky?"

"No. Well…I hate corned beef and cabbage. In fact, I pretty much hate cabbage. Uh…and beets. Oh, and brussels sprouts."

Her friend laughed. "None of the above will be on the menu, I promise." She gave Ann directions to her town house in Kent.

When Ann arrived half an hour later, delicious smells already floated from the kitchen.

Seeing her breathing in the aroma, Eva said, "Chicken curry. One of my favorite recipes."

"It smells wonderful. Way better than the frozen lasagna I was about to put in the microwave."

Eva rolled her eyes. "That stuff'll kill you. Can I hang up your coat?"

She handed it over absentmindedly. "I love your place."

The living room had all the character her own lacked. It was more feminine than she would have chosen, but suited Eva. Lacy pillows softened a flowered sofa and wing chair while end tables and coffee table were created from elaborate scrolls of wrought iron painted sage green and topped with glass. A wreath of dried lavender, framed photos of family and an oil painting of a lush bouquet combined perfectly with pretty china statues and a leaded glass bowl and a wedding ring quilt in pastels that hung over the back of the wing chair.

"Thanks." Eva smiled. "I know it's fussy, but I love a kind of overblown cottage look. I feel like the Victorians, who figured any empty spot was wasted."

Still looking around, Ann followed the slender blonde to the kitchen. Eva wore sweatpants, a T-shirt and fuzzy pink slippers. Her hair was drawn back in a clip.

"I'd just gotten comfortable when you called," she said. "I hope you don't mind the sweats."

Ann gave a startled laugh. "Are you kidding? I'm relieved to see you dressed like a normal person."

They chatted while Eva chopped vegetables for a salad. Only when they were seated at the glass-topped table in the eating space, set with quilted place mats and matching cloth napkins, did Ann say, "You haven't mentioned your marriage."

Eva looked down at her food and poked at the chicken. "Yeah, well, it still stings. Turned out he was having an affair. You know the story. But I was dense enough to think everything was fine."

"I'm sorry."

"No, that's okay. It's been a year. The worst thing about it isn't that I miss Garth, it's that I've lost faith in my judgment. You know?"

Ann nodded. "I've never been that confident about my judgment in the first place."

Looking surprised, Eva said, "But you must evaluate people's motives and character every day in your job. Don't you get good at it?"

Ann hadn't actually thought about it that way. "Maybe," she said. "But I'm not emotionally involved. That skews everything."

Eva made a face. "Boy, does it."

"I, um, wanted to ask you something."

Eva took a sip of wine. "Ask away."

"This is going to sound stupid from a woman my age, but I've never..." Oh, for Pete's sake, spit it out! She took a deep breath. "How do you know if you're in love? I mean, really in love. The marrying kind."

Eva blinked. "You just know?"

"Wow, that's a big help."

Tiny creases formed on the other woman's forehead. "I guess...it's knowing that everything else in life is better because you can share it with this one person. I mean, would your world dim a little if you don't see him again? If you can't tell him about the good things and bad things that happen to you? If..." she faltered "...you know that he's waking up in the morning next to someone else?"

Wary, Ann looked for tears. "I'm sorry. I shouldn't have asked."

Eva smiled with apparent difficulty. "No. Don't be sorry. I did love Garth. I met him in high school, you know—you must remember him—so we had quite a history. That's part of what makes it hard. It's like I have to reevaluate a huge chunk of my life. Was it really that way, or did I create a fantasy?" She shook herself. "I'm not sure anymore what I feel for him. Some days I miss him so badly I don't know if I can stand it. Others I'm furious. Then I have days when I feel detached, and I know I'll be okay. Actually, I was really glad you called tonight. I talked to Mom earlier, and she was sad, which made me sad, and..." She grimaced. "I don't have as many bad days anymore, but when one hits...pow!"

"This has not been one of my all-time great ones, either," Ann admitted.

"You know you have to tell me why you asked, right?"

For the first time, it occurred to Ann that this would have been an easier confession if she'd chosen someone who didn't know Diaz. On the other hand, Eva understood the department because of her father, as well as Ann's own history.

"It's Juan Diaz. The guy who, um…"

"Let me cry on his shoulder?" Eva grinned at her. "He's gorgeous."

"You think?"

Eva gave a small laugh. "Don't *you* think?"

Ann frowned. "Well, yeah, but I didn't at first. He's my partner, you know."

"That's awkward." Eva stuck out her lower lip as she thought. "Does he have any idea how you feel?"

"I don't know how I feel!" Ann moaned. "I mean, I do, but I don't." Meeting her friend's pointed gaze, Ann said, "We had dinner last night. He's admitted to finding me attractive. God knows why," she added.

"You know what your problem is? You didn't have a mother around to buck you up when you went through the ugly duckling phase." She paused. "Except you never had pimples, did you?"

"Uh…no."

"Lord." Eva rolled her eyes. "I had the worst acne! Do you remember? I kept telling my mother I must have leprosy. I actually have scars. See?" She jutted out her chin for Ann's inspection.

Ann scrutinized the pale skin and saw through a haze of foundation that a few faint pits marked her face.

"Antibiotics finally cleared it up."

Remembering those horrible years, Ann said, "Me, I just got buxom. I developed in sixth grade. I started wearing sacky clothes to hide my breasts, and then I looked fat. I never knew what to wear.''

"See? You needed a mother.''

"I never learned to put on makeup, either.'' Ann gave a huff that was a pained laugh. "I never learned to be a girl. I guess you knew that, huh?''

"I was too wrapped up in my own insecurities to take the time to worry about anyone else. Isn't that awful?''

"You were a cheerleader!'' Ann said it as if it were an accusation.

"What's that got to do with anything?'' Eva took a deep swallow of wine. "You knew my father. He was as bad as yours. Mom tried, bless her heart, but Dad made these constant digs. I'd sit down to dinner, and he'd say, 'For God's sake, go wash your face. It turns my stomach.'''

Ann could hear it. She drank some more wine and nodded.

"When my skin finally cleared up and I got more popular, he started telling me I looked like a slut. He saw a hickey on my neck once and slugged me. That was Mom's one gutsy moment. She told him if he ever laid a hand on me again, we were gone.'' Eva paused, expression reflective. "I wish he had. Sometimes I really thought he hated me. My own father.''

Ann didn't hesitate. "I've been looking into some of Dad's old cases. Some your father was involved in, too. The truth is, I think both of them despised women in general. They protected their own, and they respected other men who did. But I don't think it was so much chivalry as because they thought of wives and daughters as possessions. Dad'd kick somebody's ass if he messed with his truck, too, even if he always said it was a heap of junk.''

Eva stared at her. ''God, that makes sense.''

''The disturbing thing is that, when there were accusations of rape or spousal abuse, Dad always took the man's word over the woman's. The woman was a slut. Or she deserved a backhand.'' She corrected herself. ''He never actually said that. About the backhand, I mean. But that's the impression I get. There were times he should have made an arrest and he didn't.''

Eyes unfocused, Eva said, ''My father's parents divorced when he was about ten. His mother left his father for another man. He stayed with his dad.''

''And blamed her for the breakup.''

''Exactly.'' Eva gestured with her chin. ''What about your dad?''

''I didn't know his parents that well, but my impression is that they were pretty much like your dad and mom. He was an SOB, and she figured that's what men were like. Dad learned that women were supposed to be meek and men tough.'' Ann was quiet for a moment. ''There might have been more. I know there was a girlfriend in high school that he almost married, but I don't know what happened.''

''Ten to one, she screwed around on him.''

''Maybe,'' Ann acknowledged. ''But my mother was depressed. I mean, clinically depressed. She cried a lot. Dad just didn't have it in him to understand or sympathize. She probably didn't boost his general opinion of women. The two of them couldn't have been a worse match. She needed support he couldn't give, and he might have been a better man if he'd had a wife who stood up to him.''

Eva reached out and squeezed Ann's hand. Her grip was stronger than her delicate appearance suggested. ''I'd forgotten your mother committed suicide. I remember hearing my mom and dad talk about it at the time. I'd see you at school and imagine how you felt. But of course I had no idea what to say to you, so I avoided you.'' She made a moue. ''I'm so sorry, Ann. Sorry I wasn't a better friend then, and sorry you lost your mom that way.''

Uncomfortable, Ann shrugged. ''Thanks.''

''Too little, too late, you mean.'' Eva's laugh was bitter. ''Our daddies messed us up but good, didn't they?''

Surprised, Ann said, ''You look so...together. I was always jealous of you, you know. I'm so inept at anything outside work.''

''Juan doesn't seem to think so.''

How funny that Eva said his first name so naturally, and Ann hadn't even gotten so far as to think of him by it. She wasn't consciously distancing herself, but it must seem like that to him.

''I guess we've gotten to know each other working together.'' Her heart burned. Curry, she told herself. ''I *like* working with him. But one of us will have to transfer now.''

''Will that be so bad? It's not like you'd work together for the rest of your careers anyway.''

''No-o.''

''Whereas,'' Eva leered, ''you might be able to sleep with him for the next forty years or so.''

"I don't even know if a forty-year commitment is where we're going with this." As if Eva were an oracle who could tell her what might be, she asked with sudden wistfulness, "Is it possible, do you think?"

Eva's smile was sad. "Yeah, I do think. Truly happy marriages may be the minority, but I know they exist."

As she helped Eva clear the table and load the dishwasher, then said good-night, Ann found herself wondering whether Diaz had fewer doubts about marriage. Two of his sisters were married and had kids, and his parents' marriage might have been a loving one. Would the family still be so close if the parents had been angry at each other?

Probably she was the one skewed by her peculiar childhood. Driving the dark streets, it occurred to Ann that she'd always believed other girls grew up longing for something extraordinary, while she just wanted to feel normal.

In front of her apartment, she parked and turned off the car, then just sat there for a minute. Doubt still gnawed at her, but she suddenly had the thought that she might be more normal than she knew. If a woman as beautiful and assured as Eva Pearce suffered from insecurities that ran as deep as Ann's, did that mean most people did? That she just *thought* she was all alone, different?

She could learn some of the trappings that would allow her to blend in. She'd gotten used to applying a little makeup most days. Tonight, she'd put on some of her new clothes without once feeling self-conscious. She'd even been thinking she might wear something more stylish to work. If she got razzed—so what?

A funny feeling swelled in her chest. Ann rubbed her breastbone in an attempt to ease it, even though the sensation was...nice. She hadn't felt this in so long, she didn't know what to call it.

But then, the right word came to her.

Hope.

Was it possible she was worthy of love after all?

The next instant, new terror squeezed out the fragile bubble of optimism.

What if, in her inexperience, she was reading way, way too much into the way Diaz had kissed her, into his few words? What if she was imagining forever, and he was imagining sex?

Another new concept rose, a bubble as shimmery and fragile as hope had been. She could take a chance. See where this relationship went. Get hurt, or not. No matter what happened, would she be any worse off than she was now? She had spent years feeling unworthy of friendship or intimacy because of her mother's suicide, years accepting the wounds her father dealt her. Years during which she'd been unwilling to risk more pain by letting herself need approval or affection from anyone else.

Hope floated up again. Feeling a little giddy, wondering if she'd had too much wine, Ann got out, locked her car and went into her boring apartment.

Boring, she thought in amazement, not because she was incapable of choosing things that pleased her, but because she hadn't trusted herself. She hadn't *believed* she had good taste. After all, her father had heaped scorn on her every attempt to choose clothes or something pretty for the house or even a new recipe. But, damn it, he was gone! If *she* liked what she bought, what difference did it make if the whole rest of the world thought it was ugly?

Ann floated into bed. Tomorrow was full of possibilities. Full of chances to let herself be a person who mattered.

CHAPTER THIRTEEN

CHERI WAS her usual charming self when she picked up the kids at ten-thirty.

"Well, I see you survived your dad's cooking," she said, a hint of acid in her voice. She kissed first Elena and then Tony.

Diaz grinned at his children. "We had some darn good chimichangas, didn't we, kids?"

"Yeah!" Tony agreed.

Elena stole a glance at her mother and then gave a timid nod.

Diaz gritted his teeth and said over their heads, "Have a good time tonight?"

"It was great to get out and talk to adults for a change." She seemed impervious to the presence of their listening children.

"You know, they can come here almost any evening," he said mildly. "I'm capable of supervising homework."

"*And* getting Elena to ballet rehearsals, and Tony to spring soccer and making sure they get to bed on time?" She laughed as if the idea was ludicrous. "Speaking of which, it's long past bedtime right now. We've got to get going. Tony, where's your book bag?"

"Oh!" He smacked his forehead. "I almost forgot!"

As the eight-year-old ran to the bedroom, Cheri gave Diaz a look that said, *See? You can't even get them organized to be ready to go home.*

Hiding his irritation, Diaz could only wonder what he'd ever seen in her. He no longer even found her physically attractive. Cheri had kept her figure and her skin was still smooth, but since she'd become a beautician, she'd frosted and bleached her hair so many times, it reminded him of the long dried grasses that grew at the foot of sand dunes. She wore too much makeup and clothes that were too young. Discontent soured a face that had once been sweet.

How did you know, when you got married, what a person would become? Answer: you didn't.

At least, he amended, when you were both barely twenty-one. They'd been kids themselves, with unrealistic dreams of where life would take them. He remembered his swagger when he first wore the uniform, the sexual excitement it stirred in her. Neither of them imagined the sacrifices the job would demand.

He hugged the kids goodbye and watched them until the car was backing out. Then he locked the front door and headed to the kitchen to finish washing up. The phone rang before he could begin to brood about Ann.

"Hey," his brother said. "It's been a while."

"Yeah, it has," Diaz agreed. "Mama usually keeps me up to date, but I haven't talked to her lately. Been on TV this week?"

"Jeez, don't you ever watch the news? I arrested

the rapist who's been nabbing women down near the ferry terminal.''

''Seriously?'' Diaz opened the dishwasher. ''Brilliant police work? Or good luck?''

With a hearty laugh, Manuel admitted, ''Luck. I took a pretty blonde to Trattoria Mitchelli for dinner. We went down to Jazz Alley for a little music, then walked back to the car. I'd parked under the viaduct. His hunting ground. I heard a strangled scream. And like a superhero, I tore into action. By the time I caught up, he'd dragged her behind a Dumpster in an alley and was ripping at her clothes. He'd already messed her up a little. Her face is pretty battered.''

Diaz just shook his head. Manuel had always had a gift for being in the right place at the right time. ''Damn, you're good.''

''Thank you,'' his little brother said with false modesty. ''The pretty blonde thought so, too.''

''Watch it with pretty blondes.''

''Got into it with your ex again, huh?''

''She just picked the kids up. I was polite.''

''Not all women are like her. You've got to get out there again,'' Manuel advised. ''Find yourself a nice attorney who has to cancel out on dinner herself sometimes. She'll understand when you do.''

''Or another cop,'' Diaz heard himself saying.

''Yeah, or... Wait a minute. Who is she?''

He guessed he must want to talk to someone about her, or he wouldn't have hinted so broadly.

''It's messy,'' he warned. ''You know my partner is a woman. Ann Caldwell.''

His brother whistled. "You two are playing around on the side?"

"It's not like that."

"What is it like?" For a minute there, carefree Manuel sounded one hell of a lot like Lieutenant O'Brien.

"I'm in love with her."

The silence was deafening.

Diaz closed his eyes. "Say something."

"Mama met her?"

"No."

"Elena and Tony?"

"Yeah. They like her."

Another silence. Then, "You're serious."

"I guess I am. I don't know if she's in step, though. And I swore yesterday I'd keep my hands off her for a couple of weeks." He told his brother about his idiocy and the lieutenant's reaction. "One of us will have to transfer."

"You figured out what to request?"

"I'm looking around."

"What about her?"

"I think she wants to stay in Major Crimes." He told his brother about her father. "It means more to her than it does to me. I just wish…" He shut up, but his brother finished the sentence for him.

"That you knew she'd give something up for you?"

"I guess that's it," Diaz admitted. "But, hell. We'll see what happens."

"Yeah. Wow. Take her home. See what Mama thinks of her."

"She didn't like Cheri, you know." He remembered

how much it had bothered him not to have his mother's approval. "I thought because she wasn't Hispanic."

"The way I heard it, she didn't like Cheri because she was shallow and immature."

Diaz gave a wry grin. "That probably made two of us."

"You want to get together some night?"

"So you can vet her instead?"

"Did I say that?" Manuel asked in a wounded tone.

"You won't tell anyone?"

They both knew he was talking about family.

"Not a word."

"I'll give you a call," Diaz said. They concluded that both were off on Tuesday. "Tuesday night then. I'll see if Ann can come."

Hanging up, he wondered if she'd want to. She'd looked so stunned when he was stupid enough to say the word "love," he had a bad feeling they'd been kissing at cross-purposes.

Maybe it was the age difference. It didn't sound as if she'd done that much playing around. Maybe that's all she'd seen him as: an experiment. A little fun. That would sure explain her dismay at getting caught. She hadn't planned for consequences, because she'd seen no reason there should be any.

Sunk in gloom now, Diaz thought, *Unlike me.* Stodgy, middle-aged traditionalist that he was, he'd never have laid a hand on her if he hadn't seen a glimmer of a future. One he hadn't been so sure he was ready for.

Those doubts had evaporated, like smoke from the barrel of a fired gun. Diaz didn't know what it was

about Ann Caldwell. She'd irritated him in the beginning, but in a way that made him feel more alive. She
challenged his assumptions, thought creatively, stood
up for what she believed was the right thing to do. In
his experience, women used their bodies; femininity
and sexual appeal were intrinsic parts of who they
were.

Not Caldwell. She didn't seem to have noticed that
she *was* a woman. Her prickly personality and direct
manner didn't go with her lush figure—which was
why, he'd assumed, she did her damndest to hide it.

Now he knew better. He'd caught enough glimpses
of the vulnerability beneath, the confusion, the doubt.
The wistful child still lived in her, the teenager who,
he guessed, had *not* gone to her prom. Holding her
when she cried had been his downfall.

Diaz almost laughed at that. Who'd believe him if
he said he'd fallen in love because this woman who
wouldn't hesitate to kick down a door and go in ahead
of him had trusted him enough to sob against his chest
and soak his shirtfront?

Oh, hell. It had started long before that. Maybe
when he felt cramps of sexual longing at the sight of
a smile flickering at the corners of her mouth, or because that ugly damn blazer stretched across generous
breasts? Was it the night she'd said sadly that her father's cronies, sons of bitches all, were the closest
thing she had to family? Or when she had her eyebrows plucked and then tried to hide her face so no
one noticed?

He didn't know, only that this fierce desire to protect
her, to understand her, to be someone she could trust

'til death do they part, had crept up on him. And now, all he could hear was her too hasty agreement to keep her hands off him. All he could see was the shock in her vivid blue eyes when he said, "Is falling in love on your list of major screwups?"

And he was torn between anticipating morning, when he'd see her again, and dreading it.

CALDWELL WAS all business when he walked in the next morning. On the phone, she covered the mouthpiece and murmured, "He'll see us."

"Now?" Diaz asked.

She nodded, said into the phone, "Thank you, Mr. Moskowitz," and hung up. "I woke him up, he works the swing shift, but he said that's okay."

She stood, and Diaz's mouth dropped open. She'd ditched the ugly blazer, the white cotton shirt, the navy blue man-style trousers. In their place, she wore a silky royal blue blouse tucked into black slacks that actually fit her body. His stupefied gaze dropped slowly from the creamy vee of skin displayed by the open neck of the blouse to a pair of black shoes that were dainty compared to her usual sturdy oxfords.

She shot him a narrow-eyed glance that dared him to say a word. Before he'd recovered enough to say something stupid anyway, a wolf whistle from the hall sent her wheeling around to glare toward the small crowd clustered in the doorway.

"Looking good," a guy from Fraud said.

She told them where to shove it.

A newcomer craned his neck to see what they were staring at. "Wow. Caldwell? What got into you?"

"I decided to give you all a look at what you're missing," she shot back.

"Will you go to dinner with me tonight?" one guy begged.

She gave him a tight-lipped smile. "In your dreams, Lindbergh."

"Aw," he complained.

O'Brien stepped out of his office. The crowd melted away. He took in the changed appearance of his detective, but said only, "You two planning to hang around here all morning?"

"On our way, sir." She snagged a black leather jacket from the coatrack and put it on. Sleek and form-fitting, it was as out of character as the dainty shoes.

A few more whistles and shouted remarks followed them to the parking lot.

Over the top of the car, Diaz said, "You do look fabulous," and got in.

She got in, too. "Thanks."

"Why today?" he asked, knowing he risked having her take offense.

She didn't. Color spotted her cheeks, and she didn't look at him, but she answered, "I don't like being a coward. I just thought—" she shrugged "—I'd get it over with. You know?"

"Except for the fact that every single guy will be hitting on you, your transformation will be forgotten in a week."

A pleased smile curved her mouth. "Do you think?"

"That they'll be hitting on you?" he asked, irritated.

She slid a sidelong glance at him. "I don't want any of them. But the idea is flattering."

"I liked it better when you came to work in ugly clothes."

She gazed at him in apparent bemusement. "Are you *jealous?*"

His grip on the wheel was so tight, his knuckles ached. "Hell, yes."

"Really?" Ann gave him a sunny smile. "Nobody has ever been jealous over me before."

He relaxed infinitesimally. Damn it, this wasn't high school. Her idiot father had deprived her of way too much. So what if she had fun with the amazing discovery that she was a shapely woman?

"Glad to give you pleasure." He paused. "Your new look makes it even harder for me to keep my hands off you."

Her smile widened. "You know," she said, "you're the only one who thought I was worth noticing before. That's...important to me."

His fingers unclenched and he eased up on the gas pedal. "They're all idiots."

"Every man in the world?" she teased. "None of them noticed me."

"Every one."

"I think your ex-wife is the idiot."

He glanced at her in surprise. "Thank you."

"Now we're even." Ann sounded smug. "Hey, you want the next exit."

Recalled to their purpose, he asked, "Did this Moskowitz sound unhappy to hear from you?"

"No-o." She frowned. "Maybe pleased. As if he wants to give us an earful."

Diaz grunted. If Moskowitz wanted the world to hear about how the police department had failed his daughter, why hadn't he gone to the news after her suicide? Because he was busy figuring out how to pick off everyone he held responsible? Maybe. But then wouldn't he be dismayed now to find the police eye turning to him?

As if their thoughts had paralleled, Ann said, "Maybe he's playing a game with us. He wasn't sure until now that we were moving our pieces on the board."

"Could be." Diaz mulled it over. "The mother was dead, right?"

She made a sound of agreement. "He remarried. I didn't think to check to see whether he's divorced in the meantime."

"How did the mother die? I don't remember noticing."

"Boating accident. On Lake Sammamish."

Diaz didn't have to comment. Such "accidents" were easy to stage. The success of that first venture into murder would explain why killing every cop who'd failed his daughter now seemed viable.

The house was a nice one in the Renton Highlands area. The development was a tangle of winding streets and multiple cul-de-sacs, the homes all featuring three-car garages and cathedral windows looking south toward Mt. Rainier. Mature landscaping suggested the development was eight or ten years old at least.

"He's a supervisor at Boeing," Ann said, getting

out and waiting for Diaz on the sidewalk. "I guess they make enough money for a place like this."

"If his wife had life insurance, that probably helped."

From the driveway, steep steps cut through a retaining wall planted with unusual conifers, some sculpted to emphasize gnarly shapes. More steps led up to the covered front porch.

They heard the bell ring deep inside the house. After a long pause, footsteps approached. The man who opened the door was middle-height and in his fifties, at Diaz's guess, well-cut hair graying, face handsome but pasty. Bags under his eyes might be chronic, or might suggest lack of sleep. He wore corduroy slacks, a sweater Diaz bet was cashmere, and slippers.

"Mr. Moskowitz? I'm Detective Caldwell, and this is my partner, Detective Diaz."

He held out a hand, shaking each of theirs in turn. "Come in."

Too cordial? Diaz wondered.

He led them into a vast living room decorated with taste and money. Wing chairs and a couple of sofas upholstered in something sinfully soft and nubby in a pale yellow and sage stripe were clustered in conversational groups. Diaz knew enough to suspect that the cherry desk with gracefully curved legs and a subtle sheen was probably an antique.

"Coffee?" Moskowitz asked, waving them to seats.

They declined. He nodded and sat himself in a chair facing them, side by side on the sofa.

"What can I do for you?"

Ann said smoothly, "As I said on the phone, we're

following up on cases where there were complaints that our deputies could have done more. I know you were unhappy at the time of your daughter's accusations, although of course the decision not to file charges was made by the prosecutor's office, not the sheriff's department.''

Anger sparked in his eyes. "The deputies who met with my daughter were insensitive, at the very least. They failed to document bruises, so that the prosecutor's office had no proof to present in court. From the very beginning, every police officer who spoke to DeeDee sneered at her. Just what did she hope to accomplish by these accusations? they asked, with the implication that she'd made them under the belief he would buy her off. They put a great deal more effort into finding witnesses to testify that my daughter had flirted with Mr. Saffian or that she didn't protest when he put his hand on her in a familiar way than they did in interviewing family and friends who knew that for several months she'd been complaining about his advances and was unsure how to stop them without losing an internship she felt was important on her résumé.''

"Had she spoken to you about her concerns?"

His mouth tightened. "No. She was afraid I'd intervene. I wish…'' His Adam's apple bobbed. "What good are wishes? No. She talked to her stepbrother and stepmother, as well as to friends. They advised that she avoid being alone with the councilman. The night he raped her, he'd asked her to stay late, but she was under the impression that several aides were to stay as well or she would have refused.''

"We understand that Deidre committed suicide." Ann's voice was quiet, sympathetic. "Did she have ongoing problems with depression?"

"Hell, no!" He half rose in agitation, then sat again. "DeeDee was a smart, funny, popular girl until that son of a bitch raped her. She never got over it." He looked from one to the other of them, his teeth showing and his eyes dark with grief and rage. "But how could she, when the officers of the law might as well have raped her again? You know what rape victims feel? Fear, shame and helplessness. Your fellow officers dished out shame and helplessness more generously than her rapist did."

"Do you recall the names of particular deputies?" Ann asked.

He gave her a look of contempt. "How could I, after all this time? Look at your own police reports if you want to know. Or were they falsified?"

Without expression, Ann asked, "Did Deidre have a boyfriend at the time of the rape?"

Fury at a simmer, Moskowitz said, "She and her stepbrother had a relationship. Please understand. I remarried after she'd left for college. The two of them never lived under a roof as brother and sister. His mother and I saw no reason to object to their interest in each other."

"And did that relationship continue until your daughter's death?"

"No," he said curtly. "DeeDee broke up with him a couple of months after she was raped."

"Your stepson's name?"

"Ronnie. Ronald Shields."

"Did Mr. Shields share your opinion about the treatment Ms. Moskowitz received from the police? Perhaps he was even more angry, as he lost her affections as well?"

"Yeah, you can say that." He glared at her. "I'm starting to get a funny feeling about this. Like you're interested in something else."

"And what would that be, Mr. Moskowitz?" Expression bland, she gazed back at him.

"I don't know, but I'm going to ask you to leave now." He stood.

"We'd like to speak to your stepson as well. Does he live here, Mr. Moskowitz?"

"No, he doesn't. Now, if you don't mind…"

Without a glance, Diaz and his partner stood. At the door, she thanked Moskowitz for his time and cooperation, only the tiniest bit of irony in her voice.

"You know," she said, as they walked down the series of steps to the street, "this is the second time I've been booted out of someone's house this week. Very politely both times."

"Kind of eats at your self-confidence, doesn't it?"

"I feel like a half-eaten Big Mac," she agreed.

In the car, Diaz put the key in the ignition. "Shall we find Ronnie?"

"Top of the list."

The DMV reported a Ronald Shields at an address in Federal Way. The age was about right.

"He's probably not home, but we can check."

Diaz started the car. "I'm betting Ronnie has already heard from his stepdaddy. We won't be catching him by surprise."

As he pulled out onto the street, she said, "Can you believe Moskowitz didn't remember the name of a single police officer who spoke to his daughter?"

"Especially given the way he claims they treated her? Nah. I think he's the kind who'd be in their face, demanding their badge numbers."

"That's my take, too." Silence reigned for a couple miles. "He's not quite what I pictured, though."

"For a killer?" Diaz glanced at her. "Not our usual type, for sure. But these aren't our usual killings, either."

"No." She fell silent again, her expression preoccupied.

Diaz kept stealing glances to take in the effect of her changed appearance. He was used to her beside him in her mannish clothes, her hair yanked back in a bun that managed to suck the life out of hair he'd discovered was lush and full. It wasn't that he didn't know what she really looked like. But, damn it, he'd done a better job of separating their work relationship from their private one when she dressed according to her role. Now... Crap. Now, he wanted to find an alley, set the brake and neck with her.

Find the killer, he thought, *and we'll be free.*

Shields's address was Block F of a vast apartment complex. It was the kind of place where you could stumble home late at night, let yourself into the wrong apartment and go to bed without noticing unless the person whose head was on the other pillow called you on it. The B block looked like F, the layout identical, the covered parking identical, the landscaping so minimal no entrance stood out from another.

He parked in a slot marked Visitor. A feral cat darted under a stair landing when they got out. Otherwise, the place was deserted, windows blind, curtains pulled.

"Not exactly homey."

"It's nicer than my complex," she said wryly.

He cleared his throat.

"Shut up."

He pretended to zip his mouth.

"I'll move!" she snapped. "There! Are you satisfied?"

Hell, no. The last thing he wanted was for her to buy a house and settle into contented domesticity. Or even to find a really nice condo. He wouldn't be satisfied until she moved in with him. Bought a house with him.

Married him.

He was out of his goddamn mind.

The doorbell rang in the depths of unit 314. Nobody rushed to open the door and invite them in. More frustrated than he should have been, Diaz glowered at the white steel door with a peephole.

"Do we come back after 5:00 p.m.?"

"I suppose." She looked as unhappy as he felt. "I just have this uneasy feeling."

Yeah. He had one, too. A sense that, by showing their hand, they'd made somebody antsy. There was one more cop to kill: Reggie Roarke. And then, if the perp was Moskowitz or his stepson, you knew the former county councilman had to be next. The climax, so to speak.

"There's nothing we can do."

Talking to herself as much as to him, tone bracing, she said, "We can start checking out Moskowitz's background and movements. We might find out he was in South America when my father was killed."

"Does Boeing send managers to South America?"

She made a growly sound under her breath. "I don't know. I picked that out of a hat. Do you have to be so literal?"

"I was being facetious." And trying to avoid suggesting they go back to his place and make passionate love all afternoon.

"Well, you're not..."

"Hey!" a voice said from behind them. "You looking for me?"

On a flash of alarm, Diaz spun around, aware that Ann was doing the same. A fresh-faced kid stood not five feet from them. At the expressions on their faces, he held up both hands in a universal gesture of innocence and fell back a step.

"Wow! I'm sorry! I didn't mean to take you by surprise."

Diaz forced himself to relax. "No, it's okay. Are you Ronald Shields?"

"Yeah, I came home for my lunch break because Dad said you were probably on the way over here to see me."

Diaz revised his initial impression that this kid couldn't be twenty-five. He just had one of those faces: a few freckles scattered over his snub nose, pale, farmboy hair flopping over his forehead, wide blue eyes and a mouth that wanted to smile.

"Did Mr. Moskowitz tell you what we wanted to talk to you about?" Ann asked.

"Yeah, DeeDee." He gave a twitchy shrug that was almost comical, like a puppet jerked by strings. "Actually, I think he was warning me so I could avoid you, but I don't mind." He nodded at the door. "You want to come in?"

"Thank you."

Both stepped aside so he could unlock the apartment door. The interior reminded Diaz of Ann's place—furniture that could have been rented, standard cream-colored carpet, white walls, vinyl framed windows, pale wood cabinets in the kitchen visible just beyond. The difference was in the mess, which struck Diaz as pretty typical for a guy on his own. Empty beer cans, fast-food wrappings and coffee cups had been left on end tables, and a couple pairs of dirty sweat socks lay on the carpet where they'd been peeled off.

"So, you want to sit down?" He stepped over the dirty socks and settled in a recliner.

"Thank you."

Ann asked her questions.

His face stayed open, artless. Yeah, sure, he'd been real upset when DeeDee got raped.

"I couldn't believe that the cops didn't arrest him. I mean, I know rape is always a he-said/she-said thing, but, like, she had a black eye! And she'd been telling us for weeks that he kept crowding her into corners, rubbing up against her. That kind of stuff. I wanted her to quit, but she had only a couple months more to go, and she really wanted to finish the internship. So she was trying to stay out of his line of sight. You know?'' His face fell. ''Only, it didn't work.''

They established that he had been in the house when a couple of the deputies interviewed her. ''One of them had a name like yours,'' he said ingenuously. ''Caldman, or something like that.''

Noncommittal, she nodded. ''Do you recall the other name?''

''Yeah, it was Birk-something. Birkett. Birkley.''

''Birkey.''

His face brightened. ''Right! That was it.''

He'd been upset by the way she was treated. The cops had implied, according to her, that she'd had a consensual affair and was now out for what she could get. ''They were on his side from the start,'' Ronnie said in apparent amazement.

He explained that breaking up had been her idea, not his. Deidre Moskowitz hadn't liked being touched after the rape, and she'd told Ronnie Shields that she just needed space. She didn't want to hurt him by always flinching.

''Next thing I knew, she'd applied to Brown and was going back East. She said she thought she'd do better in a new environment. She got some counseling, but...'' He bent his head and looked down at his hands. ''The last time I saw her, she'd lost a lot of weight. She was kind of nervy. You know? Then, just a few weeks later, after she went back...'' He gave one of those twitchy shrugs again, although this time it was less comical, reminding Diaz instead of the peculiar movements of a crack or speed addict.

''Mr. Shields,'' Ann asked straight out, ''do you

blame the police department for your stepsister's suicide?''

He looked up, and for just a moment something dangerous clouded his youthful face. But then he grimaced, and the effect passed. ''Kind of. Yeah. Not
totally, though. That Saffian should be in jail. I was
glad to see he lost his reelection campaign, but that
wasn't enough. There's nothing we can do, though.''

Ann thanked him for his time, told him they might
be in touch, and she and Diaz left. Diaz made note of
the older, dark green Ford SUV parked in the slot for
unit 314.

Neither said a word until they were in the car. Then
she gave a deliberate shudder. ''Nobody is that nice.''

''I had trouble buying it, too,'' Diaz agreed.

''He kind of slipped there at the end.''

''I saw.''

She brooded as he backed the car out of the slot.
''Of course, there's always the possibility that he *is*
nice, and his natural anger upsets him, so he tries to
hide it.''

''Are there any people so nice, they can't let themselves be enraged when a loved one is raped and then
violated again in spirit if not body by the cops?''

''I don't know any,'' she admitted.

First droplets of rain splattered the windshield. Diaz
turned on the wipers.

''Either of them are good possibilities. It even occurred to me,'' Ann said, ''that they might be in ca-
hoots.''

He frowned. ''They're an unlikely pair.''

''Yeah, but they both loved DeeDee, and they had

to watch her plunge into depression and then kill herself because—or so they believe—the cops demeaned her instead of empowering her by arresting the rapist.''

Diaz could hear the conversation: Moskowitz, maybe, being the first one to say, ''She should be alive and every one of them dead.'' If his stepson agreed, the angry father could come back with: ''I'd like to do it with my own two hands.''

Yeah, it was barely possible. But Diaz found he still preferred the one killer theory. Shields hadn't grown up with Moskowitz as his father, so, although the relationship was clearly friendly, it wasn't as tight as a true father/son bond. What were the odds that *both* of them were twisted enough to carry their understandable fury to the lengths of serial murder?

When he expressed his doubts, Ann scowled and argued, but halfheartedly.

''Neither are registered as owners of a vehicle the right color to have left the paint scrapings on Dad's truck.''

He changed lanes on the freeway. ''If I were going to try to kill somebody that way, I'd steal a vehicle, then ditch it.''

''I should look for stolen vehicles recovered in the week or ten days after Dad's death.''

''Yeah, it wouldn't hurt, but it also might not tell us much at this point. If it was damaged, it may have been junked.''

''Still,'' she pointed out, ''we could see where the vehicle was stolen and where it was abandoned. That might be interesting.''

''Mmm.''

They threw around ideas and random thoughts on the remainder of the drive. Only as he was parking at the station did she say, "Reggie is the only survivor, except for Saffian."

"The thought has occurred to me."

"I looked," she said. "They were murdered in the order they interviewed Deidre Moskowitz. Except for the one failure."

He swore softly. "Then why not kill Saffian first?"

"Because our killer is angriest at him. He has to be last. Best."

"Which means another try at Reggie."

They looked at each other.

"Are you thinking what I'm thinking?" Ann asked.

Yeah, he was. And liking the idea. Liking it one hell of a lot.

CHAPTER FOURTEEN

"YOU'VE GOT TO goddamn be kidding?" Roarke stared like a man suffering from shock in the aftermath of a major car accident. "You want me to lie under the car and wait for somebody to knock it over on me."

"We want you to lie under the car and wait for somebody to *try*," Diaz corrected.

They were in O'Brien's office. The lieutenant sat behind his desk chomping on a toothpick and saying nothing, only his eyes moving as one after another of his detectives spoke.

Reggie growled an obscenity. "Murdered. Why didn't I start to wonder? God." Head thrust out, face crumpled in disbelief, he looked like a bulldog. "You really think somebody killed Pearce, Birkey...your dad?"

He'd asked the same question three or four times already, going from conviction to doubt and back again.

Lips pressed together, Ann nodded.

Diaz was trying not to look at her. They'd finished yesterday by persuading the lieutenant that this was a sensible plan sure to pay off, not an idiotic waste of taxpayers' money. The whole time, Diaz had been existing on two planes: the cop backing up his partner, and the man watching the woman he loved and unable to touch her.

Today she wore a variant on yesterday's getup, this one involving a V-necked sweater that fit her like a wetsuit. With her mass of hair in a casual clip on the back of her head, a few tendrils slipping down to curl against her neck, she was beautiful, classy and so sexy, he had trouble believing he'd worked with her for months before he thought much about the fact that she was a woman.

This morning, they'd moved on to Step Two in the great plan: they had to talk Roarke into tying himself out like the sacrificial goat.

"Why would anyone want to kill all of us? We all piss people off, but a bunch of us...!"

"If our suspicions are correct," Ann said, without expression, "it's because a relative of Deidre Moskowitz believes you and the deceased officers didn't give her a fair hearing. That in fact you took the accused's side from the beginning, openly stating an opinion that 'she'd been asking for it.' As a direct result of your reports, the prosecutor chose not to file charges, and Ms. Moskowitz suffered from profound depression that ultimately led to her committing suicide."

His face flushed. "You believe that crap?"

"Which part would you call crap?" Diaz asked.

Roarke snarled, "All of it! Goddamn it, I've been a cop since you two were in grade school! I know how to conduct an investigation. There never was a case. Saffian demanded the task force because his political

career would have swirled down the toilet like you
know what if he hadn't. Fact is, the girl didn't call 911
after the alleged rape, she waited a week, by which
time any supposed injuries were healed. She made it
plain that she despised police officers after having been
involved in several protests that turned violent. She
was flip, uncooperative and angry at any questions
asked in an attempt to throw light on her relationship
with the councilman. He, in contrast, was cooperative
and clearly shaken by the accusation. His staff backed
him, one aide going so far as to tell us privately that
the girl had been throwing herself at him.''

Ann waved a hand in front of his face to stop him.
''Reggie, we aren't questioning your competence or
the quality of the investigation. We're telling you what
Deidre Moskowitz's father and stepbrother believe.''

''The father was as hostile as she was! He got up
in your dad's face, ranting, spittle flying.'' He ran a
beefy hand over his crew-cut head, apparently unaware
it was trembling. ''Damn near had to haul him in for
assault. We bent over backward. Goddamn crazy family.''

''They may be,'' Ann soothed. ''That's why we're
here, Reggie.''

It took a while to settle him down. He let fly with
some of his own spittle, and Diaz began to worry about
the possibility of a stroke or heart attack, when
Roarke's face flushed purple. Wouldn't that be an
irony if they killed him trying to save him?

Still O'Brien didn't intervene. He just watched, discarding one toothpick after another without ever taking
his eyes from the little drama. The toothpicks were

beginning to irritate Diaz. Did the man need a smoke that bad?

Pretty much everything was irritating Diaz by this time, from Ann's self-possession to Reggie's offensive language. He just wanted to get this over with so he could drag her into his arms.

He finally snapped, "Damn it, Reggie, if we didn't really think you were in danger, we wouldn't have brought you in here! You can do this two ways. You can look over your shoulder until somebody tries to kill you again, or you can do your job and help us nail the bastard. Which is it going to be?"

A tic had seized control of one of his eyelids. After smouldering for a moment, he jerked his head in accord. "All right. What do you have in mind?"

They told him again.

"What if you're too slow? You know how goddamn lucky I was last time?"

"We won't be too slow," Ann said with cool certainty. "Anyway, we can block your car up so that it wouldn't go down if a wrecking ball hit it."

In the end, he agreed. What else could he do?

Plans laid, they all stood.

"Caldwell, Diaz, I want to talk to you."

Reggie nodded and left, closing the door behind him. The two detectives left turned reluctantly to face their superior.

"I can't afford for this to drag on. You've got two, maybe three days. Got it?"

"Yes, sir."

"Then get to work."

The minute they were out of the office, Ann fumed,

"Two or three days! What are the chances our guy will bite that fast?"

"If he doesn't," Diaz said in a reasonable voice, "we'll keep fishing on our days off."

"I want this done!" she snapped like a petulant teenager, before stalking off to her desk.

Diaz's mood improved immediately. So she wasn't as cool as she'd seemed. Good.

SHE HAD TO DIAL Information to get a phone number for her own grandparents. Calling them felt like a big deal, although she didn't know why it should.

A woman answered, her voice harsher even than Ann remembered, roughened by age. "Hello? Who is this?"

"It's Ann. Ann Caldwell. Your granddaughter. That is," she amended, afraid to trust her memory, "if you're Sofia Wilson."

"Ann?" her grandmother exclaimed. Muffled, as if she'd covered the receiver, she called, "Arnold! Arnold, it's Ann!" A moment later, she came back on. "I can't believe it's you."

"I should have called a long time ago," she admitted. "But I never felt like I knew you."

"Which is our fault," her grandmother said. "Ours, and your father's."

"Did he ask you not to call or visit?"

"He said—" and her voice shook "—we weren't going to ruin you the way we did your mother. As if he had nothing to do with her sadness."

"In my memory, she was always sad."

"She was a moody child. Maybe it was our fault. I

don't know. But we loved our daughter. We tried to help her. She got worse after she married, and especially after she had you. Now, I think they'd say it was hormones. Or maybe your father.'' She paused. ''Arnold says I shouldn't criticize him. He's your father. But I don't think he was a good man. I can't lie.''

''No.'' Ann's eyes burned. ''I don't think he was a good man, either.'' Saying those words felt cleansing in a way she found unexpected.

''We'd like to see you. But traveling is hard for us now. We'd pay for your ticket if you can come here, to stay for a little while. So we can get to know each other.''

Ann seemed to cry so easily these days. ''You don't have to pay for my ticket. I make plenty. I'm a police officer, you know.''

''A woman police officer.'' Her grandmother seemed to marvel at the idea. ''We don't have any around here. They're all men. Except for the state patrol. Sometimes I see a woman.''

What was she supposed to say to that? Well, I'm one of those strange creatures?

''I'm taller than Mom,'' she said. ''Stronger.''

''Lucretia would never have been a policeman. Officer, I mean.'' She paused. ''So, when will you come?''

Ann supposed she could go almost any time once she and Diaz arrested her father's murderer. Or failed. But she shied from a commitment.

''I don't know. I'll have to see when I can get time off. I'll call you.''

''We're not getting any younger, you know,'' her

grandmother told her. "Here. Talk to your grandfather."

After a rustle, Ann heard breathing. *What do I call him?* she wondered in momentary panic. Grandpa? Grandad? "Grandfather?" she finally said, stiffly.

"Ann." He was quiet. "To hear your voice."

Just like that, she began to cry again. "I wish I'd called sooner."

"You could be Lucy. The years gone." The quiet wonder in his voice wrenched at her heart. "Ann, at last."

"I'm sorry," she gulped.

"Sorry? For what? You called. That's what mattered. You called."

In the end, he was right. That was what mattered. She had family, and once she worked up the courage, she'd get to know them. Something she knew she never would have done if it weren't for Diaz.

SATURDAY MORNING, Diaz and Ann skulked through a suburban backyard, scaled the six-foot fence with the help of an old crab apple tree, and slipped through Roarke's yard to the door that let into his garage. One rap, and he opened it.

His eyes were bloodshot, his breath rancid, his temper foul. "Did you have to set off the goddamn dog?"

A hound bayed from a yard several houses down.

Diaz shrugged. "You can't tell me the dog doesn't howl when the postman comes and when the newspaper carrier throws the paper onto the porch and when the neighbors go out to barbecue. Nobody is going to think, Gosh, that dog must be barking because two cops cut through a yard halfway down the block to set up a stakeout.''

''He's gonna be looking for a setup.''

''Maybe.''

He grabbed coveralls and stepped into them. ''I had to tell Mary. I didn't want her scared out of half her life if she stepped out here and saw you two crouched like goddamn vultures in the rafters.''

''That's fine.'' Ann rocked the Corvette experimentally. ''Just so she knows to stay in the house.''

''She knows,'' he said shortly.

''Then let's get on with it.'' She used the old wooden stepladder to climb to her perch on a beam just inside the closed garage door.

Having held it steady as she climbed, Diaz moved the stepladder to the other side of the door and climbed into position himself. Reggie folded the ladder and hung it on a hook. Whatever his flaws, he kept an immaculate garage.

They'd been lucky he hadn't wallboarded in the ceiling of the garage. Instead, he used the crisscrossed rafters and beams to hold large items: a yellow rubber boat, a green nylon roll that looked like a tent, some lumber and PVC pipes, and a dusty, folded Ping-Pong table.

Once they were settled, he lifted the garage door. In the opening, he stretched, then glanced cautiously each way as if to make sure no one loitered out on the street or lurked behind his pickup, parked in the driveway. A sedan at the curb was probably Mary's. Finally, he rolled out one of those metal carts with drawers that held more tools than a surgeon would need to fix a damaged heart valve. He bent over the engine, doing mysterious things that seemed to involve clanging wrenches against metal. Eventually, he wiped now oily hands on a rag, stepped out into the driveway to narrowly eye the neighborhood, and then lay down on the creeper. Choosing a wrench, he edged under the carriage of the 'Vette so that only his legs showed.

Ann straddled the beam, checked for spiders and then peered through the slits of a ventilation register. She could see the driveway, empty but for the pickup, and the very edge of the sidewalk.

To her left, Diaz looked more uncomfortable than she was to this point. He crouched for a while, then knelt, then carefully edged around to sit sideways with his feet dangling. He was probably trying to keep limber. She knew his peekhole was even more limited than hers. As an hour crept by, then another, with no more activity than an occasional passing car or the neighbor firing up the lawn mower, she had plenty of time to study him when he seemed intent on the view of the driveway and sidewalk.

Powerful thigh muscles showed to nice effect in soft, faded jeans. In athletic shoes, he'd moved like a cat, making her feel clumsy in comparison. He'd have looked like a guy dressed for a casual Saturday with friends if it hadn't been for the shoulder holster.

Ann wore one, too. It gave them an advantage. She doubted Moskowitz or his stepson would be packing. None of the victims had been killed with traditional weapons. If the murderer took this bait, it was because he believed enough time had gone by for Roarke to believably get careless again.

She was actually a little nervous about the leaping from the rafters part of this exercise. She hadn't mentioned to Diaz that she wasn't crazy about heights. Her father used to want help putting up outside Christmas lights, and she hadn't liked climbing the ladder and then having to lean precariously each direction to hook the string of lights over nails. Now that she was settled here, she was okay; it wasn't that far down. But jumping... She stole a cautious look down. No. Better to think about Diaz.

He'd been grumpy this week. She had no idea whether he was mad at the situation, at her, at his ex-wife, or had just gotten out of bed on the wrong side every single morning. He wasn't saying, and she was afraid to ask. She had enjoyed his irritation at the reaction of the other guys to her new look. In fact, just to herself she'd admit that she'd been flirting a little bit so she could see Diaz grit his teeth. She felt petty to be reveling in a sense of power over him, but, darn it, wasn't she entitled? Other girls had toyed with boys when they were teenagers; lending new meaning to the term "slow to blossom," she'd had to wait an extra ten years.

Anyway, it seemed as if otherwise he ignored her. They talked murder, of course, but had hardly exchanged a personal word since O'Brien called them on their relationship. Okay, they'd promised not to touch. That didn't mean they couldn't *talk*, did it? Diaz seemed to think so.

Or else—and this was the part that really scared her—he wasn't that interested in talking. Except for that one oblique comment about falling in love, he hadn't said anything to make her think he was envisioning a future with her. He hadn't taken her home to meet his mother, and he'd encouraged her to look for a new place to live. On her own. Neither were good signs.

She'd wanted the past two days to tell him about the phone call to her grandparents, but had never seen an opening. She hated the sting of wondering whether he'd really care. Oh, he'd say the right things; he was good at that. But he'd been so remote when he wasn't snapping, she'd lost her faith that she mattered much to him. Self-doubt was one of her special talents.

And look at him now. With exasperation, she saw him watching the damn driveway as if the bogey monster would ooze from the concrete or creep out from under the pickup. Well, okay, she thought with a sigh, that was what they were here for. He was doing his job. She'd just feel better if he gave her an occasional smile or signal instead of acting as if he were up on the damn rafters by himself.

She realized her legs were going numb and carefully drew them under her. Gripping the beam and trying not to look down, she pulled herself to a crouch. As blood rushed into her feet, they tingled and she shifted her weight from foot to foot. The biggest excitement came when a car briefly slowed out in front, but she didn't have an adequate sightline to tell anything but that it was a white sedan. A Honda Accord, she thought, but it might have been a Toyota or another import. Probably driven by a neighbor whose foot had lifted from the gas pedal as she checked to be sure her wallet was in her purse so she didn't get to the grocery store and discover she had no money.

As any sense of suspense wore off, Reggie seemed to get engrossed in working on his skeleton of a car. He clanged and swore and muttered about parts. Mary stuck her head in the garage once, expression spooked, then retreated back into the house. Ann wished they'd thought to arrange for her to conspicuously leave the house, as she had the day somebody shoved the car onto her husband. Tomorrow.

About midday, Reggie wiped his hands, peeled off the coveralls and went into the house for lunch, leaving the garage door open. By this time, Ann was having fantasies of plywood nailed up here so she could lie down. Heck, she could have a chair! Her stomach growled, and she opened the bag of peanuts she'd brought and ate them slowly, drawing out the pleasure. The salt made her thirsty, so she sipped from her bottle of water. Even that was enough to make her start wondering whether she had to pee and how she'd last the afternoon. She'd forgotten how much she hated stake-outs.

Meantime, Diaz seemed effortlessly to be keeping his focus, stretching and changing position every twenty minutes or so. His face was sphinx-like, displaying none of her discomfort and impatience and boredom.

Reggie took his sweet time about having lunch— *and* peeing, Ann thought in disgruntlement—ambling back out to the garage, where he put on the coveralls again, took another suspicious look up and down the street, then vanished back under the engine, only his legs from the knees down in sight.

Two or three hours later, he carefully put tools away, then rolled down the garage door. Ann groaned in anticipated relief. Both the men glanced at her in surprise.

Taking the hint, Reggie brought the ladder to her side of the garage first and held it while she clambered down with stiff knees and aching thighs.

"I've got to pee," she whispered, and fled.

Mary, puttering in the kitchen, turned in surprise to watch Ann dash down the hall. She didn't actually have to go that much, she discovered. The denial had been strictly psychological, she decided, flushing and washing her hands. On the way back, she gave Mary a quick hug, then rejoined the men in the garage.

"We'd better hang out here a little longer," Diaz said. "If our guy's suspicious, he might be watching for us to leave."

"Oh, okay," she conceded ungraciously. Now she was starving.

Reggie nodded at them and disappeared into the house.

Diaz gestured to a corner where they wouldn't be seen if somebody peered in the single small window. There, in the murk, Ann shifted from foot to foot and tried to bring life back to her limbs. Diaz, of course, leaned against an exposed stud and watched her as if she were showing the first signs of some nasty disease that he suspected was contagious. After a minute, she turned her back on him so she could fidget without feeling so self-conscious.

The garage gradually got darker as the light outside faded into grayish-purple. Okay, now she was hungry *and* cold. She shoved each of her hands up the sleeves of the other arm of her sweatshirt, holding herself tight for warmth.

When a hand settled on her shoulder, she squeaked and jumped.

"Are you all right?" Diaz asked in a low voice.

"Sure," she whispered back. "Just…chilly."

"Come here," he said, and drew her back against him. Why he was still generating heat and she wasn't, Ann didn't know, but he felt really, really good. He wrapped his arms around her, and they stood there in silence. After a minute, she realized she was still rigid, and she made herself relax, letting her head fall back against his shoulder.

She wasn't hungry anymore, she wasn't bored, she wasn't cold. His body felt so good against hers. Strong. Warm. She could feel his heart beating. Or maybe it was hers. Or theirs, mingled.

She felt his penis becoming erect. What strength her legs had left deserted them. Her body seemed able to generate heat, after all, pooled in her belly. Her breathing became shallow, fast. She heard herself make a shuddery sound.

He turned his head so that his mouth was against her hair. One of his hands, splayed on her stomach, moved. Inched up, until the weight of her breast rested on it.

She made another little sound. A gasp.

He rolled his hand, so that it cupped her breast. Then he gently squeezed, rubbed, teased. Meantime he nuzzled first her hair, then her neck. She felt weak, deliciously helpless. She never wanted him to stop touching her.

But he froze suddenly, going rigid against her back. Then she heard it, too: the faintest crunch of gravel on the other side of the wall. She quit breathing, and thought he did, too. His hand still on her breast, his erection still pressed against her rump, but both strained to hear.

Another crunch. A dog? A cat exploring the woodpile she remembered being stacked against the garage wall?

But then something blocked the meager light coming in the window. The purple of dusk darkened, as if a shadow had reached in. Diaz's fingers curled, giving away his tension.

The next second, the shadow passed from in front of the window, and they heard the same faint crunch, crunch, going back toward the street.

"Damn, I'd like to go after him," Diaz murmured into her ear.

"It might have been a neighbor looking for a cat that didn't come home for dinner," she whispered.

He gave a soft snort of disbelief. She didn't argue. The shadow had felt...malevolent. The neighbor wouldn't have stopped to peer into the garage.

No, like Diaz, she believed the killer was checking to be sure he wasn't being set up. They might have slipped unseen through the backyard, but he might just as well have been watching for them to do that.

Diaz's hands fell away from her. "Let's get out of here. Now."

She nodded agreement, although she felt bereft. She stepped away, passed the darker bulk of a workbench and stopped at the door that led directly into the backyard. Feeling Diaz behind her, she opened it soundlessly, pressed the button to lock it again and slipped through. He closed it as quietly, then led the way across the lawn to the back fence, where Reggie had left an oak whiskey half barrel upended. The grip of Diaz's hands conveyed his urgency as he hoisted her onto the barrel, then boosted her to the top of the fence. She took a look to be sure the neighbors weren't barbecuing on their patio, then swung both feet over and dropped to the other side. With a soft thud, Diaz landed beside her.

Down the block, the damn dog started to bay.

"Crap," Diaz muttered. He seemed to vanish into the night.

Ann followed, watching her footing and finally reaching the front corner of the house, where she bumped into Diaz. His head turned as he scanned the street.

"Let's go," he murmured, and they hurried to the sidewalk and the car they'd left parked at the curb a couple of doors down.

Once in it, Diaz started the engine and drove away without delay, turning at the corner away from Reggie's house.

"Well, well," he said in his normal voice, "that was interesting."

Which part? she wanted to ask. *The part where you groped me? Or the part where the bad guy peeked in the window?*

"It gives me hope for tomorrow," she agreed. As if she'd forgotten those few minutes that had turned her knees to jelly.

"Cautious bugger," Diaz commented, in that same tone that suggested they were taking up the conversation left off this morning, with nothing of moment having happened in between.

"He must have been in one of those cars that passed."

"Yeah, I wish I could have gotten a better look at them." He glanced at her. "Did you do any better?"

She shook her head. "I could take a pretty good guess at some makes and colors, but no license plates."

"Damn it," he grumbled. "If one of us had been parked down the street…"

"You don't think he's driving his own car?" she scoffed.

"No, but we might have recognized him behind the wheel."

She shrugged. "We still have to wait for him to make his move. We have to catch him in the act."

"Yeah, yeah." He sounded like she'd let the air out of his balloon and he wasn't happy about it.

She spotted a Burger King ahead and her stomach growled.

"That a hint?"

She flushed in embarrassment, glad it was dark. "I can wait until I get home."

"I can't. Let's just drive through."

She pulled out the bills she'd stashed in her pocket and told him what to order. When the clerk handed over the drinks, Ann slurped at her milk shake before Diaz had even reached for the paper bag holding the burgers and fries.

As he pulled away from the window, Diaz stuck his hand in a bag. "At least you had peanuts."

So he had noticed her, at least a little. Puncturing her own moment of pleasure, she figured it was probably because she'd crunched too loudly.

"Your fault if you didn't," she told him, and took a big, satisfying bite of cheeseburger.

Eating saved them from having to talk. She was wadding up their garbage and stuffing it all in one sack when he pulled up in front of her complex.

"I want to get there at the crack of dawn tomorrow," Diaz said. "In case he's watching for us. Say, six?"

She nodded and opened the car door. "See you in the morning."

He lifted a hand and drove away without waiting until she got in her front door, the way he usually did.

Maybe that was why her apartment felt even lonelier than usual.

THE SKY was barely light when they parked in the exact same spot and stole through the yards to Roarke's back door. Diaz rapped, and a surly Reggie opened up. He wore pajamas.

"I'm going back to bed," he growled, and disappeared into the house.

Diaz held open the door, and they went in, too. The warmth of the house was welcome after the dank chill of the garage. "We can lurk in the laundry room," he said softly. "Mary put on coffee for us."

Having only had a quick bowl of Cheerios, Ann thought coffee sounded like manna.

She sat on the vinyl floor of the laundry room with her back against the washer and her legs outstretched while Diaz went to the kitchen and poured them both cups of coffee. She nodded her thanks when he handed it to her.

Remembering yesterday's obsession with peeing, Ann made herself take small sips. Even so, the warmth spread from inside.

Appearing preoccupied, Diaz did the same. Neither spoke. Ann yawned, glanced at her watch and wondered how late Reggie planned to sleep.

An hour crawled by. Ann folded her arms on her knees, laid her cheek on her forearms, and let herself slip into a half doze. This wasn't the Hilton, but it was a heck of a lot more comfortable than her rafter.

She awakened to the sound of voices in the kitchen. She had listed sideways, and her head, she realized, now rested against Diaz's shoulder. Ann sat up abruptly and mumbled, "Sorry."

He smiled at her. "You snore."

"I do not!"

"How would you know?" he asked logically enough.

"Somebody would have told me."

Diaz's smile widened. "Okay. You take very, very deep breaths."

"Hmph." She sniffed, her eyes widening in outrage. "Are they having bacon and eggs for breakfast?"

"You could have fried some bacon at home."

"Yeah. Right. At five-thirty in the morning. I was lucky to find my way to the kitchen." She sighed. "That does smell good."

Diaz, who seemed to be in an exceptionally good mood, patted her cheek. "That's one of the things I always liked about you. You enjoy your food."

"Oh, good. I'm a pig. Is that what you're saying?"

"It was a compliment."

"'Your eyes are the color of the sky at twilight.' *That's* a compliment," she snapped. "'You're a good eater' is not."

She hadn't fazed him. He smiled at Mary, who appeared in the laundry room doorway with two plates in her hands. "Is that for us? You're a sweetheart. Caldwell here was just getting grumpy. Some food'll sweeten her."

"Oh, I so wish you'd come sit at the table!" Mary fussed. "I hate to think anybody is *spying* on us."

"It's not a pleasant thought," Diaz agreed. "Maybe today will be the end of it."

Ann thanked Mary and dug in to the heap of fluffy scrambled eggs. Bacon, perfectly browned, rimmed the plate.

Diaz, she noticed, ate with the same concentration and pleasure but skipped the bacon despite the fact that he had a bigger frame and was five or six inches taller than she was. Did he have to flaunt his discipline? Feeling like a pig again, Ann hesitated, then in a spirit of defiance ate the last strip of bacon anyway.

Ann and he took turns using the bathroom, then went back to the garage. Once again, Ann climbed up first with her bottle of water. As Diaz carried the ladder to his side of the garage and mounted it, she peered through the slits.

Nada. Empty driveway, empty street. Quiet neighborhood. No mowers fired up yet. On a Sunday morning, half the people probably were getting ready for church.

Church, they had decided, would be the perfect excuse for Mary to leave the house. Half an hour later, Reggie came out to the garage, hung up the ladder, donned his coveralls and rolled up the garage door. As ordered, his wife came out the front door in a simple dress, her purse gripped with tight knuckles in front of her.

"Are you sure you won't come to church with me?" she asked too loudly. "I can wait for you."

Ann winced. Mary wasn't much of an actress.

"Nah." Her husband chose a wrench from a drawer in his rolling cart. "You go ahead. The Lord'll understand."

"Well, then," Mary told the entire block, "I'll probably go grocery shopping afterward."

"You go on then." He lay down on the creeper.

She gave him a despairing look, then marched down the driveway to her car. Ann, watching, realized Mary was near to tears. She was scared for the jerk. She must actually love him. Ann shook her head. Imagine that.

The neighborhood gradually came to life, cars coming and going. Then quiet settled again.

Now, Ann thought. *Now is when I'd do it.*

As if on cue, a hooded figure stepped into the garage right below Ann.

CHAPTER FIFTEEN

DIAZ WAS WATCHING a car backing out of a driveway a couple of houses down when movement brought his head around. A man in a hooded sweatsuit had sidled into the garage. Frozen in his crouch, Diaz felt adrenaline kick in.

A neighbor? Diaz kinda doubted it. There was the hood, shielding the face. Anyway, neighbors walked up the driveway, calling hello as they came. This visitor had to have slipped around the side of the house.

The ogre he'd only half believed in was real and had taken the bait.

Diaz lifted his gaze briefly to Ann. Their eyes met, then both watched the visitor go deeper into the garage. His head turned from side to side as he scanned the interior.

Under the car, Reggie hummed off-key. Weirdly, Diaz would have sworn the tune was *Santa Claus Is Coming to Town.* The paranoid's anthem.

The figure paused. His head swung back toward the garage door opening. A sound? Diaz quit breathing. *Don't look up, don't look up.*

After a moment, apparently reassured, the intruder continued on silent feet to the passenger side of the

Corvette. He laid gloved hands on the frame and shoved. Once, then again.

"Hey!" Reggie shouted from under the car. His feet kicked as he tried to backpedal. "Goddamn!"

The car shuddered and rocked.

Diaz snatched his gun from the holster, braced his elbow on his thigh and yelled, "Freeze! This is the police! Take your hands off the car!"

For a heartbeat, the guy went still. Weighing his options. Ten feet to the open garage door. Would the cop really fire? Then he bolted, and in the same moment Ann leaped from the rafter and crashed down on him. They disappeared behind the front end of the vehicle.

Diaz holstered his gun and jumped, too, landing with painful force. He fell, rolled and regained his feet, pulling his weapon again. Behind him, Reggie had made it out from under the car and jumped from the creeper.

"Freeze, you son of a bitch!" Diaz yelled as he came around the front end of the Corvette.

Ann and the perp fought silently. He slammed her head against the concrete floor, but she kneed him and he buckled. In an instant they'd flipped, and she was on top, his gloved hands at her throat. She was yelling at him, Diaz was yelling, and with a bellow of rage Reggie knocked her aside and flattened the bastard.

His "Try to kill me, will you" was followed by a string of obscenities.

Ann crawled back to her foe, pulling cuffs from her back pocket. She snapped one on, then the other as

Reggie rolled the perp and wrenched his arm behind his back.

Cheek grinding into the concrete, he lay belly-down, the hood still on his head. Diaz had seen his face and was unsurprised when Reggie yanked the hood down.

"I know you," he said.

Oblivious to the blood matting the back of her head, Ann stood over him. "Moskowitz."

Deidre Moskowitz's father closed his eyes.

Diaz lowered his weapon. "You're under arrest for the attempted murder of Reggie Roarke. You have the right to remain silent," he began. As he finished reciting the Miranda warning, he kept an eye on Ann. She looked like hell.

"Sit," he ordered her.

Without taking her eyes from Moskowitz, she slid to a sitting position, her back to the front fender of the car.

Diaz ordered Reggie to call for backup and medics. He'd seen Ann's head bounce off concrete. While they waited, he crouched beside her. "You okay? Stay with me."

"Yeah, I'm okay." Her face was bleached to the color of skim milk.

"No, you're not. Goddamn it, where are they?"

"Reggie just called," she murmured.

Fear grabbed him. "Maybe I should drive you to the hospital."

She turned her head a fraction to meet his eyes. "I've got a headache. Don't shout in my ear."

He could tell she was trying to sound tart. The fact that she failed scared him worse.

"I should have been on that side of the garage."

"Yeah, you should."

Reggie, back from phoning, had one foot planted on Moskowitz's back. "You scumbag, why were you trying to kill me?"

"I don't know what you're talking about," Moskowitz mumbled. "I want a lawyer."

"Oh, you'll get one, you piece of shit."

Ann was back to staring at their suspect. "You killed my father."

He rolled an eye toward her. "What in the hell are you talking about?"

"Sergeant Michael Caldwell. Remember him? He was my dad."

Moskowitz turned his head away.

Ann didn't seem to be in the mood for conversation. Once she lifted a hand and touched the back of her head, wincing at the light contact.

"You dizzy? Sick to your stomach?" Diaz asked.

"I'm okay," she kept saying. Until suddenly, in a strangled voice, she said, "I wish I hadn't eaten those scrambled eggs."

Reggie grabbed for an oil pan and thrust it onto her lap. She puked, confirming Diaz's fear that she had a concussion if not worse.

A squad car arrived first, lights flashing and siren singing. The aide car was on its bumper. Diaz was vaguely aware of neighbors gathering as the uniforms jumped out and the medics pulled a gurney from the back of the ambulance.

Diaz flashed his badge. "Take this scumbag in. Detective Caldwell is hurt. I'm going to follow her to the hospital.''

They yanked Moskowitz to his feet and led him, head hanging, down the driveway to the unit.

The medics asked Ann questions, then had her lie down on the gurney against her protests. Diaz walked beside her down the driveway, his hand resting on the gurney beside hers. Just as they reached the gaping back of the ambulance, she turned her hand and gripped his.

Her eyes were big and scared. ''Are you coming?''

''I'll beat you there.''

She licked her lips. ''Okay.'' She let go of his hand and closed her eyes.

The medics lifted her into the rear of the aide car and closed the door.

''Want me to come with you?'' Reggie asked.

Diaz shook his head. ''Will you call O'Brien at home? Tell him what happened? You'll need to write up a report, too, but I don't see why it can't wait until tomorrow. Hey, this is your day off, right?''

Reggie gave a weak grin. ''Hell, maybe I'll take Mary out for Sunday dinner.''

Diaz slapped him on the back. ''You do that.''

He followed the aide car to the hospital, pulling ahead a few blocks before they arrived so that he was waiting at the curb when Ann was lifted out.

His heart gave a thud at the sight of her, lying still as death, her eyes closed and her face waxy pale. He grabbed her hand and squeezed, and her lashes fluttered up.

"Hey," she said, her mouth twisting into a semblance of a smile.

"Hey." He grinned at her. "You know, I think our cover is blown. Holding hands in front of the whole world."

"Wanna climb on the gurney with her?" one of the EMTs asked.

Diaz gave a succinct answer that brought hoots of laughter.

He had to let Ann go when they wheeled her through the double doors. After giving the information the hospital needed, he was left with nothing to do but wait.

O'Brien called at one point to ask how she was.

"I hope just a concussion," Diaz told him. "She got her head slammed pretty good."

"Son of a bitch." He was silent for a moment. "If this bastard had quit while he was ahead, or taken a rest, he'd have gotten away with it."

"He'd have gotten away with it if Caldwell hadn't noticed a pattern."

"To be honest, I thought she was chasing a will-o'-the-wisp." For an instant, the lieutenant sounded very Irish. "She fooled me."

"I had my doubts," Diaz admitted.

"Call me when you know anything." The phone went dead.

Diaz picked up a magazine and turned pages without remembering what was on a single one of them. He tried pacing, but the room was too damn small. He sat again, picked up a different magazine, and then threw it back onto the table.

What in hell was taking so long?

"Detective?" In the doorway stood a woman in a lab coat, wearing a stethoscope around her neck. Maybe fifty, she had the leathery skin and cropped hair of a dedicated cyclist or distance runner. "I'm Dr. Venburg."

Diaz shot to his feet. "How is she?"

The doctor smiled. "She's fine. Well, she'll *be* fine. She's got a concussion and one heck of a headache. The X ray looks okay, but we want to keep her overnight. She'll be transferred upstairs in just a few minutes."

"Can I see her?"

She smiled again. "I don't know why not."

He followed her to a curtained cubicle. Dr. Venburg pulled aside the curtain so that he could slip in, then closed it behind him.

Ann lay on the narrow bed under at least a couple of white blankets drawn up to her chin. They accentuated her pallor. At the rattle of curtain rings, she opened her eyes and gazed fuzzily at him.

"They gave me something for my headache. I think I'm getting sleepy."

He watched her eyes cross and then try to refocus. "You think?"

Sounding more like her usual self, she added, "I hope he's got a headache, too."

"He's got a bigger one trying to figure out how to avoid spending the rest of his life in a cell."

"I'm glad we saved Reggie," she said, voice slurred. "But I don't care about Saffian. I think he did rape Deidre."

"Yeah." He'd read the police reports. "I do, too."

"We'll never get Moskowitz for Leroy's murder."

"Or Birkey's," Diaz agreed.

"But Dad's..." She seemed to be making a conscious effort to stay alert. "If we can find the vehicle he drove..."

"We'll find it." Diaz gave into temptation and smoothed her hair back from her brow, curved like Elena's. Tenderness squeezed his heart and thickened his voice. "We'll get him for murder one."

Her eyes fixed on his. "We can't be partners anymore, can we?"

Diaz shook his head. "Not on the job."

"I'll miss you," she whispered.

Was she saying goodbye? Fear felt like a speed bump, an unexpected lurch.

"I won't be far enough away for you to miss me."

Her eyelids sank slowly. Reluctantly. Under the blankets, her breasts rose in a long, deep breath that came out in a long sigh between parted lips. She'd fallen asleep.

He stayed beside her anyway, going along when they transported her upstairs without interrupting her nap for more than a mumbled, "What'ch'a doing?" when they shifted her to a bed in a private room.

Then he went back to the station to book a murderer.

"I FEEL LIKE a fraud riding in a wheelchair," Ann fretted. "Why won't they let me walk?"

Diaz patted her shoulder. "Hospital rules. They don't want you collapsing in the hall. Outside the door...hey, that's okay."

The orderly grinned. "We try to get you in your car, so you don't embarrass us on hospital property. We'd appreciate it if you wait 'til you're home, detective."

She glared over her shoulder at the two of them. Men. "I'm fine! That's why this is ridiculous."

Diaz hid a smirk. "Did you argue about every rule when you were a kid?"

"Probably," she muttered. Until her mother died. She'd needed her father too much to rebel. Been too afraid of him. Maybe, most of all, been afraid he'd abandon her and she'd have no one if she didn't please him. Why hadn't he guessed how his small daughter felt? she wondered now. Because he had no imagination? Or because he didn't really care?

What had once been a sharp pang was muted now. An old injury, healed as much as it ever would, instead of a fresh, seeping wound. Miracle of miracles, she had recovered.

Outside, the two men helped her solicitously into the passenger seat of Diaz's car. Her irritation increased.

Of course he was here to pick her up. Who else was there? He'd felt obligated, which made her cringe inside. This was supposed to be their day off. She wondered where his kids were instead of with him.

She grudgingly thanked the attendant, who assured her she was welcome, slammed the car door and retreated with the empty wheelchair. Diaz got behind the wheel and started the car.

"Glad to be out of there?"

She started to nod and thought better of it. "They

came in to shove a thermometer in my mouth at six o'clock this morning! I'm not sick!''

"Standard…''

"Yeah, yeah." Ann knew she was being grumpy, but couldn't seem to help it. She didn't even want to think about *why* she felt so unhappy.

He glanced at her. Even out of the corner of her eye, she knew he was assessing her.

"Headache?''

"'Ache' isn't the word for it. A jackhammer is shattering my skull so it can be repaved."

Okay, that was one reason she was grouchy. She felt like crap. That was a good excuse.

"Tell me Moskowitz hasn't walked out on bail yet,'' she begged.

"No, the judge is being cautious. Cop killers aren't popular."

She snorted. "Except in the pen."

His smile deepened the crease from nose to mouth, crinkled skin beside eyes—and flung her deeper into grief.

"He can be popular there, as far as I'm concerned."

"What's his story?'' she asked.

Deadpan, Diaz said, "He was jogging. Had chest pain. Saw the open garage door and came in to ask if he could use the phone. He was leaning on the car because the pain in his chest worsened."

She growled.

"Open to question is why he drove from Renton to Kent to jog, not on a trail, but on sidewalks in this particular neighborhood. Odds are against his having randomly chosen to ask for help at the home of a cop who he felt had wronged his daughter, too. And, heck, the latex gloves don't look good.''

''Then there's Reggie's injuries the last time someone rocked the Corvette down on top of him.''

''There is that,'' Diaz agreed.

Strategies for building a case kept them from anything more personal. Talking shop took more effort than Ann would have admitted even to someone yanking her fingernails out. Her head hammered and her stomach took an occasional uneasy roll. All she wanted was to save her pride, thank him for chauffeuring her and go lie down in her dark bedroom.

He pulled into the visitor slot at her complex, set the emergency brake and turned off the engine.

''You don't have to walk me…''

His look silenced her.

He got out and made it around to her side about the time she took a deep breath and climbed out.

''Damn it,'' he said. ''You do look like you're going to topple over.''

''I just need to lie down. I'll be fine.''

''Uh-huh.'' He wrapped an arm around her and, with his free hand, closed the car door. ''Let's go.''

She produced her key from her jeans' pocket and let him unlock. The apartment was dim and cold; she'd turned the thermostat way down yesterday morning and left the blinds pulled. It felt as if nobody had been in here in a long time. She sniffed cautiously, almost afraid food had spoiled. Maybe she'd walked through a time warp and didn't know it. This morning when that insufferably cheerful male nurse had awakened her, the first thing out of her mouth was, ''Where am

I?'' Maybe she'd been in a coma for two weeks, and neither the doctor nor Diaz had thought to mention it.

She stepped away from Diaz and turned with the best smile she could muster. ''Thanks for the lift. I really appreciate it. I'm going to down another pain pill and take a nap.''

He crossed his arms. ''I'll tuck you in.''

''For Pete's sake!''

He just lifted a brow.

''Do I really look that awful?'' she demanded.

''Yep.''

She snarled again and snapped, ''Fine!'' Aside from the damn headache and this tendency to want to cry, she *was* fine. She marched to the thermostat, turned it up to a temperature she didn't usually permit herself and continued down the hall without checking to see whether he followed. She didn't have to. She *felt* him right behind her.

Having him see her bedroom made her self-conscious. She didn't know that it said anything deep about her; it was just a bedroom. Blinds, carpet, dresser, bedside table, lamp, digital clock, double bed with a duvet covered in orange sherbet colored flannel. For some reason the color had uplifted her.

''You going to watch me get undressed, too?''

He had that blank face she knew from experience meant he couldn't be swayed. ''I'll turn my back.''

Grumbling under her breath, she snatched pajamas from a bureau drawer, grateful her best ones were clean. Not that flannel was sexy, but at least all the buttons were intact.

She sat on the edge of the bed. Before she had to

wrestle with the question of whether she could bend over to untie her athletic shoes without her head exploding, Diaz kneeled at her feet and tugged at the laces.

Looking down at his big hands gently pulling the shoes from her feet, she felt a squeeze of emotion that did make tears spring to her eyes. She imagined him teaching his kids to tie laces and looking up with a teasing smile.

When he peeled off her socks, too, and then sat back on his haunches with her shoes and socks in his hands, his eyes were dark and his mouth... No. She wasn't going to think about what his expression might mean.

Instead, Ann mumbled, ''Thank you. Now, if you wouldn't mind...''

He nodded, set down her shoes by the closet, dropped the socks in a wicker hamper she kept by the bathroom door and then turned his back.

It took Ann a good two minutes to ease the sweatshirt over her head. She had to keep pausing when her head swam. She stripped off her bra, tucked it under the sweatshirt and pulled on the pajamas, buttoning them hastily. The jeans she could just step out of and kick aside, thank goodness. Although she didn't normally sleep in panties, she left them on under the pajama bottoms.

Then she pulled back the comforter and climbed in. ''Okay,'' she said. ''I'm decent.''

''Too bad.'' He had a glint in his eyes when he turned. ''What'd you do with your pain pills?''

She closed her eyes. ''Oh, damn! I left the sack in the car.''

''That's okay. I have to go get my overnight bag anyway.''

Her eyes popped open. ''Your *what?*''

Voice implacable, he said, ''I'm staying, Ann. Don't waste your breath arguing.''

''But…what about Elena and Tony?''

''I canceled.'' On the way out her bedroom door, he said, ''I'll be right back.''

Still stunned, she heard the front door open and close, then open again not a minute later. Water ran in the kitchen. Diaz reappeared with her bottle of pain pills and a glass of water, which he handed her.

''I'm really okay.'' She accepted the pill he'd shaken out of the container and swallowed it, setting the glass of water on the bedside stand. ''Cheri'll be mad.''

''If you're feeling better, we'll take 'em out to dinner tomorrow night. Maybe go to a movie. Give her the night off.''

We?

''Uh…are you planning to move in?''

No inflection; expression didn't change. ''We can talk about that later.''

''Why not now?'' she demanded, knowing she was pouting and unable to help herself.

''You don't seem to quite be yourself.''

Her damn eyes seemed to be watering. ''I'll just worry about what you're going to say.''

A muscle twitched in his cheek. He glanced with what she imagined to be longing at her bedroom door.

Obligation, she thought again, dismally. He wished he was anywhere but here. When she'd been wounded in the line of duty, telling her that he hadn't really meant anything by his kisses must be an especially unwelcome task.

His head dipped in assent. "All right." He sat down on the edge of the bed, which gave under his weight.

Ann scooted over a little bit and tugged the comforter up to her chin as if it could protect her from heartache. He looked down at her with an odd little smile, as if she disconcerted and amused him.

"I put in for a transfer to Fraud," he said. "I'm going to start hunting white-collar crooks."

"You did?" She gaped. "I thought…"

He frowned. "That you'd be the one who had to go?"

"Well…I mean…" She groped for an answer. "You do have seniority."

"I don't mind a change of pace. I've been in Homicide and Assault for three years now." He was silent for a beat, the frown lingering. "Damn it, you assumed you'd have to make the sacrifice because no one's ever made one for you."

"You're feeling sorry for me again!" she flared. "I hate it when you do that."

"I'm right, aren't I?"

"Yes!" Tears burned her eyes now. "I know that's pathetic, but it's true. Mom sure didn't stick it out for me, and Dad didn't go out of his way to make me feel loved and appreciated. I know not everyone is like that, but…"

"But your assumptions are based on your own experience." Diaz's voice was gentle. "I get that."

She sniffed and lifted one hand from beneath the duvet to dash at her tears. "I put in for a transfer, too."

"What?" He sounded as stunned as she'd felt.

"You didn't think I would," she realized in amazement. Here she'd thought he was sure of her, that she'd been embarrassingly obvious.

"I thought…" He gave his head a dazed shake. "That being there meant a lot to you."

"It did." The next words stuck in her throat. *You mean more.* She couldn't say them. Was a coward to the bitter end.

"Tell O'Brien you've changed your mind."

Ann shook her head. "I wanted to somehow prove that I could do Dad's job. I wanted him to be proud." Dumb, dumb, dumb. "But he's dead, and I'm not so proud of him, either. And I've realized that what I like is the puzzle and the research. I'm not that crazy about blood spatter patterns. You know?"

He let out a rough chuckle. "Yeah. I know."

"I asked to go to the Domestic Violence Intervention Unit. It seems fitting, don't you think? Even if Dad never hit me. It's time for me to…oh, find my own place."

"Sweetheart, I think you already have."

"Really?" She searched a face she had come to know so well.

"You're amazing. You know you'll get a commendation for this."

"You mean, *we* will."

"Yeah." That same, faintly disconcerted smile played on his mouth. "We will."

She chewed on her lower lip. "I'll miss working with you," she said in a small voice.

He cleared his throat. "Which brings us back to the question of whether I'm moving in."

Swinging between hope and misery, she waited.

"I actually, uh, had in mind that you'd move in with me. Until we can buy a place." He spoke rapidly. "Because it's convenient for the kids, you know. They can take the bus after school to my apartment. I don't want to make it harder for them to feel like my place is home, too."

"Move in with you." She probably sounded like an idiot parroting him, but... The idea staggered her. It wasn't that she'd miss this apartment. But... She'd only been in his once. Met his kids once. And...would he and she be the butt of jokes if she was living with him?

"Marry me."

A flush burned her cheeks. "Marry you?"

"Damn it, Caldwell!" He shot to his feet and glared at her. "I'm going out on a limb here. Are you with me, or not?"

"You're asking me to marry you?" Her voice cracked.

His face softened. His eyes were a warm chocolate-brown, gentle and somehow vulnerable. "Yeah. Any chance I could, uh, hold one of your hands?"

"Oh!" She pulled both arms out from beneath the comforter so that it fell to her waist.

Diaz took her left hand in a strong, enveloping grip. "Ann Caldwell, will you marry me?"

Her "Yes," was watery but clear.

He laughed and kissed her wet cheek, then her tremulous mouth. "Have I mentioned that I love you?"

Mopping her tears with her pajama sleeve, she shook her head. "I've been so afraid…"

"Afraid of what?" he asked, with the tenderness that undid her.

"That I was making a fool out of myself falling in love with you!" she wailed.

He laughed again, and wiped tears with the pads of his thumbs. "I've been falling in love with you since the day we started working together. I just fought it."

"Me, too." She laid her cheek against his hand. "I'll have to start thinking of you as Juan, won't I?"

"I like the way you say it. But I like the way you say 'Diaz,' too."

She thought about it, and him. "Do you, um, want to get in bed with me?"

His mouth twisted. "More than you can imagine. But…not now."

She heard in his voice the grit, the desire, the kindness, and her heart swelled until it hurt.

"Maybe after you've had a nap. We'll see how you feel."

She wanted, so badly, to feel his arms around her. "You could cuddle me."

His smile was so sweet, it increased the ache and the joy in her chest.

"I'll have you know, I'm one hell of a cuddler." He kicked off his shoes, pulled his sweater over his head to expose a gray T-shirt and climbed into bed with her. He gently shifted her so that her head was on his shoulder, then wrapped her in his arms.

In a low, husky voice, he started talking about the future. A house, a yard, roses, a Christmas tree every year that would touch the ceiling. When she was ready, maybe a baby. Or two.

Eyes closed, she let his words wash over her as she imagined carrying his child. Nursing a baby that would gaze up at her with her daddy's big brown eyes. Braiding hair, helping with school projects, loving her children—and his. Loving them fiercely and forever, no matter what demons of self-doubt she herself battled.

As she would love Juan.

And he would love her. With wonder, she examined her certainty, her faith. She hadn't thought she could ever trust anyone that much. But Juan...he was different.

"You know," she murmured after a while. "My head feels a little better. And I'm not that sleepy."

He rubbed his cheek against hers. "Hmm." His voice had dropped a notch. "You're not bored, are you?"

Feeling very brave, she kissed his jaw, then his neck, tasting the salt on his skin. "No. I just started getting ideas."

"All that talk about babies, hmm?"

"Maybe." The feel of his solid body against hers might have something to do with it, too. She remembered yesterday evening in Reggie's garage, when Diaz put his hand on her breast, and she wanted him to do it again.

He moved, gently laying her on her back, and propped himself on his elbow above her. He searched her face. Sounding shaken, he asked, "You're sure?"

Her mouth trembled when she tried to smile. Her voice cracked. "Yes. Yes, I'm sure."

He kissed her, then, and wrestled with every single one of the buttons on her pajama top. But finally, oh finally, his hand was on her breast, and then his mouth was there, and if she'd ever had a headache, she'd forgotten it.

Oh, yes, she thought. She was sure. Never, ever in her life had she been so sure of anything as she was about this. About him, her partner.

HARLEQUIN *Super*ROMANCE®

A new six-book series from Harlequin Superromance.

WOMEN *in Blue*

Six female cops battling crime and corruption on the streets of Houston. Together they can fight the blue wall of silence. But divided will they fall?

The Partner by Kay David
(Harlequin Superromance #1230, October 2004)

Tackling the brotherhood of the badge isn't easy, but Risa Taylor can do it, because of the five friends she made at the academy. And after one horrible night, when her partner is killed and Internal Affairs investigator Grady Wilson comes knocking on her door, she knows how much she needs them.

The Children's Cop by Sherry Lewis
(Harlequin Superromance #1237, November 2004)

Finding missing children is all in a day's work for Lucy Montalvo. Though Lucy would love to marry and have a family of her own, her drive to protect the children of Houston has her convinced that a traditional family isn't in the cards for her. Until she finds herself working on a case with Jackson Davis—a man who is as dedicated to the children of others as she is.

Watch for:
The Witness by Linda Style (#1243, December)
Her Little Secret by Anna Adams (#1248, January)
She Walks the Line by Roz Denny Fox (#1254, February)
A Mother's Vow by K.N. Casper (#1260, March)

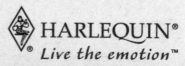

HARLEQUIN®
Live the emotion™

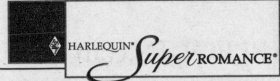

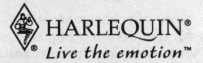

eHARLEQUIN.com

The Ultimate Destination for Women's Fiction

Visit eHarlequin.com's Bookstore today for today's most popular books at great prices.

- An extensive selection of romance books by top authors!

- Choose our convenient "bill me" option. No credit card required.

- New releases, Themed Collections and hard-to-find backlist.

- A sneak peek at upcoming books.

- Check out book excerpts, book summaries and Reader Recommendations from other members and post your own too.

- Find out what everybody's reading in Bestsellers.

- Save BIG with everyday discounts and exclusive online offers!

- Our Category Legend will help you select reading that's exactly right for you!

- Visit our Bargain Outlet often for huge savings and special offers!

- Sweepstakes offers. Enter for your chance to win special prizes, autographed books and more.

Your purchases are 100% guaranteed—so shop online at www.eHarlequin.com today!

If you enjoyed what you just read,
then we've got an offer you can't resist!

Take 2 bestselling love stories FREE!

Plus get a FREE surprise gift!

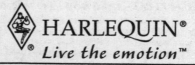